PRAISE FO:

"A pulse-pounding psychological thriller that will leave you breathless. In a claustrophobic suburban landscape that feels like a pressure cooker of secrets, Katie Sise masterfully unravels the dark undercurrents of human nature. *You Must Be New Here* is both deeply unsettling and impossible to put down."

—Kaira Rouda, *USA Today*, Amazon Charts, and international bestselling author of *Jill Is Not Happy*

"Part murder mystery, part interpersonal drama, a serviceable whodunit (or did anyone?) with a host of compelling characters . . . this novel has just enough twists to keep its readers along for the ride. Sleuths will delight in piecing together clues and untangling lies alongside the protagonists."

—*Kirkus Reviews*

## PRAISE FOR *THE VACATION RENTAL*

"With superb plotting and finely crafted characters, *The Vacation Rental* surprised me at every turn! An insightful thriller about family secrets and long-held grudges, written by a truly talented author."

—Wendy Walker, bestselling author of *What Remains*

## PRAISE FOR *OPEN HOUSE*

"Part murder mystery, part interpersonal drama, a serviceable whodunit (or did anyone?) with a host of compelling characters . . . this novel has just enough twists to keep its readers along for the ride. Sleuths will delight in piecing together clues and untangling lies alongside the protagonists."

—*Kirkus Reviews*

"A chilling thriller, *Open House* tracks a missing art student who vanished ten years prior and how her disappearance connects with a recent attack during an open house in a small university town. It also showcases the unending loyalty of close girlfriends and sisterhood in life or death."

—*Good Morning America*

## PRAISE FOR *WE WERE MOTHERS*

"Katie Sise's *We Were Mothers* expertly snaps readers to attention with its grandiose opening . . . Timing, inner discourse, and believable fiascos blend together, producing fantastic scenes . . . Her observations and vulnerability carry the read."

—Associated Press

# You Must Be New Here

## ALSO BY KATIE SISE

*We Were Mothers*

*Open House*

*The Break*

*The Vacation Rental*

# You Must Be New Here

A NOVEL

## KATIE SISE

This is a work of fiction. Names, characters, organizations, places, events, and incidents are either products of the author's imagination or are used fictitiously. Otherwise, any resemblance to actual persons, living or dead, is purely coincidental.

Text copyright © 2025 by Katie Sise
All rights reserved.

No part of this book may be reproduced, or stored in a retrieval system, or transmitted in any form or by any means, electronic, mechanical, photocopying, recording, or otherwise, without express written permission of the publisher.

Published by Little A, New York

www.apub.com

Amazon, the Amazon logo, and Little A are trademarks of Amazon.com, Inc., or its affiliates.

EU product safety contact:
Amazon Media EU S. à r.l.
38, avenue John F. Kennedy, L-1855 Luxembourg
amazonpublishing-gpsr@amazon.com

ISBN-13: 9781662507755 (hardcover)
ISBN-13: 9781662507762 (paperback)
ISBN-13: 9781662507779 (digital)

Cover design by Faceout Studio, Amanda Hudson
Cover image: © NicoleTaklaPhotograph, © Maria Dryfhout, © Iavor, © JoeEJ, © Maxim Studio, © BuseBesler / Shutterstock

Printed in the United States of America

First edition

*For Katie Clark and Jessica Clark*

# PART I

# ONE

*Sloane*

I'm standing on our front lawn with my daughter, Daisy, when a moving truck trundles up the hill. A tangerine sun hangs low in the sky, aching to set, and Daisy shields her eyes from the glow.

Her tiny hand finds mine. The bones of her fingers feel weightless, like I could crush them if I squeezed too hard. "Who's that, Mama?" she asks, her light eyes tracking the truck. It hurtles past us in a cloud of dirt and gravel.

I turn and look at my daughter, at the beautiful curves of her face, her smooth skin flushed from the early spring air. Her blond hair is pulled high into a messy bun, and there's a streak of mud across her jaw. At seven, she's still young enough to play in the dirt and doesn't mind when it leaves a mark.

"It must be our new neighbors' moving truck," I say, following Daisy's gaze back to the truck to see it nearly knock over the neighbors' mailbox. The driver stops, reverses with a series of impossibly loud beeps, and then tries again, successfully sparing the mailbox and executing the sharp curve of the driveway.

It's only our house and two others at the very top of Beckett's Hill high above the river, and the terrain is nearly impossible for a truck this size. The road widens once you descend the hill toward Sycamore Glen's tiny downtown, but here at the top, everything is tight.

I've always loved living near the cliffs. The landscape is lush and woody, and the river churns below with the promise of danger if you get too close to the edge. My daughter is a rule follower, which is partly who she is and partly because of her condition, and she won't go near the edge of our property that overhangs the river. But sometimes, late at night after she's asleep, I slip out into the dark and walk to the rocky ledge of the cliffs. There's a razor-sharp feeling of aliveness I get when I stare down into the black water. I wonder if the new neighbors felt it, too, and if it was partly what sold them on the house. A couple of months ago, when the real estate agent removed the "For Sale" sign, she saw me in our vegetable garden, and said, "A surgeon and his wife from California. Aren't you lucky to have a doctor for a neighbor?"

When she told me about the people who purchased the house, I couldn't help but wonder if she knew about Daisy's condition, and if that's why she mentioned the husband being a surgeon. Sycamore Glen is a small town, and people talk. But the real estate agent is in her late fifties, and we don't move in the same circles, so maybe she doesn't know anything about Daisy. Her words hung in the air between us like odd comments do, and she quickly added something about the new couple being *interesting* and *smart*. But then she turned away and never made eye contact again, and I wondered if there was a detail about the couple nefarious enough for her to omit. Our own real estate agent, who'd sold Dave and me our house back when we were in love, had a way of spinning things, too. I guess we all do it.

The new neighbors' house is a gingerbread castle of a Tudor with spires shooting into the bright blue sky. There's nothing McMansion about Sycamore Glen, and even though the Tudor is massive, it's also old and rambling and looks like it's full of secret doors and musty libraries. Penny, the woman who lived there until her death a few months ago, was elderly and ill, and we never went past the front door, where we dropped off dinners and holiday cards. When the weather was nice,

Penny's caretaker would take her onto the lawn, and she'd tell us stories about her husband, who passed a few years before we moved onto the street. Her stories about him were saturated with the tiniest details, like the open set of his jaw when she surprised him with a sixtieth birthday trip to Italy, or thirty years earlier, the way he'd paced the house with a wailing baby high on his shoulder, doing a two-step down the hall. Penny's stories made me sad that I hadn't had a once-in-a-lifetime kind of love with Dave, but hopeful that maybe I would have it with someone, sometime, somewhere.

*You never know,* my mother used to say about all sorts of things when I was a small girl. I could never tell if it was a warning or a promise.

Penny died in the house, just like she'd wanted. One winter morning, Daisy and I woke to sirens and we knew.

I lead Daisy to our vegetable garden, a gust of wind cold against our faces. It smells damp and earthy out here, the scent of nature gearing up for her big spring production.

In the neighbors' driveway, the driver gets out of the moving truck and heads to the back, sliding open the heavy metal door with a *clank*. There's a soft roar in the distance, and Daisy and I turn to see a dark green Range Rover round the bend and whiz toward us. "Come on, love," I say to Daisy, opening the wire gate and stepping into our garden. I pick up my head for a split second to catch a woman with wild dark hair in the driver's seat of the Range Rover, talking animatedly to a dark-haired man beside her. I lift my hand in a wave, but they don't seem to see me. Daisy copies my wave with her own. I feel the edges of my lips curve into a smile as I watch Daisy's wave gather speed until it's almost frantic; she's the daughter of my dreams—the little girl I hoped for, the one I couldn't live without.

"Daisy," I say. "Do you want to go meet them?"

# TWO

## *Clara*

In front of me are nine cake samples squared into tiny bites. Perla, the tall, voluptuous woman who owns the cake shop, hovers over me, smiling a toothy grin. She stares down at my poised plastic fork and wordlessly waits for me to start.

I smile back. I haven't had an appetite since college. I press my fork into a spongy red velvet rectangle and lift it to my mouth, unable to remember the last time I let myself have something this wonderful—edible or otherwise.

"This is *delicious*," I say.

I haven't been to a cake tasting since Evan and I were planning our wedding eighteen years ago. Or, more accurately, since my father planned our wedding. Back then, I was drowning in a sea of grief after losing my sister, and I remember barely being able to taste the cake. I picked a marble one because it reminded me of confusion, which was pretty much all I felt back then. I was only twenty-three.

"You're very talented," I say to Perla. I don't tell her how most of the parents at the school fundraiser will be too drunk to really appreciate the splendor of her culinary talent, or that most of them will be on diets. Maybe this elaborate casino-themed cake is a huge waste of school funds, but I'd rather deal with half-eaten cake than cancel on Perla.

"The red velvet is my favorite," Perla says, her grin skyrocketing toward her eyes and nearly forcing them shut. "But you must try the others."

I spear the next option, a fluffy vanilla number. The shot of sugar relaxes me, and I snuggle back into the armchair, my eyes glossing over the remaining samples. It's cozy inside this place. The walls of the cake shop are painted royal blue, and the ceiling is wallpapered in an elaborate navy-and-white print. It's like being inside a tiny jewel box.

"This one's divine, too," I murmur about the vanilla. It's intimate, eating Perla's work in front of her, and I avert my eyes. I'm about to try the dulce de leche sample when my phone rings. I dig inside my bag, retrieving the phone to see my eighteen-year-old's name flash across the screen.

"Hey, Mom," he says when I answer.

Cole was a honeymoon baby, the kind I'd only heard about in books and movies. I was entirely unprepared for what it would feel like when they passed him into my arms—the shock of all that love at once. My own mother never mentioned anything about it, which I suppose could mean either she didn't feel that way about me, or maybe she just didn't have the words to describe it. Or maybe my father was too distracting at my birth—his presence was enormous and all-consuming, and there was a chance my mom was too preoccupied to focus on her own emotions.

"Can Margaret come here tonight?" Cole asks on the other end of the line. "It'll be late. She's babysitting Daisy."

"Cole . . . ," I start, debating how to answer.

"Mom, please," he says. "She's fighting with her parents."

"Did she *ask* her parents?" I can already feel myself about to say yes.

"Hm-hmmm," Cole says, but he sounds noncommittal, like he doesn't really know. "Well, I think so," he adds. He's truthful with me, as far as I can tell. I'm sure there are things he's keeping from me, but at least he seems like he's being honest about what he chooses to tell me. I adore his girlfriend, Margaret, and he's good about staying in his room and letting her sleep downstairs in the guest bedroom. Of course, they could be having sex all over the house without me knowing, but I don't think so.

"All right," I say. "But what's going on with Margaret and her parents?"

"Can we talk about it later?" Cole asks.

I look up and see Perla staring impatiently at me. When did I become a person who talks on the phone while being helped? I used to pay so much attention to my social graces, but the more I think about leaving Evan, the less I seem to care about niceties.

"Sure, sweetie," I say into my phone, giving Perla a conciliatory smile. "We can talk about it later."

# THREE

*Sloane*

There's a waist-high stone wall separating our property from the new neighbors. So even though we're close enough that I could throw a rock and hit their car, I have to lead Daisy back along the front of our house, down our long gravel driveway, and onto the street. It's late March and only fifty-five degrees, but still sweat pricks my skin as we trek up Beckett's Hill and navigate the dips and curves in the dirt. Sycamore Glen is the kind of place where dirt roads are worshipped, and woodlands and gorges live beside the natural expanse of wild properties. We're only an hour north of New York City, and it's so very bucolic, and those two things felt like enough when we first moved here from Brooklyn. I still fantasize about moving back to New York City, or even back to LA, where I grew up and where my parents still live. But now that Dave and I are divorced, I don't think I could convince him to make that move, and I can't exactly whisk our daughter off to somewhere else. Not only because Dave's a great dad and it wouldn't be fair to him or good for Daisy, but also because I need his help with Daisy, both emotionally and financially. I do freelance editing work while Daisy's at school, but the money I make pales in comparison to what Dave makes as a derivatives trader. Usually we put my earnings directly into Daisy's college fund and use his earnings to pay the mortgage and Daisy's medical bills and every other expensive aspect of life with a child.

Ahead of us on the hill, a black mailbox marked 117 shines in the late afternoon sun. Daisy and I navigate the hill silently, both of us studying the leaf-patterned shadows dappling the dirt. The incline is steep enough to make my breath come faster, so I slow us down. I glance over and check Daisy like I always do, and she's breathing a little harder than usual, so I say, "Let's stop and catch our breath. I need it, too, baby."

Daisy has primary pulmonary hypertension. We first saw symptoms when she was five and we put her into soccer and she didn't have the endurance to run like the rest of the kids. She was always out of breath, her lips turning slightly blue, and within two months she had a diagnosis. Pulmonary hypertension is progressive, with changes in the lungs that strain the heart and often result in heart failure. Science hasn't figured out how to reverse the changes, but there are medicines and therapies her doctors use to help with symptoms, though Daisy still can't participate in gym or sports or many of the high-octane activities this town thrives on. In moments like this one, you can see the strain of a simple walk uphill all over her, and a moment later we have to stop to sit on a shady patch of grass. We stare into each other's eyes, and I model how she's supposed to recover in these moments, breathing deeply and purposefully, so she'll emulate me. I try to force myself to live in the present moment, when I'm with Daisy and we're okay. My mom always reminds me that the present moment with Daisy is full of sweetness, and she's not wrong. But we live with this every day, and while I've learned to carry it, it's hard to stay in a moment when my mind wants to circle ahead to everything that could go wrong.

I know that motherhood can be lonely and filled with worries even for mothers of typically developing children, and that even moms of healthy kids can panic over their children's present or future. So many mothers I know feel this way even without their child having a known medical condition. Which should probably make me feel less alone, but *alone* is often how I've felt since becoming a mother and living here.

I hold Daisy's hand, and she squeezes mine three times, our signal for *I. Love. You.* I squeeze hers right back.

Dave's always telling me I have plenty of friends here, but the truth is none of them feel particularly close. I joined a working moms group when I had Daisy, but my freelance work has always made me feel like more of a stay-at-home, because before Daisy went to school I was lucky enough to do work while she napped, and now I do it while she's in school. So, then I just felt like an imposter in the working moms group because I wasn't dealing with the same stressors, and eventually left it, but didn't really feel like I should join the stay-at-home moms group because I worked. There are some moms I casually text and keep in touch with, mostly Daisy's friends' moms, and they can be particularly wonderful when Daisy's hospitalized. But I don't think we'd be friends if it weren't for Daisy, and there's a loneliness to that, knowing that you wouldn't choose each other if you weren't parents cohabitating a child-centered orbit.

"I'm ready," Daisy says finally, and she looks okay as we stand together. Twenty yards ahead, the back of the new neighbors' Range Rover is in sight, and *California* is scrawled across the top of the license plate in red cursive. We walk very slowly, and the dark-haired man sees us first. He lifts a hand to shade his eyes even though he's wearing aviators. My chest squeezes a little as I take in his face and see he's quite beautiful, his jaw straight and strong, his clear olive skin marked with a sweep of dark stubble. His broad shoulders push out beneath a hunter-green quilted jacket, and his low-slung vintage Levi's are a dead giveaway that he's not from here—I don't think I've ever seen a Sycamore Glen dad inhabiting a pair of jeans in a way that implies long-term ownership. Even with the wild properties, it's more of a suit-or-khakis kind of place.

The woman turns. She's equally beautiful, somewhere in her early thirties with dark curls, pale white skin, and high cheekbones. They both smile at Daisy and me in a synchronous way, like they've coordinated how big their grins should be. It's funny how couples resemble each other the longer they're together.

"Hi!" I say when we're close enough to shake hands. Their driveway is so steep that even from a few feet away, they seem much taller. My voice is high pitched when I say, "We don't want to get in your hair while you're moving in. We just wanted to say a quick hello."

I try to smile as the two of them stare back at me, but I feel a little off balance. I used to work as a playwright, and the few times I took trips to LA to see my work put on or to have a meeting, I'd get this shrinking feeling when I saw a famous actor walking the streets or ordering a coffee in a Starbucks. I have that feeling now.

"Hello," the woman says in a gentle purr, smiling. "I'm Harper, and this is Ben."

I shake her hand, taking in the delicate curve of her catlike eyes the color of evergreens, and the way they slope upward at the corners, a combination of nature and the dark brown eyeliner perfectly smudged at her lash line.

Ben doesn't extend his hand. "Ben Wilson."

*Dr. Wilson.*

"And you are . . . ," he says.

"Oh! Right. I'm Sloane, and this is my daughter, Daisy."

Daisy smiles, and I find myself even more grateful than usual to have her by my side. She points to our house and says, "We live right there."

"What a lovely home," Harper says. A smattering of freckles adorns her cheeks, and she tucks an espresso-colored curl behind her ear, exposing a delicate gold moon earring. Her slim wrists are covered in rose-gold bangles and a tattered friendship bracelet that looks like it was made by a child. "How old are you?" she asks Daisy.

"Seven and a half," Daisy says proudly.

"Do you have any children?" I blurt. As soon as the words escape my mouth, I want to kick myself. Dave and I tried for years to have a baby before Daisy, and every time someone asked when we were planning to start a family, it felt like a knife in the gut. I vowed to never ask anyone where they were in their reproductive life, but I guess time dulls heartache, and now here I am doing it.

Harper only smiles. "We don't," she says pleasantly, gazing upon Daisy, sunshine on her face. I let go of a breath, relieved that she doesn't seem bothered by my question. I turn to look at Ben, who's also gazing sweetly at Daisy. Daisy has a way of engendering attention from adults, even before they learn how sick she is. Her eyes are the iciest blue, clear like pool water, and she holds eye contact with adults longer than most children; she's always been preternaturally interested in them. Even when she was a toddler, she had an ear cocked during adult conversation instead of focusing entirely on the neon-colored toys we scattered in front of her on a playmat.

Ben smiles, exposing a line of very straight teeth, and I wait for one of us to say something. It feels like my turn, but I can't really come up with anything. When I used to write plays, often I'd try to write a line of dialogue that was entirely unexpected, but the truth is that during most interactions, the other person says something you could've seen coming a mile away.

"I'm from California, too," I finally say, gesturing to the Range Rover's plates. "Where'd you move from?"

"San Francisco," says Ben. And then he adds, "We moved for work," as though there's no other reason anyone would leave San Francisco for Sycamore Glen. Maybe he's right.

"Ben is the new head of surgery at Phillips Memorial," Harper says.

She gazes at him with a charmed look on her face, and I force a smile. Phillips is one of the top children's hospitals in the country and only twenty minutes south of Sycamore Glen. It's where Daisy and I go for all her appointments. "It's such a wonderful hospital," I say. We stare at each other, and my stomach sinks a little thinking of what the real estate agent said about how lucky we were to have a surgeon for a neighbor. Images flash through my mind: Daisy's frequent appointments, echocardiograms, catheterization procedures to track pulmonary artery pressures, all the testing done to her little body and the endless *waiting*—waiting on hold for the next available person to help me, waiting outside in the waiting room for one of Daisy's procedures, waiting for her results.

*Dread.*

That's the feeling I get when my brain goes down this route.

"I go to Phillips all the time to see Dr. Bhatt," Daisy says. Her hand is sweating against mine, but I don't want to let it go. I never do. And normally I'd tighten up at the prospect of getting into a conversation about Daisy's medical issues, but I feel okay as Daisy starts talking. "I have primary pulmonary hypertension," she says, and Ben lifts an eyebrow. It's hard to worry a doctor, I've learned, but we've managed to do it quite often.

"Would you believe I've already been on a Zoom with Dr. Bhatt," Ben says, "and I can tell she's an awesome doctor."

I shift my weight, vaguely uncomfortable thinking about Ben talking with Daisy's doctor, and wondering if they talked about Daisy. Phillips has plenty of medically complex cases, but Daisy's might stand out enough to warrant a conversation—or maybe I just think that because I'm her mom and she's my world. Still, it's weird thinking of Ben already knowing about us.

Daisy beams—she loves Dr. Bhatt. "Oh, she *is*," she tells Ben. "She's *the best*. And her office has stamps instead of stickers. All kinds of stamps. She collects them. And she always keeps the ink pads fresh instead of all dried out."

Ben's smile is so genuine that I realize the one he gave me earlier when we first met was fake. This smile makes a dimple appear in his cheek just above his stubble.

"And you?" Ben asks me. "What kind of work do you do?"

"Oh," I stall. No one's asked me in a while. "I used to be a playwright. But now I freelance edit. Novels and plays sometimes, but mostly articles."

Harper frowns. "I don't think a playwright is the kind of thing you stop being," she says, and I'd bet she's an artist, because what she's just said is the kind of thing that another artist knows to be true. It's what I know to be true, too, and I should really stop talking about my work in the past tense.

"What was your most recent play?" she asks.

"*The Night Whisperer*," I say, the familiar feel of the words making me smile. I've always loved words: their edges, curves, and cadences, even when I was young like Daisy. And I've always liked the feel of saying that title out loud. "It was in 2019. Daisy was still a baby. I wrote it while I was pregnant with her, and it was put on at Playwrights Horizons in New York."

Harper whistles. "I know that theater. It's legit."

"It is," I say, owning it. "But I haven't had anything put on in years. What about you? You're an artist of some kind. Am I right?"

I can feel Ben glance back and forth between the two of us.

Daisy rises onto her tiptoes. "Are you?" she asks Harper, still holding tight to my fingers. "Is my mom right?"

Harper claps her hands like we've won a prize. "I'm a visual artist. Mostly a cartoonist these days."

"No *way*," Daisy says. "Like *Miraculous* on TV?"

Harper shakes her head. "I don't do any television cartoons, but I love those kinds of cartoonists. They're so talented. I do political cartoons sometimes, but mostly I do large-scale art pieces. You have to come over when they do the art install at the house, but I don't think that'll be until next week."

Ben looks back at the driver of the moving van, who's still on the phone, gesturing furiously. "I better go see what the holdup is," he says.

"We'll leave you to it," I say with a wave of my hand. "But let us know if you need anything today."

"Or any day," Daisy says, which makes Harper laugh.

"It was so nice meeting you," Harper says sweetly.

"Same," I say. I linger, which is odd because usually I'm eager to get out of a conversation—I've often felt that way ever since Daisy got sick. I make myself turn away from Ben and Harper and walk slowly away with Daisy's hand tight in mine. As I descend the driveway, I feel colder, like the temperature has suddenly plummeted.

"They seem nice," Daisy says in a whisper, even though we're well out of their earshot.

I nod. She's right. "They do," I say.

# FOUR

*Clara*

Back at home I'm fluffing pillows and humming along to an angsty pop song my daughters like. I love our bedroom now that Evan doesn't sleep here. It's pristine and zen, and I'm not only talking about the décor; it's like the entire vibe has changed now that Evan snores down the hall in our guest bedroom. He hasn't approached me for sex in nearly a year, and as relieved as that makes me, it also leaves me feeling like a wife prop for display purposes only.

Cole's in his senior year at Sycamore Glen High School, and my twin daughters, Arden and Camille, are juniors. They're all old enough to notice Evan and I aren't sleeping in the same room, but Camille, my most sensitive child, is the only one who verbalized anything. Last month, she asked me if everything was okay between her dad and me, and when I said yes, she asked, "Then why's he sleeping somewhere else?" I ruffled her dark blond hair and said something about how I couldn't fall back asleep after his four thirty a.m. alarm clock went off and needed my sleep now that she and her siblings stayed up until midnight. Which is true, but not the real reason. Camille nodded like she understood, but I could tell she didn't buy it. There are lies I've had to tell Cole, Arden, and

Camille to keep all of us intact—to keep them from knowing what their father's been up to when he's not here at home pretending to be the world's best family man.

I set a pillow down too roughly on the bed. And then I pick up my phone and call Sloane Thompson.

# FIVE

*Sloane*

I'm in the kitchen when Clara Gartner calls.

"Hi," I say gingerly, like I'm bruised and only half-ready for whatever she's about to spring on me.

"*Sloane*," Clara says, smooth as a phone operator. "Thanks so much for taking my call." She's always so proper.

"It's nice to hear from you," I say. Maybe we're all proper now; maybe it's just what happens to women in the suburbs.

"I'm calling about the fundraiser for the elementary school," she says, and I let go of a silent breath. Of course, that's why she's calling. Clara Gartner is always and forever calling about a fundraiser. This one is our annual fundraiser, each year with a different theme, and it's happening on Saturday.

"You're a saint, Clara. Your children don't even go to the elementary school anymore."

But as soon as it's out of my mouth, I regret it. It was passive-aggressive, stinking of an accusation: *Don't you have anything better to do than plan fundraisers for a school your children don't even go to?*

"Sorry," I add quickly. "I'm sure if you didn't do it, no one would."

"Something like that," Clara says coolly. And now the tone of the conversation has changed. My doing.

"Would you be able to volunteer at the photo booth from seven to eight on Saturday?" Clara asks. "It's the first hour, but we need someone to load film into the machine and organize the props and costumes."

Tension rises inside my chest. I've already said yes to volunteering at the school's spelling bee tonight. Isn't that enough? And I haven't even bought tickets to the annual fundraiser—I planned to buy them at the door if the stars aligned and Daisy felt well enough that both Dave and I could go. We still go to things like this together—it took people a while to realize we weren't going to fight in public or have an acrimonious divorce. But the tickets are two hundred dollars each, and even though it's a fundraiser for Daisy's school, sometimes Dave and I don't buy two tickets to events like these, because if Daisy's a little off, one of us prefers to stay home. And even if Daisy *is* feeling perfectly well, there's only one sitter in town we trust, a high school senior named Margaret Collins, who's preternaturally gifted at knowing when Daisy's okay, and when she needs to call us to come home; there's a very fine balance between those states, and she's never gotten it wrong. There are certain things a layperson can check for with pulmonary hypertension, like respiratory rate, pulse rate, and blood-oxygen saturation, and we're still at the stage of the disease where many of Daisy's symptoms, like fatigue, shortness of breath, and dizziness, can still be solved by Daisy sitting and resting. We could get a nurse to come, but we tried that once, and you could tell it made Daisy feel bad—like a sick kid who couldn't have a regular babysitter. And Daisy loves Margaret. She puts on her favorite outfit and earrings every time Margaret comes.

I won't express any of this to Clara. Instead, I'll go online after this conversation and purchase two tickets like the sucker I am.

"Sure!" I say, and it shocks me how convincing I've made my voice sound. I was an acting major in college before I switched to writing, and it always amazes me how often women are given the opportunity to act; I sound like I *want* to man the photo booth. "What time should I arrive?"

# SIX

## *Clara*

I hang up with Sloane and settle into a white wicker chair on our screened-in porch. On the back lawn, daffodils gather in little choirs across the grass. I wonder how Sloane would have reacted if I'd told her that the real reason I still run the elementary school fundraiser is because the years my children were in school at Sycamore Glen Elementary were the happiest in my life. I'd give anything to go back in time.

I look through the screens to see our birdbath, where two sparrows dance along the edge on twiglike legs. Sometimes I don't know how I got here; one moment we were all fine, and then the next everything was dire. Why hadn't I read my marriage correctly? Was Evan truly such a professional liar that he hid all of it? Or was I ignoring the obvious, seeing only what I wanted to?

And what would women like Sloane Thompson think about me if they really knew our situation?

I remember when I first dropped the girls off at elementary school. Cole was in first grade, and with Arden and Camille finally in kindergarten I'd felt elated and free and *happy*, knowing that they were happy, and that I'd done a good job raising them during their adorable and hellish toddler years. The kids were, by the grace of God, *okay*—all three of them—and I was gifted the privilege of time alone in my house with my own thoughts from nine in the morning until three, when I picked them up. Marlow Patel, who'd been my closest friend during the baby and toddler years, sent her youngest daughter to kindergarten at the same time I sent my twins, and we couldn't believe our good fortune and newly found hours in the day. Marlow worked part time as a therapist, but we'd often meet for coffee in the mornings at a brick-walled café in town, and then she'd go to work, and I'd volunteer at the school or at the local food pantry, where I was on the board. Marlow and I became co-class parents at Sycamore Glen Elementary and then co-PTA presidents, and as boring and cliché as that might sound to some people, I loved every second of it. I wasn't sure I could even ask for any more than what I had: time for myself during the day, often spent volunteering with friends; time with my children when they came home from school; and then time with my husband in the evenings. After growing up in a house with unhappy parents, a happy family was all I'd ever wanted. And I thought I had it.

I had no idea I was living in a house of mirrors about to come crashing down. And I remained blissfully unaware right up until three years ago when the twins were in junior high and Cole had started high school, and I walked into Cole's bedroom on the night of our annual Christmas party and found Evan fucking Marlow.

The memory singes me as I think about it, sharp and scalding, still making me flinch and curl my knees to my chest out here on a sunny porch that looks like Serena and Lily themselves came to decorate. It almost makes me laugh when I think about it too hard, what a joke the façade of our life is: a preppy backdrop covering gasp-worthy betrayal. I remember exactly how it looked to see the backside of Evan, naked from the waist down, the blue oxford shirt I'd bought him still somehow perfectly pressed. I'd stood there in the doorway to Cole's room, frozen, without Evan knowing I was there. I stood there a breath, maybe two, long enough to be sure of what he was doing, even though I couldn't see the woman on the receiving end of his athletic thrusts. Blood drained from my body and I felt cold, like I was in shock. I opened my mouth to scream or say anything at all, but the muscles that had always worked to produce speech seemed to have gone slack, and I stood there, unable to make a single sound. I'd already drunk at least three glasses of wine that night—the kids were at my mom and dad's house and being able to let loose had felt wildly decadent—and the alcohol made everything seem even more jumbled. My eyes blurred over Cole's wallpaper, and when my gaze refocused, I saw a pair of women's shoes in the blankets tossed onto the floor at the end of the bed. They were green velvet heels with a tie on the ankle; I would have recognized them anywhere. Bile rose in my throat, and as sick as this sounds, my eyes traveled to the woman's feet. I saw the dark red pedicure Marlow had gotten with me only a few days before, a color she never usually went with but picked because it was the holidays.

I pulled the door soundlessly closed. Out in the hall I felt on the verge of collapse, leaning against the wall, unable to feel my legs. But then something else took over—a feeling so visceral it reminded me of how I felt when my children were babies: when I'd first understood the true meaning of *need*. All at once, the thing I wanted most (besides my husband not to be fucking another woman) was for my husband not to know that I knew. It felt implicit and necessary, even if I couldn't completely understand it yet. I made myself put one foot in front of the other as I crept down the hall toward the stairs, a tidal wave of urgency and fear swelling behind me, propelling me forward, threatening to drown me. I gripped the banister for support, the decline of the steps suddenly too steep. One step at a time I went, cursing the heels I was wearing, sure I'd topple.

But I didn't fall. And by the time I made it to the bottom of the staircase, I was almost breathing normally again. My house hummed with cheerful, tipsy conversations and mingling warm bodies, and I slid into a throng of partygoers and let myself be swallowed whole. For hours I felt like I was outside my own body. I couldn't let anyone see me cry, so I didn't, not until much later after the party was over and I'd gathered my children from my mother's house and tucked them back into their beds. All alone in my bedroom—God only knows where Evan was—I lay down in my bed and cried until I couldn't.

My husband had cheated on me . . . *A one-time thing? A fling? A full-blown yearlong affair?* I guessed that it was the former because of the nature of it, catching them at a party and not in an emotional exchange over text or some similar clue pointing in the direction of something longer term.

Marlow was—*is*—very beautiful on the inside and out; I'd always thought so. Tall, with smooth brown skin and flowing dark brown hair, a big laugh, and an even bigger brain. But I'd never seen Evan pay her any extra attention, nor had I seen Marlow cast even a wayward glance in Evan's direction. Her husband had died years before from cancer. I'd helped her through the grief, and even when he was alive we didn't often socialize together as couples because our husbands didn't like each other. Something nebulous had gone down between them—Evan accused Marlow's husband of cheating on the golf course, and Marlow's husband said Evan had gotten up in his face while accusing him and crossed a line. When I asked Evan about this, he told me that anyone's integrity on the golf course is a metaphor for their integrity in real life. (Too ironic, right?) It scared me when they fell out, because Evan has a nasty habit of trying to take down people he thinks have betrayed him, friends and former coworkers alike. When his COO announced she was leaving, Evan sent a laundry list of complaints about her to her new employer, along with private, incriminating emails she'd sent from her work address. After Evan fought with his brother, he reported him to the IRS on baseless claims that caused his brother no financial repercussions but huge amounts of emotional distress, and they haven't spoken since. But Evan left Marlow's husband alone, thank God.

As far as I knew, Marlow hadn't dated since her husband passed away; she often said she wasn't ready. But there must have been feelings that ran between Evan and Marlow, because neither of them was drunk that night. Evan always stayed in control, and Marlow almost never had more than a glass or two. Of the three of us, *I* was the one who sometimes had too much at a party. I'd go six months without drinking and lose my tolerance and then have three glasses of wine and be just a little too drunk, and Evan would usher me out of the party with an eye roll.

So, if Marlow and Evan couldn't blame it on alcohol, did that mean there'd been something between them, and they'd finally acted on it? It was torture imagining this. And I waited for weeks for either to confess; I knew I'd feel better if at least one of them was honest with me. But neither came forward. And even worse: After that night at the party, Marlow dramatically pulled away from me, as though I'd been the one to do something wrong. The only thing I could figure was that the guilt must have been suffocating for her, and maybe she couldn't face me. Marlow wasn't perfect, but she was *good*. The kind of person who cared about everyone else nearly to her detriment. There was no way she could have done what she did and not have felt tremendous amounts of regret.

Evan acted as though nothing had happened; he was neither kinder to me nor more distant and ashamed. I couldn't discern a single thing different about his behavior, which should have been my first clue that this wasn't his inaugural affair.

For weeks, Marlow screened my calls and averted her eyes from mine when we crossed paths in town, until I finally cornered her at school after a PTA meeting and asked her what was going on, and instead of telling me what she'd done, she lied and told me she was going through a hard time and needed space. And maybe that wasn't a lie—maybe she was floundering after what she'd done with Evan. Maybe she was in such a desperate place that I came in a far second to the well-being of her nuclear family. I could understand that. I loved her, after all, and no matter how angry I was, I knew what despair felt like. After my sister died, despair was a beast inside my brain that made it nearly impossible to do anything else, let alone the right thing.

During those weeks after I saw them together, I studied Marlow more closely than ever, narrowing in on the way she acted when Evan and I ran into her at school events: first at an orchestra concert, and then at the annual spelling bee. I told no one, because who was I to ruin Marlow's reputation and the sanctity of her family? I loved Marlow's children, and I would have done anything to keep her children and mine from finding out what Marlow and Evan had done. I tried twice more to get Marlow alone—once asking her to come over so we could talk, and when she wouldn't, I asked her if we could meet for coffee at a neutral location, thinking maybe then she wouldn't be freaked out about having to run into Evan at my house. But she refused. It was clear our friendship was over without me even accusing her of anything. And now, three years later, I wish that I'd been braver, that I'd confronted her even if it meant blurting it out in a public place and waiting for her to apologize and beg my forgiveness.

I stupidly thought Evan and I could get past it. I thought that we had to—for the kids—and that the many decent years of marriage that had come before were enough reason to give it another try. So, weeks after the party, in our kitchen after the kids had gone to bed, I said to Evan, "I know what happened with Marlow." My hands shook against a cup of tea, and the air between us smelled like lavender. "I saw you together, Evan."

Evan set down the dish he'd been drying. "Oh?" he said.

It was the oddest reply. But maybe he'd intended to throw me off, because in the silence that followed his *oh*, I started babbling: "At the Christmas party. I saw you in Cole's bed, which is completely disgusting. I saw you fucking Marlow." I froze after I said it, hardly recognizing my own voice, and realizing I'd ruined any chance of trying to figure out whether there'd been other times.

Evan folded the dish towel into a perfect rectangle. He set it down on the counter and turned to face me. "I'm sorry," he said, his voice low and gravelly, sounding like he meant it. Which took me by surprise, because Evan wasn't the kind of person who apologized easily. "It was a mistake."

"A mistake? Yes, it was certainly *a mistake*," I said, and then I started crying, which was exactly what I didn't want to do. Evan closed the space between us and put his arms around me. I could feel his hands, still damp from washing the dishes, smelling like the sickly-sweet lemon dish detergent I haven't bought since.

"I'm so sorry I hurt you, Clara," he said. "Have you talked to Marlow? Is this why she hasn't been over? I've been wondering."

"You've been *wondering*?" I repeated, pulling out of his embrace. What an odd turn of phrase for the moment. And I was surprised Evan had even noticed that Marlow had been avoiding us; he usually ignored my female friends. Though I guess it made sense for him to finally start paying attention if he'd fucked one of them.

"Yes," I said. "I imagine *this* is why Marlow hasn't been over, Evan. Jesus."

He shook his head slowly. "Did Marlow tell you what happened? That she'd been pursuing me?" A red tinge flushed the skin at his hairline. He still had a full blond head of hair, the kind you see on a twenty-year-old, so thick it grows straight up and has to be combed down. I wanted to yank it out.

"*Pursuing you?*" I repeated. "What are you talking about?"

"It was subtle," he said. "But she was, Clara, I swear. I'm telling you the truth."

I swallowed over a hard lump of fear. "And you obviously felt the same."

"No, I didn't. And I *don't*. It was a stupid, weak mistake, and I swear to God, I'll never do it again." He blinked, and for a second I thought he was going to cry. But Evan never cried, and he certainly didn't that night. "Please forgive me, Clara," he said. "I don't know what I'd do without you."

I believed him. We went on, trying therapy, trying harder. The pain dulled until the saddest thing about the whole incident became losing Marlow. I could have survived the affair. Truly. But losing my best friend, the only person who'd ever been like a sister to me other than my real sister? That was deadly.

# SEVEN

## *Sloane*

I slice through juicy red flesh and pop a quarter of a tomato in my mouth. Daisy's blond head is bent over her homework at our long wooden farm table. Her papers are scattered everywhere, and an assortment of Hello Kitty pencils fan out before her. Early evening light bathes the white soapstone island, and I find myself feeling peaceful and hopeful. Spring always does this to me. There's so much to wish for.

Daisy's tiny fingers grip her pencil, scrawling her name across the next sheet of homework, but then she looks up. "Do you think I can call our new neighbor by her first name? Or do I need to call her *Mrs. Wilson?*" she asks. She holds the pencil in midair as she waits for me to answer.

"We can ask her," I say. "But I have a feeling she might be a first-name person."

Daisy smiles. "*Harper*," she says, trying it out. "I like that name." And then we hear a knock, three quick raps, like usual, making me sure it's Dave.

Our kitchen opens into the foyer, and I cross the space quickly, remembering the first time Dave knocked on his own front door years ago. We'd only been separated a few weeks then, and one morning he'd knocked instead of letting himself in. That knock had struck me as one of the saddest sounds I'd ever heard.

"Hey," I say now as I open the front door. Dave steps inside and asks, "What's up?" like someone much younger than thirty-seven. I used to think all the ways he was boyish were adorable and endearing, and maybe to a lot of people, they still are. People truly *like* Dave—he's bookish and affable, and when we were in our twenties and living in New York, he was often saying something darkly funny and a little bizarre. Now, the things Dave says are more socially appropriate; his edges have softened in the suburbs and since becoming a dad. I'm sure mine have, too, loath as I am to admit it.

"Heya, babe," he says, leaning forward to give me a hug. I fan out my arms, not hugging him back. "Sorry!" I say. "My hands are wet."

He squeezes me anyway, and I let him, standing inside his embrace with my arms sticking out like a stiff doll. I relax a little in his arms. I'm not in love with him anymore, but there's still love and affection. "Daisy here?" he asks into my hair, and then pulls away.

Daisy is almost always here—we don't do a lot of playdates—which makes me wonder if Dave has something private he needs to talk with me about.

"She's in the kitchen," I say, scanning his face. Crow's feet etch the outside of his brown eyes, but he doesn't seem worried about anything.

"She finish the science project?" he asks, wriggling out of his coat and then tossing it over the banister like a decoration. We have a coat closet, but Dave is, by nature, super messy, so even resting the coat on the banister is a step up from what he might have done.

"You can ask her yourself," I say, turning on my heel and walking over the wide wooden planks. In the kitchen, Dave exclaims, "Baby girl!" with a hint of a New York accent to his words. He grew up on Long Island, and his brothers and their wives still live there. Whenever they're all together, his accent is at its strongest. It used to bother me how hard he worked to drop it in New York City and now especially in Sycamore Glen. What for?

"Daddy!" Daisy cries, getting up from the table and throwing her arms around his waist.

"How was school?" Dave asks as I round the island and pick up a knife.

Daisy doesn't answer him. She just smiles inside his hug.

"We have the science thing next week," Dave says, gently patting her back. She's in a tank top—she's getting too warm lately, which might be the new vasodilator medication she's on. "You and Mom get the poster board?"

"Yup," Daisy says. "And we got bath salts."

"That's a good day at Target right there, am I right, babe?"

"Yeah," Daisy says, smiling.

"You guys want to hear something?" Dave asks, retrieving his phone from his pocket. "A new group out of Iceland." He presses a button, and a clash of instruments fills the air, something with a Radiohead vibe.

"Hmmm . . . ," I say, nodding like I like it. It's not that I don't like the actual music; I just don't like music on in the house while we're doing other stuff, because it always makes me feel like I'm on sensory overload, like the walls themselves are pulsing. I'm very aware that makes me sound unfun.

I throw the tomatoes into the salad and head to the fridge for a lemon.

"I like it!" Daisy shouts over the music. She's standing on the bench that lines our table, giving her hips a shake to the beat of the music, and I watch her, worried she'll fall. But she's seven, and if I say that, she's going to feel like a baby. I'm trying to be extra careful to treat her how she wants to be treated, which is like a big girl, instead of how she appears to me, which is like a small child who has a very serious medical condition. I bite my tongue and wish Dave would tell her to be careful, but he won't. Not only because he isn't overly cautious, but also because he's staring down at his phone, immersed in the music, not seeming to notice that Daisy is now on her tiptoes.

"Daisy," I say too softly, not wanting to startle her. She can't hear me over the music.

*Thump thump* goes a bass drum, followed by a guitar riff.

"Dave, can you turn that down?"

He looks up at me like I've pulled him out of a coma. "What?" he asks, disoriented, like within moments of putting on the music he's so absorbed in it he can't be a person in a kitchen.

"Turn it down!"

I've yelled so loudly that Daisy looks up and nearly loses her balance.

"Catch her!" I scream, making it worse.

Daisy rights herself before needing Dave's help. Dave looks befuddled, and then supremely annoyed. He punches a button on his phone and shuts it down.

And now the kitchen is deadly silent.

I grip the lemon like a baseball and head to the sink, my face hot. "Are you okay?" Dave asks. The question makes me want to cry.

"I'm fine," I say. I can't look up. I'm too embarrassed to even try to explain the overwhelmed feeling I get when commotion descends along with the ever-present fear that Daisy will get hurt or worse. I can feel Daisy looking at Dave and then me. I open my mouth to say I'm sorry when the doorbell rings, and all three of us look at each other. "I'll get it," Dave says, a little too valiantly. He disappears into the foyer.

"Mama," Daisy says softly. I turn on the tap, cold water rushing over the lemon and my fingers. It feels good. "I love you," she says, and I turn to look into her light eyes. Her delicate bone structure is the prettiest thing: a heart-shaped face with sharp cheekbones. Her skin is olive compared to mine and Dave's even paler skin, genes Dave always tells her are from his dad's mom, who came from Italy. Her lips are ruby red, and her lashes are deep brown, a pretty contrast with her dirty-blond hair. When I look at her, I see her as she appears now, but also as she appeared when she was a baby, a toddler, and a preschooler, like an amalgam of all the years I've known her and loved her. Looking at her is like gazing upon time itself, and there's a sharp contrast between the years pre-Daisy, when I never really understood true love, and the years following, when I understood that true love was, for me at least, laced with a dose of fear and hopefulness that it could last.

"I love you, too," I say. "So much." I turn off the tap and hear a woman's laugh.

Daisy turns toward the door. "Who's that?"

We head out of the kitchen into the foyer and see Harper standing at the door. She's changed from earlier, wearing a crisp white button-down over boyfriend jeans, looking like an ad with her dark curls and sparkling green eyes. Dave's body language has done a 180 from moments before in the kitchen when I asked him to turn off the music. He's leaning on the doorframe like he's at a frat party.

Harper spots us and says, "Sloane, hi! And hello again, Miss Daisy. This is crazy, but our hot water isn't working, and I was wondering if there's any chance I can shower here. Is that too weird?" She laughs, and it's clear she's the kind of person who could probably say anything without it seeming too weird.

"Sure," I say, hoping my bathroom isn't a complete disaster, trying to remember if I picked up my bedroom this morning. I head toward the stairs. "Come on up," I say, and then I pause and turn back to take in Dave, who's now trailing Harper through the foyer like he's going to shower with her. "I see you've met Dave," I say, trying to suppress an eye roll that Harper catches. She stares at me, absorbing the dynamic. I raise my eyebrows, and she sends me a knowing smile that makes me love being a woman with the ability to communicate inside a moment.

"Did Harper tell you her husband is the new head of surgery at Phillips?" I ask Dave.

"Wow," Dave says, running a hand over his chin.

One of the things I love about Dave is how easily impressed he is. Not that being head of surgery isn't impressive, because it is, but even if I had asked, *Did Harper tell you her husband has the largest Slinky collection in Westchester County?* he also would have been wowed. He puts people at ease with the way he's so naturally happy for their accomplishments and good fortune.

"Are you sure this isn't an imposition?" Harper asks sweetly as she clomps up the stairs behind me.

"What else are showers for?" Dave booms, starting up the stairs. Is he seriously coming with us?

Daisy laughs and so does Harper.

"This house is gorgeous," Harper says at the top of the staircase. "It's so lofty."

"Thanks," I say, smiling. The loftiness is one of my favorite things about the house. The ceilings are double height in the living room, giving the house a feeling of spaciousness and light. Soft white walls and pale furniture offset the dark floors, and there are wide windows looking out onto the wild landscape. I wonder again at the interior of Harper's Tudor, and then, as though she can read my thoughts, Harper says, "I love our new house, but it's dark. Lots of deep brown wood and some curtains they left that we'll need to switch out if we want it to be a little brighter. Once we get everything set up, we'd love to have you all over."

"We'd love that," Dave says, and when he joins us at the top of the stairs, he pauses to take in the house, maybe to see what Harper sees. Dave loves this house, even if he doesn't get to live here, and I feel a moment of true tenderness for him. He never suggested that we sell it and downsize after the divorce. The luxury of his job, obviously, but still; other men might have done it out of spite. That said, there's a chance we'll have to move at some point to a house without stairs for Daisy. Just this year I've noticed Daisy having a harder time with inclines, which makes me sick to think about. Last week we were at a birthday party, and we avoided the bounce house because there's no way she could do that kind of physical activity, but then I noticed her get out of breath even walking up the hill toward the house for cake.

Dave turns and heads in the opposite direction of the master bathroom, opening a linen closet and retrieving fluffy white towels. "Here ya go," he says to Daisy, passing them into her arms. "Can you give these to Mrs. . . ."

"Wilson," Harper says. And then to Daisy she says, "But I prefer to be called Harper."

Daisy gives me a secret grin that says, *We were right.* I've never felt so included and a part of something as I have since Daisy was born. Everyone says not to make your child your best friend, but *best friend* couldn't even begin to cover what this is—it's so much better.

Dave heads back down the stairs. At least he has the good sense not to follow us into the bathroom.

Daisy, Harper, and I wind through my bedroom and into the bathroom. On the white marble countertops, there's an assortment of nail polishes and creams I should have put away, but nothing too crazy.

"I think you're going to like living up here," I say as I pull a washcloth from the linen basket by the tub.

Harper gazes out the bathroom window toward the woods. "Us and the wild animals," she says, her face darkening.

Both Daisy and Harper look at me like they're waiting for me to say something reassuring. But there isn't much reassuring to tell Harper, because what she's said is true. It's wild up here. "I guess," I say, trying to shrug in a way that seems casual, like there isn't anything to be too worried about.

"Someone said there was a bear?" Harper asks timidly.

I pass her the washcloth. "Well, yes. But not a grizzly or anything. Just a small black bear who comes around sometimes, mostly messing with the trash and looking for food."

"You've seen him?" she asks.

"Twice," Daisy says.

"But we've lived here since before we had Daisy," I say quickly. "Eight years or so, and it's only been those two times."

Harper is tiny, and her fear makes her appear even smaller. "We had flying squirrels in the attic," she says. "When we first saw the house, we could hear them. Ben swears the other real estate agent was trying to talk extra loudly so we wouldn't hear them right above our heads, but *we did.*"

Daisy puts a small hand over her mouth, hiding her glee. She loves being inside an adult conversation that has turned into a scandalous examination of another adult's behavior. I love this idiosyncrasy about her; she's so kind she'll never bad-mouth another child, but she's fascinated by adult gossip.

Harper thanks me again for the shower, and then starts unbuttoning the top of her oxford. I feel myself get a little flustered. Is she going to undress right here in front of us?

"Let's give Harper some privacy," I say loudly to Daisy. Harper stops unbuttoning her shirt. She stares at me like she's misread me.

When did I become such a prude?

I put a hand between Daisy's slender shoulder blades and steer her out of the bathroom, shutting the door behind us. And then I hear Dave calling, "Sloane! Sloane?" up the stairs like someone died. Through the closed door, I hear the *whoosh* of Harper turning on the water.

Daisy and I hit the top of the stairs and see what's got him unnerved: Margaret, our eighteen-year-old babysitter, is standing in the foyer with a satchel at her hip, her toned arms crossed over her chest. Dave has no idea how to talk to teenage girls. He acts like this every time Margaret shows up. I didn't know Dave as a teenage boy, but it wouldn't surprise me if he never figured out how to talk to girls then, and still can't really do it now. By the time I met Dave in college, he was quirky, entirely his own person, and beloved by everyone in our theater and film studies program (he double-majored in math and film, and that meant he was basically on call to help film students with their math homework, which he relished). But sometimes eccentricities translate in college in a way they never could in high school. Dave's only ever introduced me to two high school friends from Long Island, a guy named Stuey, who teaches middle school music, and another guy named Bob, who never married and spends most of his free time at meditation retreats.

"Hi, Margaret!" I say. I check my watch—I need to get dinner rolling, or I'll never be able to leave on time for the school spelling bee, yet another event Clara Gartner tricked me into volunteering for, this time by flattering me with a compliment about my exceptional pronunciation.

"Daisy!" Margaret says. She bounds up three stairs to Daisy, and we all stand in a clump on the middle of the staircase in a way that should be awkward, but isn't, because Margaret is beaming at Daisy with total joy, and then they hug.

"I have news!" Margaret says from inside Daisy's hug.

"Spill," I say.

"I got into Princeton!" Margaret squeals.

I throw my arms around Margaret, Daisy beneath me, both of us squeezing her and making her laugh. "Congratulations!"

"Wow, Margaret. Congrats," Dave says, shoving his hands deep into his pockets.

"Thank you," she says. Her eyes well up. "I'm so relieved."

Margaret's parents are physician-scientists at Phillips. They put a ton of pressure on her, from what I can see, and it doesn't surprise me that relief tops Margaret's list of emotions.

"We should celebrate," I say. "How about Daisy and I take you out to lunch or dinner this week? Somewhere fancy." I feel a little bad leaving Dave out when he's standing right there, but it also doesn't feel like the kind of thing I need to invite him to.

"Thanks," Margaret says. "Could I bring Cole?"

I swallow. Clara's son, Cole. Would I have to call Clara and ask? "Sure," I say. "If it's okay with his parents?"

Margaret waves her hand. "Oh, they won't mind."

We move into the kitchen, peppering Margaret with Princeton questions and going over babysitting instructions for the night. When Harper comes downstairs and joins us, her pretty face is makeup-free, her wet curls long and loose over her shoulders. "Hi," she says brightly to Margaret.

Margaret has none of the stiff social reserve of her parents. She smiles at Harper, seeming genuinely curious about our guest. So am I, frankly.

"This is our new neighbor, Harper," I say. "And, Harper, this is our babysitter, Margaret. She was just accepted to Princeton today."

Harper lets out a low whistle. "Princeton, that's amazing."

Dave says, "We choose babysitters based on SAT scores," and when no one laughs, he looks a little uncertain.

"Your parents must be thrilled," I say to Margaret.

"They were hoping for Harvard," Margaret says, and I can't tell if she's making a joke. "I haven't told them yet, because I got wait-listed at Harvard, and we got in a huge fight last night, not really about the Harvard letter, but probably fueled by it. And anyway they're at work, and I didn't want to just give them the news over text." She gives us a smile that looks forced. "But I think my yes from Princeton will get us out of the fight."

"I feel bad that we're having you babysit on the day of your big acceptance," I say. Daisy goes a little red, and I wish I could snatch back my words.

"Are you kidding?" Margaret asks. And then to Daisy, "This is exactly what I want to be doing today. You know I live for time with my little woman."

I think about how lucky we are to have found Margaret, a needle in a haystack. I can feel Harper studying my face as I watch them.

"I didn't realize you were going out tonight, Sloane," Dave says.

"Spelling bee's tonight," I say. *I've told you like seven times,* I want to add, but I don't.

"Why isn't Daisy doing it?" Dave asks. There's the slightest hint of an accusation in his tone.

"Because she's in second grade, and they don't allow second graders." I'm too tired to sound snarky. It comes out exactly like how I feel: exhausted. Why is it that the school events and volunteer work are the most tiring things of all?

"Mom's the pronouncer," Daisy says proudly. "Because she has a theater degree."

"Ooh-la-la," Harper says.

"My little sister's gonna be there," Margaret says.

I freeze—is she missing her sister in the spelling bee to babysit for us? "Florence is competing?" There's a seven-year age gap between Margaret and her sister, Florence, who's in her last year at the elementary school.

"Yup," Margaret says.

"Oh no," I say. "Will she be upset you're not there? Maybe Dave could stay with Daisy, and you could go?"

Margaret shakes her head vehemently. "Nope. Florence doesn't want us there. She's brilliant, way smarter than me, but she gets nervous, especially when my parents are there. She almost lost it last year because she could see my parents right in the front row staring at her like it was the World Cup. My mother was practically vibrating."

Daisy's watching Margaret, and Margaret seems to sense her gaze, because she turns and gives Daisy a smile. "Florence would be fine with *me* coming," Margaret reassures her. She looks a little sheepish, and younger than she usually does. To me, she says, "But we realized there's no way she could tell just my parents that they weren't allowed, and that I was. So, we decided this was best." She rests her gaze back on Daisy. "And now I get to babysit *you*, Daisy. And we can send Florence good vibes."

"What a thoughtful sister you are," Harper says, studying Margaret carefully.

Margaret smiles. And then to Daisy says, "Next year, when you're in third, we can practice the spelling list. You'll slay."

"You'll be in college then," Daisy says.

Margaret blinks, looking at us like the thought makes her nervous. "Oh, that's right. I guess this hasn't sunk in yet."

We're all quiet for a moment, and something about the silence feels dark and uncertain. I turn away and head to the fridge, opening it to grab chicken, the glass container cold against my fingers.

"Dave, you're welcome to stay for dinner," I tell him. "Harper, same for you."

"Ah, no, it's fine," Harper says. "Ben ordered Italian. We did that little place in town, Lucia's? You like it?"

"Delicious," Dave says.

"Good," Harper says. "I'm not much of a cook, so you'll have to tell me all the good places to order from."

I toss the chicken into the salad and avoid making eye contact with Dave. I know he won't stay alone with Daisy and Margaret, because he'll think it's weird to hang out with Margaret without me there.

I feel him staring at me. "I've actually got to head out," he says. "Daisy, I just wanted to make sure you didn't need any help on the science project."

"Nah," Daisy says. "It's not even due until Tuesday."

"Okay, doll. Tomorrow, then."

"Margaret's getting Daisy off the bus tomorrow," I tell Dave. He looks at me, flustered, like nothing's going his way. "I thought you were working," I say easily, so that no one picks up on the tension between us. Sharing custody and figuring out schedules is dicey, to say the least.

"It's fine," Dave says, resigned. "I meant later, like dinnertime."

I force a smile at him. "Perfect," I say.

# EIGHT

## *Clara*

I'm unfolding what feels like the thousandth metal chair and wondering where my volunteers are. It's a few minutes past five, and we have to get the entire gym set up by five thirty, when registrants arrive for the spelling bee.

"You think this is enough?" asks Jeff, one of the custodians, when we've finished a row. Thank God for the custodians.

I scan the gym. Blue velvet curtains line the stage, and we've set up two standing microphones and enough folding chairs on the actual stage for the student spellers. On the gym floor, there's the long folding table for the judge and the pronouncer, and then we've got rows of chairs for the audience lining three-quarters of the gym. "I think this should do the trick," I say. "And if we overfill them, we can always add more later. Or people will grab their own, don't you think?" Metal chairs are folded conspicuously along the gym's walls, and parents won't be shy about making themselves comfortable. No matter what I do, tomorrow I'll get a slew of complaints about how the spelling bee went: *The words were too hard, your pronouncer didn't say the words clearly enough, the word you gave my kid wasn't on the study sheet* . . . and the list will go on. Whenever I get those day-after emails from parents, I sometimes imagine typing the reply THEN YOU DO IT and hitting send.

I hear the squeak of sneakers on the gym's floor and turn to see Sloane Thompson followed by one of the younger mothers who's new to the school. I always tap the kindergarten parents to volunteer at these kinds of events because they're not exhausted and over it yet, like some of the other parents with kids in older grades. Sloane's dressed prettily in the kind of outfit that matches my soul but not my life: a long, flowy skirt with slim Nike sneakers. Evan would die if I wore sneakers with a skirt. Not that I care about what he thinks anymore, but I'm trying to be exactly as I always was because I don't want him to sniff out my plan to leave.

The younger mother, Susan—Suzy? Sue?—trails Sloane, looking unsure. She glances around furtively at the three walls of the gym, the rock wall, the rope, and then a massive swing I raised money for, outfitted for children in our special ed classroom.

I make my face move into a smile for Sloane and the younger mother, and try not to let my expression show any trace of *Why are you late?* "Sloane, Suzy," I say.

"Sharon," the young mother corrects. Why does everyone's name sound so similar?

"*Sharon*," I say. "Sorry! Thank you so much for being here." I put the special beaming look on my face I used all the time when Marlow and I were co-presidents. "Sharon, I'm going to have you head right back outside the gym to where the registration table is set up. You'll help Diana register the spellers and give them their bibs."

Sharon nods vigorously, like this is all very important. Good. "Encourage the spellers to have their parent or guardian pin the bibs to their shirts," I tell her. "But if they've been separated, like if the parent is off talking somewhere or didn't get the memo that this event isn't a drop-off birthday party, you can go ahead and do it for them. But don't stab them with the pin or pin it to anything like a sweatshirt that they might take off on stage. Let them know that the stage gets warm, and then ask them if they'd like their bib pinned to a T-shirt beneath their sweatshirt or sweater." I can feel Sloane's bored edginess growing;

it's coming off her in waves. And I understand that what I'm saying is epically dull, but she's never had to wrangle kid contestants before, and it's kind of hard when they keep losing their bibs. And once one of my volunteers jabbed a kid with a pin, and the child's mother freaked out and demanded I find out whether the pins were sterile. And Marlow got fed up and joked that the pins were the cheapest thing we could find on Amazon and probably covered with tetanus bacteria. It might have been the most un-therapist thing Marlow had ever done in her life, and the mom told the principal on us.

Sharon heads off toward the registration table, and it's just Sloane and me. "Am I sitting up there?" Sloane asks, pointing toward the long folding table in front of the stage. Her voice sounds far away, like she wishes she were anywhere other than standing here with me and can't really conceal it.

"Yup," I say, trying to pretend like this is pleasant. Half of what I hate about running the school's PTA is how put out some people act when you ask them to help. Sloane approaches the table and gingerly touches the spelling word list, running her hand over the stapled stacks of crisp white paper. There's something about her, a wistfulness, maybe. She's unrushed, moving gracefully, her long fingers delicate as she flips carefully through the first few sheets of words. Her energy makes me feel like I shouldn't bark directions, because it's obvious that she wouldn't like it, that it might upset her delicate constitution.

I wait silently, moments longer than I normally would, watching Sloane take in the hundreds of words parading down the pages in columns. Her light blue eyes match her daughter's.

"You've seen these words before, right?" I ask. "I emailed them."

*Ugh. Why did I say that?*

"I didn't study the list you sent, no," Sloane answers softly.

"Of course. I didn't expect you to," I say, but then I squeeze my butt cheeks in annoyance with myself, because even that came out too huffily—like I'm making a personal judgment on the fact that I didn't expect Sloane to go the extra mile and read over the list of words she has to pronounce tonight for the spellers. "I just mean it's not a requirement of the job," I say, trying to make it better.

She flinches. "It's *not* a job," she says. "So yes, hopefully there aren't too many requirements."

Oh my God, fuck my life.

"We're very grateful you're doing it," I say, and then, to make everything worse, Marlow flounces into the gym carrying a drop-dead gorgeous flower arrangement, her dramatic turquoise-and-yellow dress swirling around her ankles. Marlow has a charmed way of entering a room, a Glinda the Good Witch vibe like she just arrived on a cool night breeze. She lost her magic a little in the year following her affair with Evan, and I always wondered if the guilt was crushing her and snuffing out her light. But then, slowly and surely, she came back to herself. A part of me was so relieved to see her turn bright again, which made me realize that what I had with Marlow was true friendship, the kind of love that means you only want the best for the other person, even when they've hurt you in one of the worst ways humans know how to hurt.

Marlow's dark hair curls long and loose over her shoulders. Her sandals pat the floor as she heads toward us, her smile like a sunrise. She's so luminescent I avert my eyes, which I've found myself doing whenever we cross paths at school or at a party. It's too hard to look dead-on at everything I've lost.

"I thought these would be pretty on the table," Marlow says when she reaches us, setting down the flowers on the corner of the table. She doesn't exactly look me in the eye, either. It's hard to believe this is the same woman I used to spill secrets to over coffee.

"Yes, thank you," I say formally. "They're very pretty."

Marlow crosses her arms over her dress and stares at the flowers, as though the tulips are about to put on an exciting show.

"I don't think we've met," Sloane says to Marlow.

Marlow breaks her trance and glances up to look at Sloane, considering her. Is it possible they haven't met yet? Marlow is nearly as involved in the school as I am.

"We've met," Marlow says simply. "Last year at the holiday sing-along."

I suppress a smile. That's Marlow for you. Never forgets a face, and not shy about letting you know.

A soft pink flush appears on Sloane's fair skin. "Oh, sorry, that's right," she says.

"So, listen, with this list," Marlow says to Sloane, leaning forward to scan the spelling word list on the table. "If the kids keep spelling everything correctly, and the night starts dragging, and you can feel *all* hope that it will *ever* end draining from your soul, it's okay to skip forward a few pages and give them harder words."

"Okay," Sloane says, letting out a surprised laugh. This is one of the things I miss about Marlow—the way she just says whatever and makes people feel comfortable. I wish I knew how to do that. It was always Marlow doing it for us.

Marlow joins in laughing with Sloane, and then says, "I was the pronouncer last year, and I literally went from asking the third graders to spell *math* to asking them to spell *rambunctious* in a single round, because I couldn't take it anymore."

Sloane laughs again, and I want to shut all of it down because it's too hard to be standing on the outside of the Marlow Show, pressing my hands against the glass and trying to get back in.

"The judge will also help you decide when to do that," I say flatly, buzzkilling everything.

Sloane stops smiling. She glances between Marlow and me like she's missing something. Marlow shrugs. "Okay, well, good luck," she says. She gives Sloane a wink. "I'm gonna go see if they need anything at registration."

# NINE

*Sloane*

The spelling bee goes off without a hitch until about an hour and a half in, when Margaret's little sister, Florence, gets up to the microphone. Florence and another fifth grader named Danny are the last ones standing, battling it out for first place. We've already crowned the winners for third and fourth grade, and all the adrenaline has flushed from my system. My jaw is sore from trying to pronounce everything perfectly—*saturated . . . scientific . . . systemic*—trying to slowly give each letter its due as I say the word into the microphone. The parents are tired, too. I can't see them, but I can feel them fatiguing behind me. At the start of the night, there were sharp intakes of breath before their children spelled words, followed by crisp exhalations and the rustling of paper programs and candy wrappers. Once, a phone went off, quickly silenced, an apology uttered. But we're nearing eight o'clock, and Florence and Danny have been in a standoff for the last thirty or so words. It's time for this evening to be over.

Florence steps up to the microphone with her hands clasped, and I think of Marlow telling me to jump forward a few pages to make it harder. My fingers are sweaty against the papers as I debate what to do. Someone coughs behind me and it makes me flinch, but then I do it: I flip forward five full pages and spy the words at the top of the column. My heart rate picks up: They're noticeably tougher.

Florence wears Converse sneakers and a tutu, the outline of her face like a young Margaret. The only sign of her nerves tonight has been a slight twitch in her lips before she spells. Otherwise, her lanky form is relaxed, and she looks like she belongs up there, like competing academically is what she was born to do. She reminds me of Margaret in this way, so utterly sure that she's been blessed with intelligence, and resigned to allowing the world to witness it.

I lean toward my own mic and lock eyes with Florence. Locking eyes with each small child who's about to spell has been by far the best part of the night. The moment is like a confidence shared, and their trust is so poignant and all-consuming that I find myself unable to turn away from their searching eyes.

Florence blinks at me, waiting for me to deliver her fate. I hope I haven't made a mistake by jumping forward to the harder words, but I have a feeling both spellers can handle it. And really, how else is the night going to end?

"Your word is *humorous*," I say into the microphone, and Florence repeats it carefully.

A soft-spoken, short-haired woman named Judith sits beside me. Her kids are Clara's kids' ages now, and she and Clara have been doing the spelling bee for a decade. Judith is the official judge, the one who's supposed to decide, after a child repeats her word into the microphone, that the child has heard and understood the word correctly. Judith nods after Florence repeats *humorous*, and Florence begins spelling.

"H-U-M . . ."

Florence takes a big breath. Her knobby knees peek out from beneath her tutu, and she shifts her weight.

"E-R-U-S."

A few members of the audience let out their breath. Florence repeats her word when she's done spelling, and my stomach drops, and I realize, not surprisingly, that I'd been hoping she'd win.

"I'm sorry, Florence," I say, "that's incorrect."

Florence's eyebrows arch. I expect to see her face fall, or for her to look like she wants to cry, but she doesn't. She looks shocked, as if it couldn't be so, and then there's the sound of a metal chair scraping over the gym's floor.

"It's not incorrect," comes a man's voice.

I whirl around in my chair. Judith does, too. I see the audience—nearly two hundred parents—some gaping at me, some turning to locate the male voice.

In the very back of the gym stands Margaret and Florence's father. He's nearly obscured by an oversized easel, as though he's trying to hide, and I think of Margaret telling me Florence asked him not to be here tonight.

"The word," he says loudly, stepping farther away from the easel. His voice echoes through the gym. "The word Florence has spelled is not incorrect."

Now everyone's talking in hushed murmurs. Blood has rushed to my face, and I feel a little ill.

"She's spelled *humerus*," Florence's dad says. "The longest bone in the arm." And here he gestures to his upper arm. "I suppose you may have been trying to get her to spell *humorous* as in comical or funny. But audibly, that's indistinguishable from *humerus*, the bone that runs from your shoulder to your elbow."

I hate myself for doing this—I turn to look at Judith. *Save us*, I think. *You're an older mother. You know what to do, don't you?*

Judith lets out a sigh. And when neither of us says anything, when we're so quiet we might as well be invisible, Florence's dad says to me, "You're a *writer*, aren't you?" He emphasizes it like a dirty word, and everyone turns from staring at him to staring at me. A beat passes, and then Florence's dad starts talking again, and they all turn back to him like their necks are on a coordinated swivel. "So, you must know *humorous* and *humerus* are homophones," he's saying, "and that neither belongs on a spelling list."

My heart pounds. He's not wrong, of course, but the way he's speaking sounds like he thinks he's the most intelligent human ever to grace the gym.

Judith turns off her microphone so the entire gym can't hear what she's about to say. She leans in close to me and says, "Give her a new word."

My face is burning, and I imagine things I could say to Florence's dad over the mic. But then I turn away from Florence's dad's murky shadow and see Florence again, and her sweaty, mortified face stops me in my tracks. She looks like she's about to cry, like she wants to be anywhere other than on that stage. It immediately grounds me. This is my role—to make the spellers feel as comfortable as they possibly can be. Or at least it's my interpretation of my role, whether or not that was what Clara had in mind for me when she asked me to be the pronouncer.

"I'm so sorry, Florence," I say into my microphone. "We gave you a homophone. Let's start again with the next word on the list. Are you ready?"

Behind Florence, Danny, Florence's competition, is fidgeting. He's got a misshapen blue stress ball in his tiny hand, and he passes it back and forth, giving it a few squeezes while he waits for Florence to have another go.

But Florence is still. And the set of her face has changed: She no longer looks like she's going to cry. She looks furious.

"I'm ready, Mrs. Thompson," she says to me, steel in her voice.

I swallow. "Your word is *preposterous*," I say, in the same calm and clear tone I've used all night.

"Preposterous," Florence repeats.

Judith gives a small nod beside me.

"P-R-E-P-O-S-T-E-R—" she begins spelling, but then stops. And she no longer looks at me. She lifts her gaze and looks toward the back of the gym, where her father is standing. She pauses, staring hard at him. And then, into the microphone, she spells, "U-S . . . ," leaving out the final *O* in her word. She repeats her word with a chilly snap, sealing her fate:

"Preposterous."

A gasp or two sounds from the audience.

I blink. There's no way Florence doesn't know how to spell the ending of that word. I open my mouth, thinking of the small quiver I'd seen her display all night when she'd tried her best to spell the words correctly. Not this time. "I'm sorry, that's incorrect," I say softly, realizing that she's thrown the spelling bee, losing on purpose.

A hush has fallen over the gym. No one shuffles their chair or unwraps candy; no one scolds a child or gets up to use the bathroom.

Florence gives a small shrug as Danny grows visibly excited behind her. She looks up once more toward the back of the gym and smiles at her father. I turn—I can't help it—and spy Florence's dad's shadowy form in the back. The fury on his face sends a chill over my skin.

# TEN

## *Clara*

Trust me, I'm all set," I say to Sloane as she gathers her things. She still seems a little shaken, even though I've assured her that every year at the spelling bee there's always some kind of small drama. Last year we caught one of the fathers mouthing the letters to his child on stage, and I'd made the mistake of being the audience monitor that year (never again) and had to ask him to stop in front of everyone. And after that night, the child's family took me off their holiday card mailing list.

"You're sure you don't need me to help clean up?" Sloane asks again.

It's still hard to hear in here. Parents are high on the feeling of being released from the clutches of a school event, and now they're all standing around talking too loudly.

"I'm sure," I say. "It's just the folding chairs. It's late. Get back to Daisy." She smiles appreciatively. "And take these." I nod toward the flower arrangement Marlow brought.

"Oh no," she says. "You should take them." She gestures vaguely around the gym. "You planned the whole thing."

I shake my head. I don't want Marlow's flowers sitting on my kitchen island, beautiful until they wither. How is the sting of losing a female friendship this achingly sharp?

*"Darling,"* comes Evan's voice behind me. I see Sloane catch sight of him first. Her eyes scan his handsome face, female behavior I'm quite used to, but then she looks away, unimpressed, like she can't be bothered. Good for her.

"Sloane, how are you?" Evan asks in his charming baritone. We used to invite Sloane to the parties we held. Years ago, before she had Daisy, I'd met her in town at the library one morning with my twins; she seemed lovely, and we exchanged information. For maybe a year or two she came to our parties, but for the next several years she declined, which I'd assumed was because she was busy raising a new baby. But even when Daisy was eventually a toddler and then a kindergartner, she never said yes to an invite, so finally I stopped asking.

"I'm fine," Sloane answers Evan, not bothering to ask the question in return.

"Stellar job on your pronunciation tonight," Evan says, slick as oil. My eyes scan the map of his handsome face, the fault lines I know so well, the dips and valleys, the ridges and flat planes, all of it adding up to something quite beautiful.

Sloane turns to me. "You're right. I should get back to Daisy," she says, swooping up Marlow's flowers without any further protest. She folds into the crowd with her head down, seeming to truly want to get out of the gym without any more conversation.

"Something up her ass tonight?" Evan asks crudely.

"Evan, shhh. Someone could hear you."

"She was a little unfriendly to me, didn't you think?" But he's smiling, like he's enjoying it. Children are literally climbing the walls around us—the rock-climbing wall we raised money for last year. Their little hands and feet blur over the rainbow-colored plastic stones.

"She was probably just thrown off by Florence and Margaret's dad," I say.

"That guy's a prick," Evan says, retrieving a pack of Breath Savers from his pocket. He's had a dedicated mint habit since college, and the wintergreen breath to match.

"He's arrogant and aloof, but he wasn't wrong," I whisper, double-checking that the microphones on the table are switched off. Publicly announcing my distaste for an elementary school parent, especially the father of the girl my son is dating, is the last thing I need. "And it's so annoying, because I looked over that list to make sure there weren't any homophones. But who would have thought of *humerus?* Not me. I'm not a doctor."

Evan pops a mint in his mouth and starts working on it. "You're definitely not a doctor."

I let out an overdramatic sigh. "That's right, Evan, I'm not. I'm a housewife. Just like you like me to be."

"That's not what I meant," he says, cracking the mint so loudly it sounds like he broke a tooth. I imagine his molars falling out, one by one, in front of everyone, and how satisfying it would be to watch him cover his mouth and hide in shame.

"Whatever," I say. "See you at home."

He's in his golf clothes, which means that when he was finished with a round of golf and dinner at the club, instead of going home, he came here, even though we don't have a child in the spelling bee. He did this because he's a pathological socializer. No one likes being adored more than Evan, and he'd rather be out in a swarm of people from our community than home alone with his own thoughts.

He kisses my cheek. "That's not what I meant," he says again. He tries to hold my gaze, but that's gotten so much harder for me to indulge, so I tell him goodbye. Mercifully, he leaves, which doesn't surprise me, because he certainly doesn't want to get into a conversation about my career hopes.

I used to work as a librarian before the kids were born. I adored the job. Our library had a vibrant membership with plenty of book clubs and author events. It was easy to book authors because so many of them lived an hour south in New York City, and because our patrons were so involved, we drew a good crowd. I stopped working when I had Cole. I loved being home with my kids; but there was a window when

I should've gone back to work, and I didn't. I was so involved in the school, so swept up in my job as a mother, that I just kept at it instead of trying to figure out a way to work while mothering, too. Which I realize is easier said than done, but other women do it, so why couldn't I? And now, with what's happened to my marriage, it seems so obvious how much wiser it would have been to get my career back in place.

Still. It's never too late, is it? This past year I've begun volunteering at Sycamore Glen's public library with the goal of turning that into a full-time librarian position somewhere else. And what Evan doesn't know is that next week I have an interview at a library halfway between Sycamore Glen and New York City in a town called Harrison. If I'm planning to leave him next year, I'll need a full-time job with benefits lined up, because God only knows what he's going to do when I break this news to him. He's the type who would try to take the kids away. I know that's an awful thing to say about someone—but I also know it to be true, and it's the entire reason I'm waiting until Arden and Camille turn eighteen next year, so we'll no longer have to worry about custody. Evan's biggest fear in life is being embarrassed or ashamed. A public divorce in front of all his friends would be his version of a massive embarrassment, even without me telling everyone what he's done. And I don't plan to tell anyone what he's done, because I don't want to hurt the kids, but he won't believe that.

I finish with the folding chairs and think about what things might be like when I'm finally free of him. A sweep of goose bumps crosses over my skin, the knowing there's no way it'll go down easily.

Still, I have to try. For the kids, for me. People start over all the time, and they survive. Surely, I can do the same.

# ELEVEN

*Sloane*

My headlights bear down on Route 22, the road glistening from an earlier rain shower. I curve right and drive carefully up my street, winding all the way to the top, where my house and Harper's are standing sentinel. Through the windshield I can see that Daisy's light is off, which means she's no longer reading and already asleep. I glance up to Harper's house, where all the lights are on. The stunning flower arrangement from Marlow sits in my passenger seat, and I imagine showing up at Harper's door and passing them into her arms. Or would that be too strange at this hour?

I park my car in my driveway and turn off the ignition, sitting there for a moment and staring at the flowers. I finally decide to head toward Harper's, and my pulse picks up as I get out of my car, making me wonder if my life has really become so dull that dropping off a flower arrangement sets my heart aflutter.

I cradle the arrangement carefully as I walk down my driveway and onto the road, curving left onto Harper's driveway. Branches loom above me in the dark. Harper's property is much more wooded than ours, and it gives it a storybook vibe, like you're sweeping beneath a canopy of pines to get to her doorway. Inside the house, I can see the outline of Harper and Ben silhouetted behind a second-floor window.

Harper's arms are gesticulating wildly, her ponytail fluttering as she talks, like maybe they're fighting.

The night still feels wet from the rain, as though the air itself is soaked. I balance the flower arrangement in the crook of my arm and step gingerly up the driveway. There are small, jagged holes in the gravel, not quite potholes, but close enough, which is kind of funny when you consider how high the listing price was.

I climb stone steps and ring the doorbell. It lets off an old-fashioned series of chimes, and then footsteps pound the stairs, and Ben swings open the door.

"Sloane, hi," he says, words clipped. He doesn't seem surprised to see me standing there. And he looks a bit of a mess, but in the world's most handsome way: He hasn't shaved, and his dark hair is disheveled. He messes it up even more when he tries to run a hand through it. Behind him, a massive wooden staircase zigzags along the side of the house, and a crystal chandelier plunges into the center of the expansive foyer, like something out of *Phantom of the Opera*.

"Sloane, hey!" Harper's voice trills. She bounces down the stairs like someone much younger than thirtysomething. "We still don't have hot water, if you can believe it."

I turn to look at Ben. His deep brown eyes are so intense, and the smile he wore earlier today when we first met is gone. "Do you need to use our shower?" I ask him, feeling my face warm as his eyes hold mine. "You're welcome to."

Harper sidles up beside him. "Oooh, pretty flowers," she says.

"They're for you," I say, glad for an excuse to break Ben's stare. I pass the flowers into her hands.

"Really?" she asks, delighted. "Come in, come in."

But Ben just stands there, and I don't want to brush past him into the doorway.

"Actually, Harp," he says as Harper sets the flowers down on a dark brown entry table. "I think I'm going to take Sloane up on the hot water offer." His voice is hard, and I wonder if Harper did something to make him angry before I got here. But if she did, she certainly doesn't seem bothered. She doesn't look up from the flowers, arranging a few large coffee-table books beneath them, shifting the whole thing toward the center. "What a great idea," she says pleasantly, still not looking at us.

"You should come, Harper," I say, because I don't really want another woman's husband in my house taking a shower without her there.

Harper glances up with innocent, blinking eyes, looking like it never occurred to her. And again, I feel like a prude. "Oh, sure!" she says. "How fun. Let me bring a bottle of wine and we can chill."

"We don't have any wine," Ben says.

"Oh, right," Harper says with a quick snap. And then to me, "We didn't have any special bottles worth packing, you know? I mean it's not like we're the kind of people who hold on to some special vintage bottle we inherited from our parents."

Ben flinches like she's said something rude.

"When did you get into Sycamore Glen?" I blurt, wanting to fill the silence with words. Their dynamic is making me anxious. "Not just today, right?"

"Ben was here for a month in an Airbnb in Scarsdale," Harper says. She moves toward a coat closet and opens the door to reveal a neatly organized line of coats, shorter ones toward the left and longer ones on the right. I marvel at how quickly everything got unpacked today. Did the movers do all this? There's a line of standard coats: raincoats, a khaki trench, and a few fleeces. Harper bypasses those and picks a delicate gray cashmere coat with a sequined leather sash. It's the kind you'd wear with an evening dress, but Harper's wearing a Pearl Jam T-shirt and black leggings, and as she shimmies into the coat and then slips into rain boots, the whole picture is charming. "Let's go," she announces, and we head out single file onto the driveway, with me leading the way. "Do we need a flashlight?"

"Use your phone," Ben says, still sounding peeved.

"I don't know where it is," she says.

"Harper," Ben says beneath his breath. He takes out his phone and shines it near her feet.

My eyes take a little while to adjust to the dark again. We walk carefully down the driveway, the call of a spring peeper making Harper glance about, and all of it seems a little surreal. It's been tricky making friends in Sycamore Glen. Many people who live here grew up nearby, and even the ones who are transplants already seemed to have a solid crew in place by the time I got here. There's an element of aloofness, and often I find myself feeling like a newcomer, even though we've been here for nearly a decade.

"My art's coming on Monday," Harper says, picking up her pace to pass Ben and walk beside me. Ben eventually turns off his flashlight, and Harper is sure-footed in the dark, moving like a dancer. "Thirty pieces or so. They'll spend all day putting it up, like a proper install. You should come over Monday night and see it. Or are you busy?"

I'm not busy. "I'd love to," I say. An animal cries out in the woods and Harper flinches.

"Oh, jeez," she says. "What was that, do you think?"

"It's just a bird, Harp," Ben says.

It wasn't a bird, but I don't say anything. We walk silently along the road to my house and down my driveway. "Your house is so pretty," Harper says as we climb the front steps. There's awe in her voice, even though she saw the house just hours ago when she was here alone.

"Thanks," I say as I unlock the door. "We really like it. Daisy especially. There's a secret cabinet in her closet, and a little hideaway under the stairs. Can't beat an old house, right?"

"So true," Harper says.

Ben's quiet beside us.

"How was Scarsdale?" I ask him.

"Fine. Much busier than here, though."

"Sycamore Glen is so quiet," Harper says. "But Ben likes that kind of thing."

I wonder how the busyness of San Francisco was for him, but I don't say anything. I stick my key in the lock and open the door. Inside, we're flooded with light. The foyer opens to the kitchen, where Margaret sits at the long wooden table. She shuts her laptop and looks up at us, smiling. She's so darling, and I feel fondness seeing her here, in my house. We've gotten close over the past two years of her babysitting for us, and sometimes she'll even text me random stuff during the week unrelated to babysitting in a way that makes me think she enjoys my company, like she's not just pretending. Maybe all mothers want to feel that way, to be a part of the magic of young life again, to feel like they're not invisible. But with Margaret it feels genuine.

"Hey, Margaret," I say. "You remember Harper, and this is Ben, her husband."

"Hi!" Margaret says, standing from the table. Her sweatshirt falls off her shoulder, exposing the thin strap of a tank. I see her eyes catch Ben's, and right away her cheeks blush.

"Hi, Margaret," Ben says, extending a hand. "Ben Wilson."

"Nice to meet you," Margaret says. Her skin is still flushed, but she sets her shoulders and stands up straight as she shakes his hand. And she holds Ben's gaze confidently, suddenly seeming much older than eighteen. A beat of silence transpires between them. It feels noticeably awkward to me, and maybe to Harper, too, because she blurts, "Good job getting little Daisy to bed."

Margaret looks away from Ben. She waves a hand like it was nothing. "Daisy's an angel," she says in a cool, confident voice.

Harper and I simultaneously shift our weight. I haven't witnessed Margaret around many adult men. Only Dave, and he's so busy acting dodgy that I'm not sure he counts.

"Margaret just got into Princeton today," Harper says to Ben. "How amazing, right?"

Ben's dark eyebrows shoot up. "Princeton, wow," he says.

Margaret grins, looking more like herself again. "Yup. I can't believe it."

"You don't have to be humble in front of us," Harper says sweetly. But then there's an edge that creeps into her voice when she adds, "We're not into that." I turn to look at her, and so does Ben. "What?" Harper asks us with a laugh. "It's *true*. Why do women always have to be so humble about their accomplishments? It's like a sickness." She gestures toward Margaret, but she's looking at me. "Look how young it starts, am I right?"

Margaret crosses her arms over her chest and squares herself, like she's on one team and Harper's on the other.

I say, "You're not wrong, but—"

"How old are you, Margaret?" Harper snaps. "Eighteen?"

"Yes," Margaret says steadily. And then, "My parents are intellectually arrogant, and I'm making a purposeful decision to be the opposite. So please don't mistake my humility for weakness."

I blink at Margaret, surprised.

"Oh," Harper says with a little laugh. "Well, that I can allow." She smiles, seemingly happy now that Margaret pushed back. "But maybe there's a happy medium, wouldn't you think?"

Margaret shrugs. "Maybe. But you haven't met my parents, and if you did, you'd realize that not even a happy medium would cut it."

"Please excuse Harper," Ben says softly to Margaret. "She often acts overly familiar with someone she's just met. And in this case, she spoke before knowing your parental circumstances."

"*Ben*," Harper says. "I didn't say anything *that bad*."

Ben smiles. "You didn't. Not this time." He turns to me. "Do you mind if I take that shower now?"

I swallow, uneasy. "Sure," I say. "Follow me."

And for better or for worse, I leave Margaret and Harper alone in the kitchen.

# TWELVE

*Sloane*

A short while later, the sound of Ben's shower thrums above Margaret, Harper, and me. We're sitting around the kitchen table clutching mismatched mugs of chamomile tea.

"Your parents," Harper says, softened by this point. "How bad are they?"

Margaret's mouth twitches. Her straight dark hair is parted down the middle and falls over her shoulders in two shiny sheets. "Not as bad as they could be," she says. "They feed us and keep us safe, for one. That's a privilege many kids don't have."

Harper reaches a hand across the table and pats Margaret. "This isn't a college interview. I'm really asking you, and no one's recording it. I'm certainly not going to tell your parents what you said."

Margaret looks off to the French doors that open onto our deck. I follow her gaze to see a silvery moon in a black, cloudless sky.

"My biggest problem with my parents is that, at their core, they're not all that kind," Margaret says. "Academic medicine is cutthroat, and they're myopic about it. They're obsessed with their publications and their *impact*. And they *are* contributing to the world, don't get me wrong. But sometimes I see the way Clara—Mrs. Gartner, I mean—is with Cole. It's all softness, like he's enough for her just by existing. The conversations they have meander without an end in sight, whereas with my parents, it's like every time we talk, they're pushing an agenda." Margaret smooths a hand over her hair again, her hot pink nail polish even brighter against her near-black locks. "Florence and I love playing piano," she says softly. "And we have an old one from my grandmother, and nothing about playing piano feels like something I want to compete in. I just really like it, and all I want to do is play that stupid piano and think of my grandmother. But because of my parents, I can't just play piano because I love it; I have to play with the goal of participating in a musical competition because that's tangible. It's something that can be put on a college application. We argued all year about it, until I finally gave in and signed up for a state-wide competition, and I hated every second of it. They forced me to practice when I didn't want to, which made me hate piano." She takes a breath and looks at us like she's worried about what we're thinking. "Maybe academically high achieving is who I would have been anyway, even without them breathing down my neck. But it would have been nice to come to that on my own terms, because now all I feel is completely burned out and sort of . . . I don't know . . . *dull*, I guess. All of this is over, high school, college acceptance, and it's like I got to the finish line, and now I barely feel anything at all."

She's never told me any of this before.

"Parent-child relationships are complicated, aren't they?" Harper asks, her voice gentle.

"I guess," Margaret says with a shrug. She looks so disillusioned. "Mine are."

"Mine, too," Harper says. Her fingers tighten against her mug, and she looks like she wants to tell us something but says nothing.

"How so?" I finally ask her in a quiet voice.

Harper takes a quick breath. "They were just so cold," she says. "They barely touched my brother and me, no *I love you*s, or bedtime stories, barely any eye contact." She looks at us thoughtfully, her head cocked to the side. "I think, looking back on it, that they were clinically depressed and untreated, but they died before I was grown up enough to realize that it wasn't me making them that way; that it was mental illness. I always thought there must be something deeply wrong with me for them not to love me. Even though I knew, logically, that that couldn't be true, because my brother was more typically perfect—a straight-A student, and very polite, all those things—and they didn't take a shine to him, either. And then they died in a car accident the year I went off to college. All of it is just so . . . sad."

It is. "I'm sorry, Harper," I say. "That's tragic."

"Awful," Margaret says, her eyes misty.

Harper shrugs. "I know, right? A tragic story, and it's mine. Sometimes I look back on my childhood, and it feels like such a blur." She turns to Margaret. "You're an adult now, officially, and you can decide exactly who you want to be when you go off to college. And I bet even though your parents are academic snobs, or so it sounds, they probably deeply love you."

Margaret swallows. "They do."

I think of Margaret and Florence's father tonight at the spelling bee, jumping into the fray to defend his daughter as though the homophone was a bear. I'd seen it as an act of pride and control, but maybe if I'd looked with a more generous interpretation, I would have seen shades of love and protection.

Harper gives us both a small smile. "The things that happen to us as children are right there, aren't they, pushing up against the edges of our skin." Margaret nods, and I think of my own parents, healthy and alive in California, and I imagine calling them tomorrow and thanking them for my perfectly lovely childhood.

Upstairs, the shower turns off, and I picture Ben getting out of it and padding barefoot across the floor. I blush at the thought; and it's moments like these when I know I need to get out more. I've dated a few times since Dave and I divorced, but everything felt too lackluster to pursue. Most recently there was a nice guy named Sam, but he spent so much time talking about gaming, and it got tiring constantly trying to steer the conversation onto different topics.

"I should go," Margaret says. "It's getting late."

"And you haven't told your parents about Princeton yet," I say.

Margaret's eyes travel to the French doors again. "They'll be so happy," she says wistfully. She gathers her things and can't find her phone, and when Harper tells her she does that all the time, she sounds so young and carefree.

"Are you sure tomorrow works?" I ask Margaret when she finally finds her phone in the bathroom. "Daisy will get off the bus at three fifteen. You're sure you can grab her?"

"Of course," Margaret says.

"Because I can reschedule this thing . . ." I've never had anyone get Daisy off the bus before. "It's actually your boyfriend's mom, asking me to do yet another volunteer thing at school . . ."

Margaret laughs. "Mrs. Gartner has a good heart." She says it like that's all that really matters about Clara, and she's probably right. "All right, then," I say.

"Good night, Margaret," Harper says. "It was nice getting to know you. Sounds like you've got quite a bright future ahead."

Margaret smiles at us, but there's doubt on her face, like she doesn't really believe what Harper says is true. She gives both of us a small wave before heading out into the dark night.

# THIRTEEN

*Sloane*

Harper and I talk for a while longer before Ben finally emerges in the kitchen, his hair nearly dry. I can't even imagine what he was doing up there after the shower was turned off. Rummaging through my things? Checking out the rest of the house?

"Thanks so much," he says.

His stubble is gone, and there's a smear of blood where he cut himself. It's the kind of thing you'd think Harper would notice and clean off, but she doesn't. She just smiles at him pleasantly. "The hot water guy is coming tomorrow," she says to me. "So hopefully this was the last time we have to crash your house to clean ourselves."

"It's no problem at all," I say. *I like having you here,* I want to add, but I don't.

"He's not a hot water guy," Ben says to Harper, but unlike earlier, when he seemed annoyed by her, now he only seems relaxed, as though the shower drained the last ounces of irritation from his system.

"Call him whatever you want," Harper says with a wave. "He's going to make the hot water work."

Ben manages a smile, shoving his hands deep into the pockets of his jeans. "Thank you, Sloane," he says. It's late, a little past ten, and I assume he's going to gather Harper and go, but instead he comes to sit with us. "As if I haven't helped myself enough in this house, is there any chance you have a beer?" he asks gently. His tone is so unassuming and polite, and my thoughts flash to his work, and I wonder what he's like with his patients. I imagine that in the operating room he's the opposite of unassuming.

"I do," I say, grateful that Dave always keeps beer in the refrigerator even though he barely drinks it.

I stand up and feel Ben's eyes on my back as I head to the fridge. "This okay?" I ask, grabbing a Red Stripe.

"My favorite, actually," he says. His smile is so lovely.

"My ex-husband's, too," I say, handing Ben the beer.

"Dave's your ex?" Harper asks as I sit back down at the table. She leans forward, like she smells something delicious and wants to follow the trail. And I don't mind it, not really. The divorce doesn't hurt like it used to.

"Yup. Four years now. Daisy was three. It was before she got sick," I say. I always think of the divorce in terms of Daisy's age then and now. It was about Dave and me, of course. But the entire reason I tried to make it work was for Daisy, and when it didn't, she was the one I worried about. There was a time when Dave was my whole world, and then something happened, something so dark it still takes all the oxygen from the room when I think of it. After everything went down, I couldn't look at him the same way or feel what I'd once felt, and maybe even worse, I couldn't respect him. It was like a curtain had been pulled back, and I saw him for who he was. Or who he wasn't.

"What happened?" Harper asks.

Ben sucks in a breath. "Harper," he says.

"It's fine," I say. I take out my hair tie and rewrap my bun, centering myself. I always want to be cautious during these kinds of conversations because Dave lives right down the road, and I don't want to paint an unfair picture. "After Daisy was born, we stopped working as well as we once did," I say. "And Dave would have tried harder, but I reached a point where I was done, which I take full responsibility for . . . Maybe other couples could have gotten through it, but we didn't."

"Did you fall out of love?" Harper asks.

"I fell out of love with him, yes," I say carefully.

"Was it something in particular?" Harper asks.

My stomach drops. No one's asked me that point blank. Usually, I can fudge my way through this conversation with the kind of general stuff you hear people say when they talk about the demise of their marriages. "Um, well . . . ," I say, stalling. *Yes, it was something in particular,* I imagine myself saying. What would it be like to finally tell someone? What would it be like to have a friend here that I could trust with my darkest secret? "It was a lot of different things," I say instead, feeling guilty, like the liar I am.

"I'm sure all marriages have their very specific inner workings," Ben says, and I'm grateful to him for jumping in. "Intricacies and such. Things you can't even begin to understand unless you're inside of it. And even then . . ."

"Right," I say. "And no one can predict the things that will befall a marriage over time. Things that could break it; things that could hold it together."

"And something that could break one person's marriage could strengthen another's," Ben says.

"Exactly," I say. "Like Daisy being sick. I think everyone somehow thinks her illness put too much of a strain on Dave's and my marriage. But we separated before she got sick. And if anything, Daisy is the uniting force. If we were ever going to make it, it would have been because of her. But like I said . . . we couldn't . . . or *I* couldn't."

As the three of us talk, the feeling of being able to confide so many things—not everything, of course—is like something electric zinging through me, like a switch flipped in a dark room. I'm not sure the last time I've felt so connected, and the feeling is molten, something I want again and again.

When we finally say goodbye, I crawl into my bed, but I can't sleep. I toss and turn for hours, finally slipping into the murky thickness of early morning sleep. I dream of Ben, of his hand on mine and his dark eyes heavy as he listens to me tell my secrets. In the dream, nothing I'm saying makes any sense. But still Ben leans forward and presses his lips against my cheek.

I wake, startled, reorienting myself to my room. The patter of Daisy's footsteps sounds in the hall.

I untangle myself from the sheets and go to her.

# FOURTEEN

*Clara*

I spent the morning fielding parent emails about last night's spelling bee, and now I'm on the second floor of the Sycamore Glen public library, reshelving books, when a low voice behind me asks, "Excuse me?"

I turn to see a guy with dirty-blond hair pulled into a man bun. His hazel eyes blink behind thick black glasses, and he looks so familiar that I try to place him, but can't. I don't think he's local, because I would have noticed him before; he looks more artistic than most of the men around here, like he belongs in Tribeca, writing a film, rather than on the musty second floor of our suburban library.

"Can I help you?" I ask softly. I'm a volunteer here, not staff, but he seems lost.

"I heard there was a quiet workspace up here," the man says, his voice low and reverent. It's a certain kind of person, maybe my favorite kind of person, who respects the library's quiet rules. So many people pass the sign for quiet at the top of the stairs and keep chattering loudly, but not all of us. I've always loved libraries and churches for their dependable pockets of quiet space, the peacefulness of it all. "Are there desks somewhere?" he asks.

"There *are*," I whisper. "But only a couple. Come, follow me."

I pass him in the narrow space, smelling the scent of books mixed with his woodsy cologne.

"I'm Cal, by the way," he says as we curve left out of the aisle and head toward the library's back windows.

I introduce myself as we arrive at the simple wooden desk and chair. We both look out the window to the back garden, and Cal's eyebrows lift when he sees the view. "Wow. Yeah. This is really something."

There's a gentleness about him that wakes something up inside of me. I shove it down. "Have you not been to the library before?" I ask, curiosity getting the better of me.

He shakes his head. "I haven't. I'm new to the area," he says. "I'm doing an artist-in-residency at Sarah Lawrence College, and I usually write there, but . . ."

"Oh, *wait*," I say, realizing why he looked so familiar. "You're Cal Graham." I want to clap my hands together and squeal, because I love his writing. "I've read your books."

"Oh," he says, his voice still so quiet. "Did you like them?"

"What's not to like?" I ask, feeling a smile curl my lips. His work is gothic and atmospheric, mostly taking place over generations and often involving a supernatural element. And the supernatural element is never cheesy; it makes you understand the characters more deeply rather than taking over the whole plot. "My favorite is the one with the woman who meets the older version of herself in Italy," I say. "*Time Again.* Wasn't that the title?"

He nods, his smile seeming genuine. "That one was the hardest to write. I'm not sure why."

"They always say that about sophomore novels, don't they? I've heard so many authors say something similar on podcasts."

"Yes, definitely. Plus, I kept having nightmares about meeting an older version of myself."

He's wearing one of those heavy wool sweaters that looks like it was knitted in the 1800s by a fisherman's wife. It's been chilly, even for March. You can see how broad his shoulders are beneath the sweater, and he shrugs now, looking sheepish. "Maybe knowing the future has always scared me, and that's probably why I wrote the book in the first place."

"To go there?" I ask.

"To go there," he says.

"I don't know that I'd want to meet an older version of myself if I had the choice," I say. I think of what a future version of me without Evan might be like, and the ways things could go sideways if I wasn't careful.

"I know I wouldn't," Cal says. "What if he's the same as I am now, and hasn't learned anything along the way, and just looks older?"

I laugh. "I think you gain wisdom. You must. Doesn't everyone?"

"Maybe," he says. "I hope." He holds my gaze, and I avert my eyes and let them settle on a small replica of the library someone built as a gift for an anniversary year. It sits proudly on a display beside an ancient red leather atlas.

"I should let you work," I say, wanting the opposite of that.

"It was nice meeting you, Clara," he says. He pulls out the wooden chair, sits at the desk, and retrieves his laptop. I turn to leave, trying to remember in which aisle I was reshelving books. I pad over the carpet and an unsettling feeling descends upon me, the gut instinct that it's the wrong move to wait inside my marriage, missing every possible connection with anyone who could ever mean something to me. It's not like I'm going to pursue a friendship with a handsome writer while I'm married. And not that I'm jonesing to date someone—I'm not. But it would be nice to one day find a romantic soulmate instead of just obsessing over the soul connections I feel with my children.

When I find my stack of novels, I pick them back up and stare at the shelves. I tap my index finger against the spines of the books, traveling the length of the shelf, until the alphabet matches the spot I'm looking for. I'm about to slide one into its proper slot on the shelf when the cover image catches my eye. It's a couple locked in a cheerful embrace, staring into each other's eyes like everything's okay now that they've found each other. I consider the couple, the girl with her curvy blond ponytail and even curvier hips. The man is tall and trim, and he gazes upon her like he'll never leave. Were things ever that simple between Evan and me? Even in our early days, our best days, didn't I always know he had this in him—the potential to be unfaithful? I did—of course I did. But don't most women feel that way? That there's a chance everything could go haywire? Or do some women rightfully and implicitly trust their husbands?

It wasn't just Marlow, and that's the part that stabs me in the gut at night when I lie awake, thinking about it.

Two years ago (almost a year to the day after I walked in on Marlow and Evan in Cole's bedroom), Evan and I were out at a restaurant socializing with a couple from his work. The lighting was dim, the music was low, and I was starting to relax a little after a glass of wine. I was still deeply bruised from Marlow and Evan's affair, and any moment that didn't feel exquisitely painful was a gift. That night at dinner was one of those moments: I wasn't on high alert, or analyzing everything Evan was doing; I was simply me, a woman at a restaurant in a flowery dress, who felt mostly okay. The kids had texted to tell me they were starting a movie, and I was enjoying a conversation with the new woman who worked at Evan's company. I'd heard everything about her from Evan: how talented she was, how Evan had valiantly lured her away from a Fortune 500 company. Evan had gone on and on about her one night while I was in the kitchen making Cole a sandwich, and I remember reminding myself to listen, because the truth was that in the year since Evan slept with Marlow, I'd become less interested in what he had to say. Instead of listening and engaging when he spoke as I'd always done before, I burrowed between his words and tried to find a morsel of what I'd once felt for him. I often wondered if he noticed the difference, if he realized that instead of my truly being in any conversation with him, I mostly watched him like he was on display at a museum, an exhibit for me to understand and decipher. I no longer felt like his lover; I felt removed a few steps, as though someone had plucked me out of my marriage and dangled me like a marionette as everything unfolded in front of me.

That night at the dinner, the woman said, seemingly out of nowhere, "And how lovely that you and Evan are heading to Miami next week."

I made myself force a smile at her. I certainly wasn't heading to Miami. Evan had told me he was going for work, and when I asked him what was happening there, he was evasive about the details. So, I was already primed for suspicion, and instead of seeming surprised or confused, I decided to play along and see if I could figure anything out. Evan was deep in conversation with the woman's husband, their voices much louder than ours, and he wasn't paying an ounce of attention to what we were talking about. So, I said, "Yes, we are. I need some warm weather. Gosh, I can't even remember if this one's a work trip. Are you all doing business in Miami? We've booked so many trips this winter to get out of this dreadful cold I can't remember which ones are work and which ones are purely vacation."

The woman assured me it wasn't a business trip, and I changed topics and made it through dinner without giving away what I'd learned. I spent the next few days purposely avoiding any talk about Miami with Evan, because I knew there was no way I'd catch him doing anything if he knew I was onto him. So off Evan went to Miami on his fake business trip, and I waited until the kids were at school and scoured his email. We had a shared password, crazy as that sounds, and there was absolutely nothing out of the ordinary in his emails. But I'd checked his email after his affair with Marlow (before he knew I knew) and couldn't find anything then, either.

Evan had left the name of his hotel with me in case of emergency. So, on the same morning he left, I asked my parents to stay with the kids and booked a flight to Miami. I showed up at five p.m. to the glitziest hotel I'd ever seen, the kind of place no one in their right mind would book for business. The all-glass exterior shot up straight into the sky like an erection. Glistening pools surrounded the building, and women in heels and bikinis carried trays filled with drinks. Music pumped, making the entire place vibrate, making me miss the library.

I sat in the interior lounge dressed to the nines and sipping a seltzer, and waited like a lion stalking her prey, scanning everyone who went in and out through the hotel's entrance. If I hadn't already known about Evan's affair with Marlow, I might have been sadder, devastated even. But this felt more like a chase, like something primal I had to do. I'd done my best to try to repair our marriage after what I'd thought was a singular mistake. But a secret planned trip to Miami? If Evan was here to have another affair, then we weren't making it out.

I sat there for hours with fear and adrenaline coursing through me, but no one except the bartender seemed suspicious of my shaking hands or my solo status—by my fourth seltzer the bartender asked if I was *waiting for someone*, but by eight p.m. he'd clocked out and a new bartender took over, and by then the bar was too busy for anyone to notice me.

Just past ten, Evan sauntered through the lobby's door, looking smug and handsome. From my angle, I could see there was clearly a woman on his arm, and though her face was partially obscured by his body, I saw striking red hair pulled high into a bun.

I didn't hesitate. I stood from my stool and started walking toward them, but I'd been sitting for so long that one of my feet had pins and needles. I limped gingerly until the feeling came back into my foot, bumping into a few people who jostled for my spot at the bar. The music thrummed inside my ears as I pushed through the crowd at the bar and stepped onto the marble floor of the lobby, mere feet behind Evan and his date.

My husband's *date.*

How had my life come to this?

My legs shook as I followed them toward the elevators. I had no idea what to do—pull the woman off Evan's arm and confront him there, in the lobby of the hotel? He would have talked his way out of it. He'd tell me the woman was a business associate, or a friend, or a real estate agent helping him find us a house in Florida as a surprise for me. Could I stop at the front desk and try to sweet-talk my way into getting a room key so that I could catch them having sex? Would they give me a room key if my name wasn't on the reservation? Unlikely.

I needed to keep following them. If I lost them, then I'd never have proof. I felt a burning inside my chest as I tracked Evan and the woman past sleek-looking receptionists, trying to look like I belonged there, like I had a key card to a room, too, and like what I was doing made perfect sense. I watched the backs of their heads as they boarded a crowded elevator, and then I ducked out of sight and made my way to the staircase. I sprinted up the first flight, and at the top, I opened another door onto the second floor and listened for the ding of elevator doors opening. Nothing. I slipped out of the swinging door onto the third floor at the same time I heard the elevator. There was a woman's giddy laugh, too shrill and high pitched. But maybe that was what he wanted: someone who laughed at his jokes, someone who was *fun*.

The hotel was carpeted with a plush white wool, and I couldn't hear their footsteps clearly enough to know if they were heading toward the wing where I was standing or making their way farther down the opposite hallway. I knew if I rounded the corner there was a chance I'd run smack into them, but so be it. I'd come this far, and I didn't want to lose them. I wanted to catch their body language, their intention; I wanted to know who I was married to.

I raced past the elevators and peeked my head around a corner into a long wing and there they were: backs to me as they receded down the hall, his arm around her waist, her head against his shoulder. Evan fumbled for his key card, never seeing me. I stood there watching Evan let himself and the woman into his room, and I fought the urge to stalk down the hall and scream and throw things. Because what I wanted more than that moment of confrontation was to *win*. And the only way to win—to leave Evan without him turning his powers of destruction upon me—was to stay one step ahead of him.

I turned back to go the way I'd come, my mind racing. Evan had gone down to Miami at least three times that year. Had he met someone while on business, and then continued to see her? I let go of a breath, knowing that no matter what, I'd seen enough to be sure my marriage was over.

In the lobby, I pulled my hair up into a topknot and called an Uber back to the airport.

# FIFTEEN

*Sloane*

The temperature's dropped into the high thirties, and I'm freezing as I exit the elementary school and walk a block to where I parked in town. As I near my car, I see Harper standing outside the post office, pulling stamps off a roll and holding a letter in her mouth. It's a funny picture, because she's dressed so stylishly in a wool trench and chic leather flats, but she's fumbling with the stamps and biting into a letter. My mood lifts a notch seeing her there.

"Need some help?" I ask.

She looks up, her green eyes shining. I get closer and realize she's a little teary, likely from the cold, biting wind. It's one of those early spring days that takes you by surprise.

"Hey!" she says, still holding the letter in her mouth. She passes me the stamps and grabs the letter. "Everything is blowing everywhere!" she says as a gust of wind splays her dark curls across her face.

I pull off a stamp and pass it to her, and she carefully presses it onto a letter addressed to someone in Spokane, Washington, and drops it into the royal blue mailbox. "So whatchya up to?" she asks, turning toward me.

"Not much, just volunteering at Daisy's school. I thought I'd get out of it by agreeing to do this photo booth thing at the fundraiser, but then Margaret's boyfriend's mom, Clara, roped me into more of it. At least it ended early, but I really have to start saying no, because I'm behind on a few editing projects."

"It's hard saying no," Harper says matter-of-factly. "And how lovely is this town?" She glances around at the post office, the library, and an old historical building that used to be a courthouse in the 1800s. I see it through her eyes, what it must be like to see all of it anew. And the truth is that Sycamore Glen's picturesque beauty isn't lost on me, even after nearly a decade of living here.

"It really is," I say, letting my gaze settle on the hyacinths and purple crocuses in front of the library. Hopefully this cold isn't too much for them.

Harper snaps her fingers, like she's in a sitcom and communicating that she's just had a great idea. "Do you want to grab coffee?" she asks, gesturing toward a new bakery a few spots down from the post office.

I check my phone. It's 3:04. If I leave now, I can get Daisy off the bus. But I *do* already have Margaret in place, and Margaret's coming all the way here, so maybe it would be better not to show up at my house and tell her I don't really need her to babysit. And really, besides the rare trip in NYC to visit an old writing friend, I haven't had coffee with a friend in a long time, which is why it was so nice to stay up talking with Harper and Ben last night. And even though we covered a lot of ground, I still feel like there's so much more to talk about.

"Sure," I say to Harper. "I'd love to."

She smiles sweetly, and there's a bounce in her step as we walk toward the coffee shop.

"It's *freezing* out," she says. "Tell me this isn't normal for spring."

"It's not, I promise. A few cold spring days, sure, but this feels more like the dead of winter." I open the glass door of the coffee shop and step onto the white-tiled floor. The shop is dressed in chrome and pale wood, more modern than most of the small shops we have in town. Harper and I order at the counter and take our lattes to a tiny round table in the back. I fire off a text to Margaret: Hi! Having coffee with a friend in town. I can come home right away if for any reason Daisy gets off the bus not feeling well.

"So," Harper says, "Ben and I would love to have you and Dave over one night for drinks. I mean, if you guys socialize together. Do you do that?"

I love how frank she is. "We do," I say. "It used to be kind of awkward, but now it's easier. Some other couples seem a little uncomfortable when Dave and I are hanging out together at school stuff. I have a theory, actually, that the more secure the couple, the less freaked out they are by the prospect of socializing with divorced people. Some couples seem to shy away from us, as though they don't want to spend time with us because Dave and I are an advertisement for the divorce option."

"How interesting," Harper says. She takes a sip of her latte and winces. "Jesus, this thing's *scorching*."

I pass her an unopened water bottle from my bag. I always carry them for Daisy. She takes a grateful sip, and I say, "So maybe it's kudos to you guys that you actually want to do something with both of us."

Harper glances away, shrugging. I stay quiet, waiting for her to say something about her marriage, good or bad, but she doesn't. And then she surprises me, asking, "Do you ever feel like you're outside your body just watching stuff happen to you, like you're watching a movie about yourself?"

I sit up a little straighter. "Oh, I guess, yeah, sometimes. Especially with the monotony of things, sometimes I feel like I'm just going through the motions on autopilot, which feels a little out-of-body, or like I'm not connecting to anything real."

"*Exactly*," Harper says. "I'm having one of those days today. Like I just want to *feel* something, for God's sake. I'm practically glad they made this coffee too hot because at least the burn is something I can feel in my body, like it's real." She rolls her eyes and I laugh a little. Not at her, but at her demeanor, saying these things and then rolling her eyes like someone much younger.

"Maybe it's just the new setting," I say, swirling my latte with the tiny wooden stick. "You just moved across the country. Maybe that's why you're feeling off."

"San Francisco is more frenetic and in motion, for sure. And I think a part of me needs that energy. I mean, I have appetites, you know. It's kind of why I chug coffee all day, I think. I like a lot of stimulation and adrenaline, or else I just feel sort of dull. Like what Margaret mentioned last night, actually."

"Maybe that's why I miss the city so much," I say, considering it. "I haven't thought about it in those terms, but there's an energy I miss for sure. I miss how you'd be out in the intensity all day, the people everywhere, the noise, the constant movement, and then you'd come home to your apartment and feel spent, like your skin and your bones had properly been wrung out. I never slept better than I did in the city, even with the sirens."

Harper nods. "*Exactly* what I'm talking about." She adds a splash of water to her latte, then takes a careful sip. "It was Ben's idea to come here, and I mean this with no offense—your town is so bucolic—but I'm just a little worried that I won't be able to figure it out here. We've only ever lived in cities."

I try to smile, but suddenly I feel incredibly sad, partly at the prospect of her leaving if it doesn't work, but mostly because I get what she's saying about Sycamore Glen. "I understand, I do, because it *is* incredibly beautiful, and I love so many things about living here, like how the community has rallied around Daisy. But I miss the city, and mostly I stay for Daisy. This is where her whole world turns."

"I can tell that you understand," Harper says. "That's why I'm confiding it." There's a darkness in her tone that sends a shiver over my skin, but then she blinks and quickly lightens, her voice higher pitched when she says, "So, thank goodness we're neighbors! I mean, what a lucky coincidence, right?"

Our conversation turns to more mundane things for the next twenty or so minutes, and I'm just about to tell her I need to get back to Daisy when my phone buzzes and I see the name of a neighbor down the road flashing across the screen.

"Mrs. Larsen?" I answer. She's nearly eighty, and I hope everything's all right. We exchanged numbers years ago, but she's never called me before.

"Sloane? I've got your daughter Daisy here."

My heart drops. "What? Why? Is she all right?"

"Well, she's all right, but she's *freezing*. I think you may want to hurry home and see if you think she needs a visit to the doctor. I've got her sitting down at my table drinking hot chocolate, but the poor thing got off the bus and your door was locked, and she couldn't get inside, and she had to walk all the way down the hill to my house . . . No one was home at the Sullivans—I think she tried their house first . . ."

"Oh *no*," I say, gathering my things and shooting up from the chair, motioning to Harper to follow. My muscles are on fire as I tear across the café—the walk to Mrs. Larsen's is way too far for Daisy. "Our babysitter Margaret was supposed to get her off the bus," I blurt, my heart pounding.

"And she's not really dressed properly," Mrs. Larsen adds unhelpfully.

It's so cold outside, and Daisy wanted to wear her puffer vest this morning instead of a down coat, and I'd caved. "I know, I *know*, I'm so sorry, I'm right in town, and I'm just going to get into my car, and I'll be there in a second. Please tell Daisy I'm on my way."

"Of course, dear," she says. We hang up, and Harper asks, "What happened?" as we push open the front door of the café.

"My God, Margaret never got Daisy off the bus," I say. My face stings with an icy slap of wind that feels like January. "And she's wearing this stupid puffer vest that Dave got her, so she's completely freezing." I have tears in my eyes now, which is embarrassing, and I can feel them falling over my cheeks. And then Harper does the most unexpected thing: She grabs my hand and holds it like we're schoolgirls. We race together toward my car. "I'm just so mad at myself," I say, fully crying now. "There's a key I told Margaret to use to get inside, but it's up on a high shelf in the shed. I either should have put the key where Daisy could reach it, or left the door unlocked, or I should've had a backup plan for Daisy if Margaret didn't show. It's just that I'm always the one getting her off the bus, so I never really thought of it before, which is so incredibly stupid of me—"

"And Margaret seems like the most responsible person in all the land," Harper says.

I appreciate her trying to get me off the hook, but it's my fault. "I should've—" I start again as we stop in front of my car. But Harper whirls me around to face her.

"Hey, *Sloane*," she says, her voice firm. "Daisy's okay. And she'll always be okay, deep down, because she has *you*, and you love her like crazy. And she knows it." She opens my car door. "It's all she actually needs. Maybe it's all any child needs." And what she says helps, it does, it makes the guilt recede just a little. "So go get your daughter." She smiles.

I slide inside and start the engine. As I pull away from the curb, I catch the image of Harper in my driver's side mirror, watching me. She gets smaller as I drive away.

# SIXTEEN

## *Clara*

I finish restocking books at the library and drive home at sunset. When I open the back door to our house, I hear the chatter of my kids, one of my favorite sounds in the world. Arden's laughing at something either Cole or Camille has said, and then I hear Camille say, "You can't *possibly* believe that, Arden. Please, tell me you're joking."

I curve into our kitchen and smile at the sight of the three of them. Camille and Arden are sitting on stools at the island, and Cole's standing, leaning against the island with his tall frame, looking just like Evan. He's holding a seltzer, seeming relaxed.

"Hi, sweethearts," I say, hugging my girls. Camille holds on extra tight, and I squeeze her back. "Hi, Mom," she says into my hair. At least I have them. That the three of them came from this sham of a marriage is what keeps me going, and we'll exist, all four of us, as a unit, even when I leave Evan. At least that's what I tell myself.

"Did you work things out with Margaret today?" I ask Cole, because last night they got into some kind of argument, and Margaret never came over.

Cole shrugs, staring down at the seltzer. "She didn't answer any of my texts today. And she wasn't in school. Kinda weird considering she probably wanted to tell everyone about Princeton."

"Is she sick?" I ask, heading to the sink. I turn on the faucet and pump lavender soap into my palm.

"I dunno. She's obviously pretty pissed if she's ghosting me."

"What'd you do, Cole?" Arden asks, barely suppressing her delight in her perfect older brother doing something wrong.

Cole shoots her a look. "I didn't *do* anything. Not that it's your business if I did."

"You should check in on her if she wasn't in school," I say, drying my hands on an ikat print hand towel Evan brought back from Morocco.

"I've texted her like ten times," Cole says. His features draw into something hard and impassive, a face I usually only see from him on the baseball field. I remember when he was six or seven and Evan signed him up for baseball, and we saw that he was much more competitive than we realized, that he hated losing almost as much as Evan. I saw a side of Cole I'd never seen before, and I couldn't decide if I loved it or hated it.

I head to the fridge, and then there's the sound of Evan on the stairs, his heavy thudding unmistakable. I brace myself, and I swear Cole does the same thing. Not the girls. They both look up with big blinking blue eyes at Evan when he enters the kitchen: their dad, their protector.

"I didn't realize you were working from home today," I say, trying to sound pleasant. I open the fridge and busy myself finding the flounder Camille bought. "Thanks for getting this, baby," I say to her, shutting the door and putting the package on the counter. The girls just started driving, so now all three kids share the car that formerly only belonged to Cole. They spend more time fighting over it than driving it, but at least it's easy to get them to run errands.

"You're welcome," Camille says, "though I can*not* stand in that fish section again. It smells like day-old death."

"Camille," Evan says, smiling as she pinches her nose.

After I saw Evan with the woman in Miami, I lost every last desire to fight for my marriage. I cancelled the marriage counselor we'd been seeing, telling Evan that I really thought we were on the right track now. I faked my way through everything—knowing I could absolutely do this until the kids were out of the house. Cole leaves at the end of August, off to Bucknell to play baseball, and the girls leave the following August. One more year and a few months. I can do it, and it's the safest way, to have the kids off at college when I drop the bomb that I'm leaving. Evan will be shamed beyond belief when I leave him, his little-boy ego burned and embarrassed, and every volatile bone in his body triggered. I've thought about going back to the marriage counselor when it's time to break the news, so we're somewhere neutral, but Evan's a pro at keeping things cordial and appropriate when he needs to, socially. And then who knows what he'll do.

Arden steps away from the island to grab a water glass. Her wide-legged jeans are so much bigger than her skinny frame; I'll never understand the particulars of this current style. I'm about to unwrap the flounder when my phone rings. "It's Margaret's mom," I say to Cole, looking down at the screen. "Do you want to take it?"

"I certainly don't," Cole says with a smirk, and I don't blame him; Margaret's mom, Deb, isn't all that friendly. I swipe the bar and hold the phone to my ear. "Hi, Deb," I say, bracing myself.

"I'm sorry for the urgency," she says. "I just received two voice mails that I somehow missed earlier at work—the service is so spotty in the hospital—one from Sloane Thompson, because Margaret never showed up to babysit Daisy, and then one from school, delivered even earlier, because apparently Margaret didn't make it there, either." Her words fly at a quick, hammering clip, and there's disgust laced thinly through them rather than worry. "I can't reach her, and I was wondering if she's still at your house. If perhaps she and Cole skipped school together today?"

The hair on the back of my neck wakes up. "Still at my house?" I say, repeating her phrasing back to her. "Margaret didn't stay here last night. And Cole went to school today."

Evan flips through the mail like nothing's wrong, like he's oblivious to my side of the conversation. But over the kitchen island, I meet Cole's big eyes.

"Excuse me?" Deb asks. "Are you sure?"

"I'm sure," I say. And then to Cole, my voice sharp, "When was the last time you talked to Margaret? Deb, I'm putting you on speaker." I put the phone on the counter and watch as Cole's mouth drops an inch. He looks scared, and then, in the awkwardly loud and clear voice reserved for speaker phone, Cole says, "I haven't talked to Margaret since last night, Mrs. Collins. She said she didn't want to sleep over here, and she was sleeping at your house."

"Margaret never came home last night," Deb says, loud enough for all of us. My girls exchange a glance, and Cole's gaze narrows at the phone as Deb goes on, "Her dad spoke with her, and asked her to come home to speak with him about a private family matter, but she blew him off." And then, more accusingly, "We thought she was with *you*."

This makes Evan look up. I can feel his gaze, heavy on Cole.

"Deb, what can I do to help—" I start, but she cuts me off.

"I'm going to go now," she says, her voice hard and tinny in our kitchen. "Cole, please have Margaret call me the minute you hear from her. I'm going to make a few phone calls, and then . . ." Her voice trails off, and in the silence, I can feel my heart thudding against my chest. Deb lets go of a breath, and she sounds like she's talking more to herself than to me when she says, "Well, I don't know. I don't know what to do . . ."

"We could call the police," I suggest.

"The *police*?" Deb's voice bellows. Cole stands up straight, his hands falling against the kitchen island. The seltzer topples and spills, and all at once, everything takes on a chaotic sheen. Arden and Camille are white faced, and Evan is all sharp edges, his light eyes glaring at Cole. "I'm sure she's fine," I say quickly, more to my kids than to Deb. "I'm sure it's just a misunderstanding. But just to be safe, we could . . ."

"I have to call my husband," Deb says, and then she disconnects.

Cole, Arden, Camille, and I stare down at the phone on the kitchen island between us like it's contaminated. Evan crosses his arms over his chest.

"Mom," Cole says softly. I see the fear all over him. "The *police*? Do you think something bad happened?"

"No, I don't. Of course I don't." I move around the island to comfort him.

"Should *we* call the police?" Arden asks, watching us carefully. "Even if Mrs. Collins won't?" She's been no-nonsense since she was a toddler.

I wrap my arms tightly around Cole's shoulders, but he tenses, flinching like my nearness is hurting him. "You said she was fighting with her parents," I say. "Maybe she just needed some space."

"But she's always fighting with her parents," Cole says. "She wouldn't take off just because of that."

"Would she have gone to another friend's house? Ashley's, maybe?" I suggest, scanning my brain for the names of Margaret's friends, and realizing that's the only one I know. Does Margaret have a lot of friends? I'd always assumed so, but there's so much about these kids I don't know.

"Ashley's? Maybe," Cole says, but he looks doubtful.

Evan says, "Cole, if you know anything Margaret's up to, you need to tell us."

Camille looks down at her hands, biting her lower lip like she might cry. Arden stares at Cole like she's trying to read him.

Cole doesn't look at Evan. His body arches forward, like he's going to run a race, or leap onto the kitchen island. "Can I take the car?" he asks me. "I want to go look for her."

# SEVENTEEN

*Sloane*

That night I'm upstairs lying with Daisy in her bed, fretting over Margaret and fielding texts about both the fundraiser tomorrow night and whether Daisy's okay. I don't know who my elderly neighbor Mrs. Larsen talked to about Daisy getting locked out in the cold earlier, but now everyone at school seems to know. Texts came in from moms I didn't even realize had my number, all in the name of Daisy's health, and while my most generous interpretation of that scenario would be to think they were truly worried and wishing her well, I'm not so sure. There was a phone call from one of the second-grade moms who made Daisy getting locked out sound scandalous and vaguely thrilling. And then she said something to the effect of "It's *so* crazy, because you're usually *so* careful," and I got the sick feeling she'd been waiting for me to somehow mess up; and now that I had, she was enjoying it. I had to remind myself that Daisy's a child and everyone here wishes her well, and that maybe due to the stress of the day I was overreacting. I just feel so guilty about letting her get locked out in the cold I can't think straight. Her pulmonologist said that if her oxygen readings and other stats were stable, we didn't have to come in, and I must have counted her respiratory rate a dozen times, making extra sure her breaths were below twenty-two per minute. She hasn't been out of my sight since.

And where is Margaret? Her mom called me this evening, frantic after talking to Clara. Apparently, Harper, Ben, and I were the last ones to see Margaret last night, and she never turned up to Cole's house or her own. I've called and texted several times—but Margaret's phone goes straight to voice mail, and she hasn't replied to any texts.

I snuggle closer to Daisy, and we take turns reading her favorite Mercy Watson book, a go-to for when she's tired and can't handle a new book. The cover, featuring a dolled-up pig in a tiara, is torn and well loved, and I try to relax into the feeling of my daughter beside me, safe and warm, but I can't stop thinking of Margaret. Clara and Cole don't know where she is, and neither does Margaret's mom, and the last place Margaret was before disappearing was my house. It makes me so unsettled I can hardly lie still. I just can't imagine a universe where Margaret would have forgotten to pick up Daisy, and then not be in contact with me or anyone else.

"Can you stay with me while I fall asleep?" Daisy asks, setting her book onto her night table and taking a sip of water.

"Of course, baby," I say, kissing her temple.

I lie there in the dark while she falls asleep, feeling sick to my stomach thinking about what could have happened to her if Mrs. Larsen hadn't been home. The next house was another quarter mile away, and the descent down Beckett's Hill isn't an easy one.

Daisy's breathing slows, and I try to shake off the guilt. When I'm sure she's asleep, I inch my legs over the side of the bed and walk to the window to shut the shades. I put a hand on the heavy fabric of the curtains, and then spy a light on inside Harper and Ben's house. Once the trees fill in, I won't be able to see them, but through the bare branches I can make out Harper standing very still in the middle of what I imagine is her bedroom. It almost looks like she's staring straight at me, but I can't be sure. I feel too weird shutting the shades on her if she's truly looking at me, so I quickly bend as though I'm picking up Daisy's room, but there's nothing there to clean, so I'm just awkwardly miming a fake chore. I stand up too quickly and get a head rush, and then rapidly move out of view. My heart is pounding. What is wrong with me?

*Ding dong* goes the doorbell, and I nearly faint, because who could possibly be ringing the door at nine p.m.? Daisy's still fast asleep beneath the covers. I creep through her open doorway—I always leave her door open because I find myself waking each night to check on her—and walk down the dark hallway, turning on lights as I go. Times like these are when I wish I had a dog.

Downstairs, I peek through the peephole and see a tall man with salt-and-pepper hair wearing dark clothes.

"Can I help you?" I ask loudly without opening the door, hoping he can hear me through the wood.

"Paul Delaney," the man shouts back. "Here to ask you some questions about Margaret Collins."

Jesus. "Uh, okay," I mutter to myself.

"Good evening," he says as I undo the chain and open the door. "Retired police detective Paul Delaney, formerly with the Atwater Police Department. I'm a family friend of Margaret Collins's; her grandfather and I went to high school together a few towns over in Bedford Hills. Margaret didn't come home last night, and I'm here for a little chat, because my understanding is you were the last one to see her, as far as Deb and Justin Collins know."

I try to slow my breathing. It's not that I'm scared to talk to him; I'm scared something awful happened to Margaret. Was it cold enough for her to freeze to death if she fell last night on the trail and broke her leg and no one found her? "Margaret was here last night," I quickly say, "with my neighbors and me." I nod toward Harper and Ben's house, and the detective follows my gaze. Harper is still in her room—you can see her from our spot on the front steps. She's no longer standing so eerily still; now she's moving across the room with Ben at her heels, like they're looking for something.

"Those neighbors right there?" the detective asks, watching them through their window.

I nod, and when he doesn't take his eyes off them, I say, "Yes. That's them."

He finally turns back to me. "Well, how about you give your neighbors a call and let's see if we can get them over here, yeah?"

He reminds me of my uncles, affable and laid back in the way he talks and carries himself, even if it might not match his interior life.

"Sure," I say, because what other answer can I possibly give him?

I dial Harper, hoping she'll pick up, and when she does, it's eerie, because from our vantage point on my front step, we can see her leaving her closet with her phone pressed to her ear. It looks like she's striding topless across her bedroom, but maybe she's just taken off her sweater, and her T-shirt is beige. The detective immediately averts his eyes.

"Sloane," Harper says into the phone. "How's Daisy?" She's been extremely sweet and neighborly today, checking in on Daisy and me and making sure we didn't need anything.

"She's okay, sleeping now, thank you. I'm calling because there's a detective here, a friend of Margaret's family. Apparently Margaret hasn't been seen since leaving here last night, and he's wondering if you and Ben are possibly available to come to my house to speak with him now, all of us together, because we were the last ones to see her as far as her parents know."

Harper lets out a muffled sound on her end of the line. "Oh *no*. Yes, of course, we'll be right there."

We get off the phone, and the detective and I stand awkwardly outside. My palms are sweating as I slip the phone back into my pocket.

"Did Margaret exit this door when she left?" he asks.

I nod, thinking of Margaret standing at the door before dipping out into the night. The detective is looking up, and even before he asks, I realize he's probably looking for cameras. Which we don't have.

"Any interior or exterior cameras here?" he asks, looking dubious.

"No," I say, inexplicably embarrassed, like I've failed an important test.

"Did you see Margaret get into her car?"

For a quick second, a flash of a possibly nonexistent car in my driveway pops into my mind. And this is one of the things that tips me off to how nervous I am to have this detective standing on my front step, that I can't even remember if Margaret was driving last night. She has a car, but she usually runs the trail through the woods if she's going home and it's not late. Last night was late, so maybe she brought her car? She also always drives if she's going to Cole's after, because his house is on the other side of town. Once, when she didn't have her car here, she changed her mind about where she was staying, and Cole picked her up, his baseball cap lowered and the sun glinting off his SUV.

"Um," I say, "I'm sorry, I can't remember whether she had her car last night. I think she was on foot."

"On foot?" he asks. "Your road doesn't seem friendly for travelers."

It strikes me as odd phrasing—if I'd written dialogue like that in a script and shared it with a writing critique group, one of the writers would have noted it as archaic and suggested I change it.

"There's a trail through the woods that cuts directly to her house," I say. "It can't be more than a quarter mile. Margaret grew up in these woods, and she's a runner, so she does it all the time."

The detective fires off a text and then says, "Problem is, Margaret, or someone else, turned off her location tracking last night. So anything you can remember about which way she might have gone would be helpful."

"I'm sorry," I say, embarrassed again. "I honestly have no idea."

"So, let me get this straight. Margaret was babysitting for you, and you returned to your house at what time?"

"Maybe around eight thirty? Or nine? I was at a spelling bee, and it ended later than I thought it would."

"And your neighbors were at the spelling bee, too?"

"They weren't, but when the spelling bee finished, I had a flower arrangement and decided to drop it at their house. To be welcoming, because they're new to the neighborhood as of this week." I'm surprised by the very real instinct I have to distance myself from Ben and Harper in the retelling of this story. It's just a flash of a feeling, and it quickly fades as I see them exit their front door. Harper's wearing a huge sweater that she hugs over her chest, and Ben's in the same green jacket he was wearing when they moved in. Their pace is brisk as they descend the driveway, disappearing in a few spots behind the hedges, and then emerging onto the street. Ben's long legs mechanically stride over the road, and Harper keeps up with him by breaking into little bursts of a trot. The detective unabashedly stares at them, his eyes following their every move in a way that both unsettles me and makes me look closer.

"Harper and I were sitting at the kitchen table," I say softly as we watch them. "We'd been talking with Margaret for some time, having tea, and talking about college, and that kind of thing. So, I know she left through the front door, and I didn't see her get into her car. Though obviously, if she had one here, it was gone later that night."

"Notice anything out of sorts about the state she left your house in—or did what you walked in on seem par for the course?"

"Par for the course."

"Did she seem like she was in a rush to get out of here?"

"Not at all—she stayed and talked with us in the kitchen for a half hour maybe?"

"Do you know of anyone who was here while she was babysitting?" he asks, his eyes leaving Harper and Ben and landing on me.

I shake my head.

Now Ben and Harper are on my property heading toward us. Both have matching worried looks, but Harper looks excited, too, horrible as that sounds. "Is Margaret all right?" she asks, breathless as she approaches and climbs the front steps.

"That's what we're trying to figure out," the detective says. And then he introduces himself to Ben and Harper, and asks me, "Mind if we go inside for a chat? It's buggy out here."

It's cold and not buggy at all, but I lead them inside anyway, and we sit at the kitchen table. I think of Daisy earlier, right here on the bench, me warming her up with chamomile tea while she assured me that she was okay, and that she wasn't even scared when Margaret wasn't there to meet the bus, only cold.

"Did Margaret tell you where she was going when she left last night?" the detective asks us. Ben's large hands are folded together on the table. Harper leans forward, her small shoulders hunched, her body seeming tiny and meek. "No," she says quickly. "Well, not me. Did she tell you, Sloane?"

I shake my head. "She didn't. Sometimes she goes to her boyfriend Cole's house, after she leaves here," I say to the detective. "I'm assuming you've already spoken with him?"

"I haven't, not yet. And you?" he asks Ben, his voice sounding harder than when he first asked us to join him inside for a chat. "Did you speak with Margaret?"

"I only spoke with Margaret for a few moments, and then I went upstairs to shower," Ben says. He sounds confident and eloquent, even though he's talking about showering at his neighbors'. "That's why Harper and I were here last night. We just moved in, and our house hasn't had hot water until today."

Harper takes in Ben's profile, studying him like he's a painting, like she's curious about the shape his face is taking while he speaks.

"I only met Margaret for a short period of time," Ben says, "and without knowing her parents, but based on what Harper relayed to me last night when we returned home, I'd say the pressure being put on Margaret from her parents sounds unhealthy, with the potential for long-term damage."

I blink. Did he seriously just say that?

The detective lets out a snort. "Is that your professional opinion?"

"It is," says Ben, seemingly unbothered by the detective's tone.

"Are you a family therapist?" the detective asks.

"I'm not. I'm a pediatric surgeon. And I see a lot of parent-child dynamics," says Ben.

I fidget on the wooden bench. The entire mood of the kitchen seems to have shifted. "Would anyone like something to drink?" I ask, but everyone ignores me.

"You can feel free to pass along my concerns to Margaret's parents," Ben says.

"And why would I do that?" the detective asks.

Ben shrugs. And then, in that same calm, unemotional voice, he says, "Or you could pass my concerns along to any officer who's eventually assigned to work on the case in an official capacity."

The detective's mouth tightens, and no one says anything. And then Ben leans forward until his abdomen is nearly pressing against the table, and says, mock-conspiratorially, "I'm assuming you're not working on the case in an official capacity. You never showed us a badge, maybe because you don't have one anymore. Is that correct?"

I watch Ben, my pulse picking up. The air between all of us has an electric snap, like something's about to blow.

"I'm not sure what your problem is, Mr. Wilson," the detective says. "I've already told your neighbor exactly what capacity I'm here in, and I don't appreciate your tone."

"And I don't appreciate being interrogated without a full picture of what's going on," Ben says.

Harper puts a hand over Ben's and gives it a quick squeeze. "Ben," she says, her voice shrill. "He's only trying to help Margaret. So, stop, please." And then she locks eyes on him like she's trying to communicate something. "Everything's *fine*," she says.

The detective clears his throat. There's a moment when I think he's going to excuse himself and leave us sitting there, but then he seems to gather his composure. "Walk me through your night with Margaret," he says.

We do. We tell him everything we remember. He asks us all kinds of things, like whether the door was locked when we arrived—it wasn't—and whether Margaret was on the phone with anyone at any point while we were in the kitchen with her. He asks what she was wearing and if she'd had any visible injuries or if anything about her appearance or demeanor was out of the ordinary. When he asks whether anything Margaret said made it sound likely that she might run away, I tell him what Margaret told Harper and me about feeling dull lately after all the burnout of gearing up for college applications, but that I still didn't think she'd ever run away and not let me know she wouldn't be able to get Daisy off the bus, and that I didn't think she'd ever purposely scare her sister or her parents. And when Harper broaches the topic of Margaret's parents again, the detective seems to listen.

An hour later, when the detective excuses himself and tells us he'll be back in touch, the three of us watch him walk out the front door. When he's gone, Harper and I stare at each other. Ben looks down at his hands. "Hopefully nothing happened to her," he says, seemingly more to himself than to us.

"It's only been a day," Harper says. "She could have run off to get some attention, maybe?"

"She just got into an Ivy League school," Ben says. "Wouldn't that garner enough attention?"

I stare out our French doors to the woods, where the edges of green-black trees are silhouetted against the sky. I feel like I'm underwater and unsure which way is up. Is Margaret all right and everyone's just overreacting?

"What if something terrible happened to her?" I ask into the still air of the kitchen. It lands like I know it will, and Ben and Harper stare at me, their gazes hot and penetrating. "There's no scenario I can think of where she'd take off and scare everyone, especially her little sister."

"Unless she told her sister what her plan was," Ben says.

The doorbell rings, and Harper says, "Oh God, more questions?"

"It might be Dave," I say, standing. "He's furious with me, I'm sure."

"Why?" Harper asks.

"Earlier," I say. "Daisy getting locked out."

"Wasn't your fault," says Harper.

"Should we go?" asks Ben.

"Maybe he'll be nicer with us here," says Harper.

"It's open—come in!" I call.

When Dave makes his way into the kitchen, his eyes are wide, his brown hair ruffled. "What's going on?" he asks when he sees Ben and Harper, an edge in his voice.

I cross my arms over my chest, already feeling defensive. "Margaret's missing," I say, feeling a little guilty for exaggerating the facts so that he'll be less mad at me about Daisy. Margaret *is* missing, I guess, but it feels self-serving to announce it like that to try to get myself out of trouble.

Ben stands to shake Dave's hand, and I watch their eyes meet over the handshake. It feels quieter in the kitchen now, even with Dave's agitated state. Ben seems to have softened since the detective left, and his body language comes off as deferential to Dave. "We can go, if that's better," he says. "I know you've had a scare today with Daisy."

Dave's face changes, morphing into something more vulnerable. "Can I see her?" he asks me.

Emotion rises in my chest. "Of course," I say. "But she's sleeping. She's okay, Dave, I promise."

He nods. And then, softly, he asks, "What happened to Margaret?" He's usually so laser focused on Daisy that his disquiet over Margaret catches me off guard.

"We don't know," I say. "A detective was just here, asking us questions."

Dave's face pales. "Seriously? Asking the three of you questions?"

I nod. Ben is still standing, watching Dave carefully. Harper's the only one sitting, and out of nowhere she looks tired and drawn. "We should go," she says to Ben, gingerly getting to her feet.

"Please let us know if you hear from Margaret," Ben says.

We walk them to the front door and say our goodbyes. When the door is closed, Dave looks at me. "You're spending a lot of time with people you just met," he says.

"What's wrong with that?" I snap.

"You don't know them very well."

"Most people don't know their new neighbors before they move in. I'm being friendly. And I like them."

"Well, Margaret's disappeared, and possibly from our property."

"How do *you* know that?"

"Because I just saw Evan at the club, and he told me that Cole's out looking for Margaret, and that the last place she was seen was at our home. Pretty fucked up, wouldn't you say?"

Goose bumps sweep over my skin. "Then why did you act surprised when we all just told you she was missing?"

"Because I'm not giving those two any proprietary information about a girl who disappeared fifty yards from their house."

"*Disappeared*," I say, trying out the word, my heart racing. All of this has to be a mistake. "Are you actually implying Ben and Harper had something to do with it?"

Dave shoves his hands deep into his pockets. "Nope. But until we know for sure that Margaret's okay, maybe we should be keeping a careful eye on Daisy, rather than letting her roam the neighborhood alone."

Fury descends upon me. "How can you say that?"

"I'm not saying you—"

"No one's more careful with Daisy than me. Not you—not anyone."

"I know, Sloane. I know."

We're quiet for a moment, standing alone in the foyer.

"But if anything ever happened to her," Dave says.

"I'd die."

"Me too."

*But we face this reality all the time,* I think to myself.

"Then we won't take our eyes off of her," I say. "Which means I'll need you here, tomorrow night, watching her while I'm at the fundraiser."

"Can't we just skip the fundraiser? We could take Daisy out for dinner and a movie instead, try to take our minds off this thing with Margaret."

Margaret has to be home by tomorrow—it would be too terrifying otherwise. "We already bought tickets," I say. "And I promised Clara Gartner I'd run the photo booth."

"Oh, right. And no one says no to Clara Gartner," Dave says, rolling his eyes.

"Not if they want to show their faces in this town again," I say, a pathetic attempt at a joke, something we've learned to do to avoid an argument. What's the point now that we're divorced?

"Can I see Daisy?" Dave asks gently. "Just for a few minutes. I won't wake her."

"Of course. C'mon," I say, starting up the stairs.

# EIGHTEEN

## *Clara*

By Saturday evening, the event space we rented has been transformed into a glamorous casino with evenly spaced velvety tables featuring blackjack, roulette, baccarat, craps, and poker. A disco ball hangs from the ceiling and scatters light over the game tables, and little flecks of iridescent streamers dot the floor, catching the disco light and making the floor sparkle. Smooth jazz plays over the speakers, and the entire thing feels magical, despite the uneasy feeling inside me.

Margaret is still gone. All day I've held my breath as I worked alongside parent volunteers and the company we hired to deliver the casino game setup. I must have checked my phone a thousand times, hoping to hear from Cole that Margaret had been in touch, or from Margaret's mom. Or from anyone.

The caterer has set up the food; the bartenders are in place behind tables filled with glistening bottles of alcohol; and we're only moments away from opening the doors to guests. I'm standing in the middle of the event hall and scanning everything to make sure nothing's out of place, when Sloane Thompson strolls in with a strikingly beautiful dark-haired woman on her arm. Their elbows are linked like paper dolls, and the picture they make together is so pretty that for a second, I stop worrying about whether tonight will go off without a hitch, or whether Margaret will be found, or whether, when I leave, Evan will find a way to enact revenge on me in a way I can't withstand. I just stare at them. Sloane says something, and the dark-haired woman throws back her head and laughs, like they're in a commercial featuring women who share deodorant. I can't place the dark-haired woman—maybe she's a new mother at the elementary school I haven't yet met?

"Excuse me," I say, slipping past a cluster of volunteers smoothing a tablecloth. (How many women does it take to smooth a tablecloth, honestly? And why do the dads barely ever volunteer?) "Sloane?" I call out as I walk toward her. It's the oddest thing: Sloane and the woman are staring at each other, talking like there's no one else in the room besides the two of them. And is the dark-haired woman drunk? I smell fruity white wine as I approach them, and Sloane turns to me and looks happier to see me than usual.

"Hi," I say. I almost tell Sloane's friend she needs to wait outside the event hall until seven when we start letting guests inside, but seven is only a few minutes away, and I don't want to be a jerk. Instead, I stick out my hand to her. "I'm Clara."

"Harper," she says warmly, and extends a tiny, delicate hand to take mine. She's young—early thirties, maybe?

"You must be new here," I say, dropping her freezing fingers. "Do you have a child in the elementary school?"

"I don't," she says. "I'm Sloane's new neighbor."

"And I'd already bought two tickets," Sloane says, brushing auburn hair from her face and tucking it behind her ear. Friendship bracelets collide on her wrist as she goes on. "And of course, Dave couldn't come with Margaret being gone, or running away, or going missing, or whatever is happening . . ." Sloane's voice trails off, her entire being seeming to deflate.

"I was actually hoping you'd heard something from her," I say, softening. I want to cry, honestly; can't they just hurry and find Margaret wherever she's gone?

Sloane shakes her head. "I was hoping you had."

Harper's eyes bounce from Sloane to me.

"I haven't," I say. "And neither has Cole. No texts, no calls."

"God," Sloane said. "You don't think—"

"I don't know what to think," I interrupt. I can't really manage my own feelings about this. Are we all going to be irritated when Margaret comes home, having worried everyone for no reason? Or are we going to be devastated because something terrible happened to her? "I'm hoping maybe she just ran off to make a point or something with her parents. Her parents aren't easy on her, I'm sure you know."

Before Sloane can say anything, Harper chimes in. "I would have done something like that when I was young." Her words are a little slurry; they're both obviously buzzed. Not that it matters, I guess. It's a party, after all.

"I would've been too scared of my dad to do it," I say, unsure why I'm divulging that when my dad still lives in town. But Sloane seems like the kind of woman who doesn't share confidences, and it's not like I said anything all that bad. "I'm sorry Dave can't be here," I offer, trying to change the conversation.

Sloane shrugs. "He just dropped us off. He and Daisy are going to a movie, which will be good for her. We're trying not to freak her out about Margaret, but she knows something's up." She glances around at the card and game tables, her pretty face spattered with disco light. "It looks great in here, Clara," she says. "You did good."

I smile despite myself, despite the growing sense that something awful happened to Margaret. And then Evan enters the event hall in a perfectly tailored navy-blue suit. He looks gorgeous—even I can't deny that—and I see Harper notice him as he walks toward us.

Sloane tugs at Harper's arm. "We should go to the photo booth. That's our job, remember?"

"Yeah, yeah," Harper says with a little smile, like maybe she thinks the whole thing is silly, but not in a condescending way. She comes off as sweet, actually. And then she looks at my husband again, her head tilting coyly. "Who's *that*?" she asks, but Sloane is already pulling her away.

I brace myself for Evan. He's giving a wave to a few women he recognizes, two of whom go to our club, and another who has a son in class with Arden and Camille. I watch him bestow his attention upon them and wonder how someone who comes off as so noble could be so dishonest. The contrast always startles me. Do the other women see through him?

"Looks great in here, babe," he says as he approaches me, loud enough for others to hear him over the jazz. He puts an arm on the small of my back and kisses me on the mouth. I try not to pull away.

"I'm about to open the doors," I say, glancing around. Sloane and Harper are hurrying toward the photo booth, arms linked again. "I think we're ready."

# NINETEEN

*Sloane*

Halfway through the fundraiser, Harper and I are decidedly drunk, and Dave's warning for me to stay away from her is easier to forget now that I'm loose with alcohol. I'm not a big drinker, but right now I'm grateful for it—it's taken the edge off my worry about Margaret. And most of the parents here don't know Margaret, so it's easier to lose myself in this particular crowd. Margaret just needs to come home tonight, and then tomorrow everything can go back to normal. Even a boring normal sounds like a mercy right now.

Dave was furious when I said I was giving Harper the extra ticket, and even more annoyed when we had a glass of wine together before he drove us here. Harper pretended like she didn't pick up on the tension between us on the drive over, but when we got out of the car she said, "Oh my God, I think he hates me," and we both burst out laughing like teenagers.

Now we're trying to adjust our props correctly in the photo booth to get a proper photo without the disguises falling off. Harper grabs the film being printed and says, "Oh, this is it; this is the one!" We tip out of the photo booth, a tangle of limbs. "Can we dance now?" Harper shouts over the music. Somewhere in the last few minutes, jazzy casino music morphed into Top 40 songs. There's a makeshift dance floor, and some people are barefoot, which makes me smile. It's nearing the end of the school year; spring is here; and as soon as Margaret is found, maybe things will start looking up. I have a new friend—something I haven't been able to say for a long time—and I can feel the zing of friendship in every cell in my body. I've always liked having one or two very close friends, rather than a big group, even when I was young. I was that way even in elementary school, and though I'd often have a wider circle of female friends, it was always that one friend who kept me tethered and helped me get through female adolescence mostly unscathed. I haven't found that one true friend in Sycamore Glen. I'm not saying Harper will be that person; but she might be.

I'm high on the wine, and I let Harper tug me away from the photo booth and toward the cluster of dancing adults. We've been sequestered near the photo booth, sneaking drinks, and now working the booth seems sort of pointless. I feel like a caged animal set free as Harper pulls me into the warm mass of bodies on the dance floor. I recognize a few parents, most of whom stare at Harper. She doesn't really seem to notice them. She mostly just focuses on me, not really giving anyone the time of day, even one woman who's clearly trying to dance with us. I try to let the woman in, but Harper cuts her off and starts doing wild dance moves, both of her arms circling high in the air, her hips gyrating like she was once a professional dancer.

Harper and I dance for a while, both of us giggling at her increasingly outrageous moves, but it's earned us too much attention: I feel the stares of other parents like something physical. And then a man walks by us and shouts over the music to a woman I know from volunteering at the school store: "They haven't found her; of course, her parents aren't here. They're working with the cops. Do you know them?"

Harper must overhear the man, too, because she stops dancing and grabs my hand. A woman named Kitty with a daughter in Daisy's class is fully staring at Harper and me, nudging the woman next to her and whispering something. And suddenly everything feels sad again.

"Let's get out of here, don't you think?" I shout to Harper.

"What?" she shouts back.

"Let's go! Let's go to my house?"

"But what about the photo booth and that lady . . . Clara? . . . Don't we have to do it?" Harper turns around and eyes Clara, who's standing on the fringe of the dance floor. Clara's holding a water bottle, looking like she's having zero fun. She's staring at her husband, who's staring at Harper.

What must that be like for a man like Evan, to have snagged a perfectly beautiful and appropriate wife like Clara? Maybe she's all he ever wanted in a woman, someone lovely who did and said all the right things; someone who raised his children, stood by his side, and showered him with attention; someone who ignored any wrongdoing. I think of their parties, how glitzy they were, the antique wallpaper and sparkling china, the endless drinks and catered food, the sheer *socializing*. When I think of Clara and Evan, I think of prom queens and soap opera businessmen with thick, parted hair; I think of two people who know their place in their community because they've made it so. They've fought tooth and nail for it, and now they're comfortably sitting on their laurels like fatted pigs.

As soon as Evan sees me catch him staring at Harper, he turns away. I watch Clara strike up a conversation with one of Margaret's neighbors from the bottom of Beckett's Hill. Suddenly I can't stand the sight of them for a second longer.

I take out my phone and open the Uber app.

"Who cares about the photo booth?" I tell Harper, scheduling us a ride. "I need some air."

# TWENTY

*Sloane*

I have an idea," I say to Harper. We're snuggled inside our coats and slumped against the Uber's leather seat. "Instead of my house, what if we go to the cliffs? Daisy's sleeping already, and I don't really want the night to be over yet."

Harper sits up straighter. "The cliffs?"

For a split second, I doubt myself and think of Dave's warning. But if anything, it has the opposite effect—it makes me want to run even faster toward Ben and Harper.

"Behind our properties. Haven't you been back there?"

"Ben has. He went with the real estate agent. But not me."

"It's beautiful," I say. "Like a hidden gem. Your property line goes right up to the edge."

"What about the bats and coyotes," Harper asks, "and the *wolves?*"

"No wolves," I say, trying to suppress a smile. "But bats everywhere."

She's quiet for a moment, and I can feel how real her fear is. But then she lets out a little laugh. "Okay. No wolves. That's good."

"I go back there all the time, I promise. There's a trail I'm pretty sure we can get to from your lawn that intersects with the trail from my house."

Harper leans forward and says to the driver, "Can you take us to number 117, please? Keep going past this one . . . and then, yeah, this one, thanks."

The driver cruises toward her driveway and slows on the gravelly incline. "You won't be disappointed," I tell her as he takes us to the top. We climb out of the car carefully into the chilly night air and stand on the gravel while he pulls away. When we're all alone, I ask, "You sure?"

She nods, pulling her coat tighter over her chest. Behind her, the house is entirely dark. "Is Ben sleeping?" I ask.

"He's at the hospital." Even in the dark I can make out the roll of her eyes. "He's always there. In San Francisco it was all the time. I'm hoping here his hours will be a little better, but he's a perfectionist about work, so I don't know how much of it is the hospital and how much of it is *him.*"

Harper walks tentatively toward her backyard. I trot along beside her, my eyes adjusting, praying a rogue owl or coyote doesn't take this moment to cry out and change her mind. "He obviously loves you," I say softly, because two nights ago, even when he was clearly exasperated with her for losing her phone and pestering Margaret, it felt clear to me that he loved and cared deeply for her.

"Oh, he loves me," she says, moving easily over the cold, wet ground. "Yes. That's true."

The way she says it is odd, but I don't push. She's drunk, and I don't want to take advantage of her state to satisfy my curiosity and get her to say something she might not say sober.

"And he's a good person," she adds as we creep along the side of the house toward the woods.

We're quiet for a moment, and when Harper sees the opening to the trail, she asks, "What if we get lost? It's *cold*, maybe dangerously cold, if we get stuck out here."

"Our phones get service," I say, holding mine up and turning on the flashlight. "It's okay, Harper, I promise. I know these trails like the back of my hand. And the cliffs aren't far off. Maybe a football field away."

I don't look back as I plunge into the yawning mouth between the trees, hoping Harper will follow. "You okay?" I ask when I hear her behind me, twigs crunching.

"Um, I think so," she says, her voice small. There's just enough room on the trail for us to walk side by side, but Harper stays a foot or two behind me, like she doesn't want to get too close to the trees and bushes pressing in upon us. She's slightly out of breath, which I imagine is more from fear than lack of being in shape. She's a muscle-y little thing, tight like a spring. "Do you do yoga?" I ask, trying to distract her.

"Yeah. I do. You?"

"No. I should."

I think we're going to go on like that, talking nonsense, when Harper says, "I started doing it as a teenager to deal with some sexual abuse that happened when I was a little kid."

I stop dead and Harper smashes into me. "Oh! Ow!" she says.

I turn to her. "I'm so sorry," I say, the darkness making it hard to see her features, to read her. "That you went through that."

"Oh God, yeah. It was awful," she says. And then she takes my hand, and we start walking again, this time together. "It was our neighbor in Spokane—that's where we grew up. He did things to me no one should ever do to anyone, let alone to a child. It nearly ruined my brother and me. My poor brother, honestly. The man didn't do anything to him, but my brother knew it was happening to me. But we were both too young to know what to do about it." She's walking quickly now, navigating the trail easier than I thought she would. I hurry to stay by her side, still holding her hand. "We didn't tell our parents," she says, "because they probably wouldn't have believed us, and we didn't really have the right words, because they'd never talked to us about anything like that. I mean, maybe that's not fair. Maybe they would have believed us; maybe I should give them more credit. But either way, we never told them. It continued until, oh, well, until I turned twelve and bashed his head in with a rock."

I stop dead again. "What?"

She turns and looks at me. I can see the whites of her eyes in the dark now, the outline of her heart-shaped face against the black woods behind us. "I bashed his head in with a rock," she says plainly.

"You killed him?" I ask, my stomach twisting.

"Would it be that bad if I did?" she asks.

A heavy silence falls between us, and I can feel cool air come to rest against my face. "Um. I-I . . . ," I stammer, feeling sick, like everything I ate and drank tonight is threatening to find its way out. "Well, I . . . ," I start again, but then Harper cuts me off.

"Shhh," she hushes me. "Never mind, Sloane." She pats my back, and I realize that I'm hunched over a little. "You feeling okay?" she asks.

"I'm fine," I say. "And I'm sorry about what your neighbor did to you."

"I didn't kill anyone," she says softly. "I'm sorry I upset you. Ben says I do this all the time." Her words are quick and remorseful. "He says I say things that make people upset. That I don't know how to read a room and just blend into it. I'm really sorry."

We're still just standing there, staring at each other. I take her hand and squeeze it. "You don't need to be sorry," I say. "You didn't do anything wrong. It's me. I think the story took me by surprise, and then my stomach has been a mess anyway. All that wine we had . . ."

"I feel pretty sober now," Harper says.

"Oh, okay. Well, you didn't say anything wrong. Trust me." I imagine standing with her at the edge of the cliffs and looking down at the black, churning water. And I say again, because no number of times seems like enough, "I'm really sorry that happened to—"

"Yes, let's keep going," she cuts me off, but I don't want to stop talking—I don't want her to ever feel like I can't handle something she tells me. Isn't that supposed to be what true friends do for each other: Hold the space between them for the thing that needs to be spoken aloud? "And I don't agree with Ben," I say. "Not that I've known you for a long time, but I don't think you need to start reading a room."

She says nothing as we start walking again.

"So you bashed his head with a rock, and he stopped?" I ask.

She squeezes my hand. There's more energy in her pace now, like she's glad I brought it back up. "Yeah, I did," she says. "That was it for his wandering hands. That trusty old rock." She lets out a small, sad laugh that sounds like the end of something. And then she goes on, "I carried the rock back to our front lawn and put it next to the steps, kind of like a warning. Not even a warning for other people. More like a warning for myself, a reminder, so that I'd know what I was capable of, and that I didn't have to take anyone's shit. And after that, I didn't." We emerge onto the clearing before the cliffs and Harper stops to take it all in, nodding appreciatively. And then she turns to me and asks, "What about you? Did anything ever happen to you?"

I take a breath. I need to do this—to drop the guardrails I usually put up around this awful truth. What is it now—one in every three women sexually abused or assaulted by early adulthood? And most of us feeling like we can barely talk about it? "Can we sit first?" I ask. I gesture to a patch of rocks about ten feet back from the start of the cliffs.

"Sure," she says, and we lower ourselves to sit on the rocks' worn edges.

"I've never told anyone this," I say, "because the memory of the night is so incredibly confusing and unclear. Maybe if I remembered it perfectly, if it weren't so hazy, I would have told everyone—or maybe that's an excuse and I'm a coward who never would have told anyone, even if the memory were crystal clear. But eight years ago, at a party held at Clara Gartner's house, I got really drunk, and I have memories that came back in flashes of Clara's husband, Evan, raping me."

Harper's light eyes widen, and her small hands ball into tight fists. "*No*," she says, the word like a low, feral growl.

"Dave and I had been trying to get pregnant with Daisy for years, and we never could. The timing of me getting pregnant that month . . ."

Harper's starting to sway, even sitting on the rock, like she's overcome with emotion and can't sit still. She reaches forward and takes my hand, and I can feel that the words I'm about to say, to have found someone I can say them to, will be a tiny grace, a salve on the deepest wound of my life.

"I'm pretty sure that Evan is Daisy's biological father."

# TWENTY-ONE

## *Clara*

After the fundraiser, I'm outside the event hall getting some air, leaning back against the white-brick wall, feeling the odd desire to smoke a cigarette, which I haven't done in twenty years. Maybe it's something about the setting—hiding outside a party for quiet. I stand there, gazing up at the dark sky spattered with sparkling stars, my legs tired and feet aching in too-small kitten heels, and think about the way things were when Evan and I first got married. That time in my life feels like a cloudy memory, maybe my brain's way of protecting me from how devastated I was after losing my sister, Natalie, the year before. She died the summer before her senior year of high school (Cole's age—which makes me shudder every time I think of it). A drunk driver struck her while she was walking our road in the dark, just a mile down the road from where I live now. Natalie didn't have a habit of walking the streets at night; she only went out for the walk because my father had called her *ungrateful* and smacked her cheek in the kitchen. He'd never hit either one of us, and we were stunned by what he'd done. We stood there speechless, staring at each other as a red mark came to life on Natalie's beautiful face. Had I said anything at all—had I fought for my sister in any small way—she'd likely still be alive. But I'd remained quiet. The sad part is how much I'm still like that now—I can barely say anything controversial, even when the thoughts are right there in my brain, dying to scratch their way out. It's how I was raised by my parents, to always be palatable; it's what I learned. And the things you learn are hard to escape. If that's an excuse, it's also something true.

On the night she died, Natalie came sailing into our driveway on the back of a motorcycle driven by a kid our father forbade her from seeing. She'd disobeyed him, and then paraded into the house, calling our father old-fashioned and controlling.

And even when Natalie was dead and gone and our family irreparably broken, my father never once said he was sorry for slapping her, for driving her from the house to her ultimate demise.

Sometimes I think I picked Evan as a reaction to my father. Evan was nothing like him, which was exactly what I wanted. My father was a judge, relentlessly moral, hard on himself and on others, whereas Evan was okay with bending the rules, just like Natalie had been. And even though I hate this about him now and feel foolish for ever being attracted to it, when I was twenty-two, it felt thrilling. My father was cold with my mother, almost never showing her affection in front of my sister and me, but Evan was constantly touching me, and when we were first married, he was consumed with me. He'd cup my face and kiss my lips and make love to me every night—sometimes mornings, too—and I took it as a sign of how in love we were. There didn't seem anything untoward in his desire for me—his sex drive felt entirely within the bounds of normal for a twentysomething. But then I had Cole. At first, Evan stayed away from me. The doctor told us we couldn't have sex for six weeks anyway, and I'm nothing if not a rule follower. But by week three, Evan was nearly beside himself. I thought it was just the stress of having a newborn, so I told him I could manage Cole by myself. I didn't really want Evan there with us in the middle of the night, anyway, lurking around and seeming agitated during our feedings. I adored the sleepy midnight hours alone with Cole, and I didn't need Evan there, sucking the life out of the room. Cole was magic. He was my new love, and in some ways, I knew that the space that had always been wide open for Evan would never be the same now that Cole was here. Evan must have felt it, too, and maybe some new fathers meld seamlessly into their new role, but Evan bucked against it, demanding that we make time alone without the baby. And I suppose I was wrong for not giving that to him, but I wasn't ready to separate from Cole. During the day, I forced myself to part with Cole so Evan could hold him and try to bond. But Evan didn't bond with him the way I thought he would; instead, he seemed like he wished things would go back to the way they were, with just the two of us young and newly wed and, frankly, having sex all the time. Our marriage suffered, and then I became pregnant with the girls while I was nursing Cole and stupidly thought I couldn't get pregnant. (Not that I'd trade Arden and Camille for the world—I wouldn't—but the surprise of a twin pregnancy and delivery when Cole was only a year and a half did nothing to help the chasm that had opened between Evan and me.) We pushed through the baby and toddler years, keeping our heads down and putting one foot in front of the other. I knew Evan wasn't happy, but I had zero energy left to do anything about it.

By the time the kids were in elementary school, I thought we were reasonably okay again. We started having more sex, and I played the part of a good, cheerful wife; I threw parties because Evan loved them, shuttled the kids wherever they needed to go, accompanied Evan to work dinners, and did whatever else was unspoken and required of me. The kids were my true loves and my entire world, but I thought I did a fine job of making Evan feel important, too, because I *did* love him, and I certainly loved our life together.

I hear the clack of heels against pavement and turn to see Marlow rounding the side of the hall, walking toward me with her head down. I'm instantly nervous, wondering if she meant to find me, or if she's stumbled upon me by accident and this is going to be awkward. I straighten, and when she looks up and smiles at me, I feel the full force of her sunshine. Adrenaline floods my system, the split second of hope that things could ever be right again between us.

"Hey," she says, coming closer. But then she stops a full body length away, like I might bite. "Tonight went great," she says, and I can hear in her words that she's a little tipsy. She stopped drinking after her affair with Evan, and I'm not sure what made her start again. She's not fully drunk, but I can tell by her soft movements and how easy she seems around me that she's not sober, either.

"It did go great," I echo. *And I'm glad it's over.* It was so much more fun doing this kind of thing when she and I were working together, but now she mostly volunteers at the high school and leaves me to do the elementary school fundraiser by myself. She's on the board of ed and comes to a lot of events here, too, but we're no longer co-conspirators planning things side by side. It feels like another way that she's moved on, and I've stayed stuck.

"How are you?" she asks. She hasn't asked it like this in ages, with proper eye contact and a tilt to her chin that means she really wants to know the answer.

"I'm okay."

"Just okay? The event was a success."

It's funny the way she says it, like my okay-ness would be determined by how well an event I planned has gone. Maybe years ago, that was true. But not anymore.

We're quiet for a moment. I know I could comfortably steer the conversation to something surface level, but instead I say, "Yeah. Just okay."

"What's up, then?" she asks. "Something wrong?"

*All I can think about is leaving my marriage,* I want to say. *It's permeating my every thought.*

"Cole's girlfriend, Margaret, has been missing since two nights ago," I blurt.

"I heard," Marlow says. She crosses her muscular arms over her chest. "Strange. Do you think she's run off?"

I shift my weight. My shoes have been pinching my toes all night, making them go numb. "I don't think so, but don't they always say adults barely understand what kids this generation have to deal with?" I break Marlow's stare and gaze off for a moment. A meadow backs up to the play area, and tall grasses sway with the wind.

"What does Evan think?" Marlow asks.

It's the first time I've heard his name come out of her mouth since the affair, and the sound makes me nauseous. There were many weeks following the moment I walked in on them that I spent imagining it: the things she said to him when they were having sex, what she must have looked like beneath his gaze. I tortured myself with all the ways sex with Marlow could have been different from sex with me. In our early marriage, Evan always tried to get me to talk to him during sex, which I found to be a complete turnoff. I tried a few times, but I felt so ridiculous I had to stop. But what about Marlow? Did she say the things he'd always wanted to hear?

"I think Evan thinks what everyone else thinks," I say dryly. "Which is that the police will eventually find her. That she's hiding out somewhere."

"Or she's dead," Marlow says.

I swallow. "Or she's dead," I say, anxiety edging up my throat. It's not like I haven't considered it. It makes me feel frenetic, and then I snap, "Yes, Marlow. That's the other option."

Marlow raises her eyebrows. "You don't have to be snotty about it."

"I'm not being snotty." I hate how childish I sound. And maybe that's why I say what I do. "Why did you come back here to find me tonight? Usually, you avoid me."

"I don't avoid you," Marlow lies.

"You've avoided me ever since the night you slept with Evan."

We both freeze, because there they are, smack between us now: the words that have never been spoken.

For a moment, everything seems to still and fall silent: Nothing moves in the brush, no voices sound from the front of the event hall, and no engine roars to life from the parking lot.

My fists clench, not only because I'm mad, but because I need something to hold on to, a physical sensation to ground me inside this horrible moment. Everything suddenly feels sharp and foreign and nothing like the familiar grounds of a town where I know my footing.

"You always think you know everything," Marlow says.

"I know enough," I say.

"You *don't*," she says.

"Then *what*?" I spit. "What else do I need to know? That you were in love with him? That you couldn't help yourself? That you were going through something outside the bounds of what I could ever possibly understand, and Evan was right there, and you couldn't resist?"

Marlow no longer looks angry—she looks shocked. "In *love* with him?" she repeats. "With *Evan*? Is that what you think?"

"Well, I don't know what to think. Because you've never thought our friendship was worth enough for us to talk about what you did. You slept with my husband and then dropped me like a stone. Like it was my fault."

"I never thought it was your fault," Marlow says. "Never. Unless . . ."

"Unless what?" How could this *ever* be my fault?

"I wasn't sure if maybe you knew about some of his proclivities. If maybe he'd done something like this before, and you never reported him."

"If he'd ever had an affair before?"

Everything feels wrong and menacing. Nearby flowerbeds appear tangled and overgrown, and the red-and-blue play structure in an adjacent yard looks jagged and dangerous. Nothing feels like it's supposed to, especially Marlow.

"Well . . . ," Marlow starts, and then everything gets quiet again.

"I don't understand," I say. "You had an affair with my husband, and now you want to know if there were other women besides you? How self-centered can you possibly be?"

Marlow shakes her head, and she suddenly looks so incredibly sad. "Clara, I'm so sorry, trust me, I am . . ."

I feel like I've lost the thread of the conversation, like it's spun entirely out of my control. "If you're so sorry, then why didn't you ever apologize before this moment, nearly two years later?"

"I'm not sorry for anything I did," she says.

And now it's my turn to look shocked. "How can you say that to me?" I ask, barely able to get the words out.

And then Marlow says the thing that tilts the world sideways and opens the ground beneath me.

"*Evan raped me, Clara,*" she whispers, the words like tiny knives. I hear it in slow motion, acutely feeling the way the words make the blood course inside my ears and my skin go clammy and cold.

"No," I say slowly, trying to get a breath into my lungs. "I saw you, Marlow. I walked in on it." My heart races. I thought I'd seen consensual sex—but have I gotten everything backward?

Tears have started in Marlow's big brown eyes. "I had no idea," she says. "*God,* that's even worse, somehow," she says, wiping her tears with shaking hands, a gold cocktail ring glittering on her index finger. "I don't know what you think you saw, but here's what I *do* know: I'd had one or two drinks that night at your house. I was a little buzzed, that's for sure, but then suddenly I was the drunkest I'd ever been in my entire life. I'd been in a corner talking with Evan, and I know what this is going to sound like, but I'm almost sure he put something in my drink. Because all of a sudden, I could barely stay upright. He asked if I wanted to lie down, and I stupidly told him I did, and the last thing I remember is him trying to get me up the stairs. I could hardly make my legs work by then, and I don't remember what happened after that—I have no memories of the actual rape. I don't even remember how I got home, but the next morning, I had blood in my underwear."

My stomach falls, my heart pounding against my ribs. I'm trying to follow every word Marlow says, but my brain feels like it's gone somewhere else, like I'm hearing everything through a tunnel. If I had heard the story without seeing the rape, there would be room for another ending, like Evan helping her up the stairs to lie down and someone else raping her. But I saw the rape. I'd never even considered the possibility that she wasn't in her right mind to consent—because I'd seen her minutes before, laughing with our friends, nothing awry, drinking no more than her typical self-imposed two-drink limit.

Marlow tilts her head, looking at me like she knows I'm barely standing, like she's worried. I reach out an arm to steady myself, but there's nothing to hold. Her voice is softer when she says, "Apparently, your garden club friend Julie found me upstairs and took me home, but I don't remember that part. The only reason I know how I got home is because Julie said something about it to me in town on Monday, and we shared a horrible, fake laugh about how drunk I'd gotten. And here's the stupidest thing: The next morning, I never went to the hospital for a rape kit. I was all alone when I woke up, blood in my underwear, dealing with the kids by myself, my head completely swimming, but those memories of Evan helping me get upstairs breaking through. I was *fucking terrified*. I wasn't sure whether to go get the morning-after pill, because God forbid I got pregnant, and I felt like I was having an endless panic attack, with no one there to help me." Tears run over both of our faces, and then, just when I think nothing can get any worse, Marlow says, "There's never anyone there to help me. That's what no one tells you about early widowhood. That you'll deal with nearly everything having to do with you or the kids all by yourself. You have friends, of course, and extended family. But it's not the same. And even though I have this feeling deep in my bones that none of this ever would have happened if John were still alive, I still shudder when I think about how, if he were alive, he would have killed your husband."

The words land like a slap, and then Marlow starts sobbing. Hands that don't feel like my own reach out and grasp her shoulders, pulling her into an embrace. "I'm sorry," I say, and then I'm sobbing, too, and we're both just standing there, holding each other. *"I'm so sorry.* Please forgive me, Marlow. I had no idea."

Mascara streaks across her cheek as she tries to wipe her face. "There's nothing to forgive you for, not as far as I'm concerned," she says.

"But isn't there?" I ask. "Shouldn't I have considered the possibility?"

"That I'd been too incapacitated to consent? You'd just been downstairs with me. You knew I'd only had a drink or two. And after, you kept reaching out to me to talk and I wouldn't let you. I didn't give you the chance."

We stand there, still half hugging, and it takes me a minute for my thoughts to go straight, for me to go from confused and terrified to a feeling that feels a little better: *determined.*

I pull away to look her in the eye. "But now what do we do? Don't we need to tell someone what he's done? Because what if he fucking does it again? What if he already *has?"*

I hate him more in this moment than I ever have. The feeling spirals inside me like a storm, ready to break free from my body and destroy everything I've ever known, but Marlow only shakes her head. "I've already asked a lawyer about pressing charges," she says. "Weeks later, when I put myself together again, I went to a lawyer, not only because I knew there should be repercussions, but also because I felt so horribly guilty at the thought of it happening to another person. But the lawyer told me it would be nearly impossible to have Evan convicted. We had no DNA, I was drinking, and there were no witnesses that we knew of. And most importantly, I couldn't remember a single thing about the actual rape I'm sure occurred. The last thing I remember was him helping me up the stairs. But anyone defending Evan would say that he helped me up the stairs to lie down and sober up, and that another man could have come in and taken advantage of me."

It doesn't feel real, to be hearing these words about my husband, to try to absorb them and understand them as my reality.

"*I* saw him doing it, Marlow—we can still go to the police. I saw everything."

"I can't believe you had to see it," Marlow says, her voice cracking.

"I wish you'd told me," I say, but then I feel awful, because the last thing I want is to blame her for her reaction to being raped. Isn't that what happens to women all the time, victimizing them doubly? "Sorry," I manage to say, and then I can't stand any longer. I sit down right on the pavement, and to my surprise, Marlow does the same.

"I'm so sorry, Clara. I'm sorry I never told you."

I reach forward and grab her hand and give it a squeeze. "I'm sorry he did this to you," I say, even though there aren't really words to convey the depth of my sorrow. "And I'm sure I should be saying so much more, but I feel so sick I don't know what to say, and I don't even know what I'm supposed to do. I'm married to a fucking rapist? Now the fuck what, Marlow? I'm sorry to make it about me."

"I've been dealing with this for two years," Marlow says gently. "I've gone to therapy. I've had some time to process it. You're just hearing it tonight, for the very first time. We can make it about you right now."

She gives me a small smile, and what she's just said to me is the perfect example of what it was like to be friends with her. We were both so giving to each other, always trying to be there for each other in new and bigger ways. I supported her endlessly when she lost her husband, because where else would I be? I loved being there for her—sometimes it felt selfish, like I got as much from giving her comfort as she got from receiving it.

I wipe tears from my eyes and ask her, "Did you know I knew—or suspected—that something had happened between you and Evan?"

"I figured," Marlow says. "Because I knew you'd have fought harder for our friendship if you thought I was just pulling away for some unknown reason."

"I still don't understand," I start, trying to phrase this carefully, trying to choose my words correctly so that I don't make anything worse. "You're like the world's greatest feminist; I can't imagine a universe where you wouldn't tell me what had happened and want me to know the truth about him."

Marlow lets out one of the saddest laughs I've ever heard. "Yeah, it's kind of funny, isn't it? You're the world's greatest feminist until something like this happens to you. It wasn't black and white. I mean, the fact that it was rape was black and white. I was drugged and unable to consent. But I was buzzed to begin with, and I kept doubting my memory of all of it. I can't even remember *anything* past the walk up the stairs, and even to this day, I vacillate on what happened to me. I can't figure out when or how Evan would have drugged my wine. I poured it myself, I think. And he was the center of attention at his own party, everyone wanting to talk with him."

"Everyone always wanting to talk with him," I say.

"Exactly. But if he drugged me that slickly, without anyone noticing . . ."

"Then it likely wasn't his first time doing it," I say, and Marlow looks relieved that I said it first. "There was another woman he slept with. Or raped," I tell her, nearly choking on the words. "She's the only other woman I know about, though I'm sure there've been more."

Marlow leans forward and puts a hand on my knee. "We could both report him," she says. "Me, again, with that night. And you, with what you saw happening to me, and with what you know about the other woman. Do you think he raped her?"

"I only saw them entering a hotel room." I feel like I have the flu, like my body is flooded with aches and chills, as my memory scrolls back to that night in Miami. "I saw them walking down the hall, and I didn't see her face, or read anything weird in her body language."

"Maybe he does it both ways. Maybe he has consensual affairs when he can. But that night, for God's sake, we were in our own *town*. He knew I'd never sleep with him. Maybe he did it on purpose because you and me were best friends, and he wanted to stick it to us, for some fucked-up reason." Marlow looks at me like she can't believe any of it. "And my *wedding ring*," she goes on, despairing. "I don't know if he took it off me, but it was *gone* after that night." She shakes her head, staring down at her shoes. "I guess maybe I could've just lost it . . ." Her voice trails off, and I can tell she doesn't believe that. "I've thought about all this way too much, alone, late at night. It plagued me for so long. It still does, but it's softer now."

"Why did you decide to tell me tonight?" I ask.

She looks up again. "Did you see that woman with Sloane tonight? Harper, I think her name was?"

I nod. She wasn't really the kind of person you could miss. She was dancing sexily enough to give one of the older dads a heart attack.

"Evan was watching her in an almost predatory way," Marlow says. "Maybe I'm reading too much into it because of what I know about him, but it scared me. Enough that I kept an eye on her all night and felt relieved when she left with Sloane."

My heart beats a little faster. I'd seen what Marlow had. At first, I thought maybe Evan recognized Harper from somewhere, because he was looking at her with this intense look on his face, almost like he knew her and was trying to place her.

Marlow says, "I guess it kind of put it right up in my face, everything that was at stake. That he could do this again at any point. I've always known that. But something about his energy tonight felt off, like he was salivating for her. You know him better than anyone . . ."

"Apparently I don't."

We sit there in silence for a moment, and I wonder what I'm supposed to do next. Warn Harper that my husband is a dangerous man, and that she should stay away?

Or do I take it a step further: Tell him that I know everything, and then go to the police?

# TWENTY-TWO

*Sloane*

Out on the rocks before the cliffs, I tell Harper everything I remember about the night with Evan at his Fourth of July party. Her body grows increasingly agitated as the story goes on, like she could spring from the rock and demand justice if there were anyone here to grant it to us. At one point, when she angrily asks me why I didn't press charges, I get defensive, telling her that the memories came back in flashes over the next few weeks, too tenuous to feel real, too scary to face for a while. "Most people don't report sexual assault, Harper," I say. "Especially when it happens with someone they know, and especially when they were drunk. The statistics are terrifying."

"But what did you tell Dave?" she asks, her body hunched forward, her hand clasping mine. We're sitting on the rocks like schoolchildren, like we come back here all the time, like it's always been our place for secrets.

I swallow over the hard lump in my throat. It's the thing that haunts me, the thing that ended my marriage. "I can't be sure," I say, starting slowly, trying on the words, waiting with bated breath to hear what they sound like spoken aloud, "because everything from that night feels so fluid. What I remember is Dave walking into the room as Evan was tucking his shirt back in. I remember Evan saying he was looking for someone's coat, and then commenting on how drunk I'd gotten, like it was funny. And Dave either believed him or felt too unsure to accuse him of anything, because he stood there and said nothing."

The outrage on Harper's face could kill someone. And it's exactly what I never knew I needed—it's maybe even what I've been waiting for all these years: pure, enormous rage shared by another person. Maybe I was afraid to tell the story and not see on someone else's face exactly what I see on Harper's.

"That's disgusting," she growls. "*Inexcusable.* What a fucking coward."

Adrenaline zips through me, the feeling of being validated like fire in my veins. "Do you want to hear the *really* disgusting part? Evan was sponsoring Dave for membership at his golf club. I didn't want to do it, but Dave was so into it. After the party, the last thing I wanted was to join a place where I'd have to see Evan and Clara, so I really put my foot down, fighting Dave on the cost and whatever else I could come up with, waiting for Dave to do something—anything—that distanced us from Evan . . . because wouldn't you think Dave would at least pull his membership application after he saw his sponsor possibly assaulting his wife at a party? Nope. The week after Evan raped me, there was a cocktail party for new members. And Dave *went.*"

Harper gasps. "*Are you fucking kidding me?*"

I shake my head. "I'm not."

"Do you think Dave knows you remember seeing him there in the room after Evan raped you?"

"I have no idea. Half the time I doubt my own memory of the whole thing—I doubt I even saw Dave in the room. But, in a weird way, it's like my body knows it to be true. I could never look at Dave the same way after that night. I couldn't stop wondering how it was that he didn't fight for me. He dragged me out of the party like I'd done something wrong, and things were weird between us for weeks after, and then slowly but surely, I could feel our marriage failing."

Harper shakes her head like she can't believe it. "And you're sure Evan is Daisy's father?"

"Not one hundred percent sure, but Dave and I couldn't get pregnant before Daisy, and we'd tried for *years*. A part of me thinks Dave knows it's a possibility that Evan is Daisy's father, certainly if my memory is correct and he saw Evan rearranging his clothes while I was passed out on the bed. And Daisy looks so much like Clara and Evan's kids, so much so that I'm increasingly terrified Clara will see the resemblance. It's like watching a ticking time bomb the way every year Daisy looks more and more like Clara's girls. And don't mothers intuit these kinds of things? I feel like Clara's going to figure it out one day; she'll catch a glimpse of Daisy in the schoolyard, and she'll just *know* Daisy is her children's half sister. I once saw an old yearbook at school that had photos of Arden and Camille, Clara's daughters, when they were in fifth grade, and it completely terrified me. Daisy looks just like them."

Harper shakes her head like she can't believe it. "And you're never going to tell Daisy who her real father is?"

"Definitely not while she's a child," I say. "I'm going to let her believe she's the child of two parents who consensually conceived her, who love her, who might not be together, but who aren't rapists. Can you even imagine what her life would be like if she found out that Dave wasn't her real father, and that her real father was a man who lived in her town, who raped her mother?" I shiver at the thought of it. And then I say to Harper, "And that's why you can't tell anyone—not even Ben."

Harper puts a hand up like she's in court, swearing on a Bible. "It's your truth, not mine. I'll never tell *anyone*." She says it deadly serious. And maybe I'm a fool—but I believe her.

We're quiet for a moment. Sharing the secret with the person I believe is the right person to share it with has freed a tiny something inside of me—like something tight has loosened and slipped from between my cold, trembling fingers. We sit a while in silence, until we hear a branch snap.

Harper's eyes dart nervously. "What was that?"

"*Hello?*" I call, but no one answers. "It's probably just an animal," I say easily. "Sometimes even the small ones make a lot of noise out here, and they sound so much bigger than they are."

Another crunch sounds, and then a few more, until I'm sure it's not a small animal.

I brace myself as a tall man bursts into the clearing, and Harper lets out a scream.

"Oh my God," I say, more about Harper's scream than anything else.

"Ben!" Harper exclaims. "You scared the shit out of us!"

Ben looks as surprised to see us as we are to see him. "What are you doing back here?" he asks Harper gently.

"What are *you* doing back here?" she snaps.

"Trying to find you," he says, but Harper calls him on it.

"Really?" she asks. "You thought I'd be back here with all the nature?"

Ben's wearing navy hospital scrubs with a gray hooded sweatshirt, and the way he moves into the clearing and how comfortably he sits beside us makes me think the real estate agent took him to this exact spot. The bluffs overlook the rushing water; the trees dance in the wind; the moon glitters—it's all too breathtaking not to be in awe if it were your first time. But this is his property, it's not like I'm going to accuse him of sneaking back here.

"What were you guys talking about?" he asks.

"We will actually never tell you," Harper snips, and the confident way she says it makes me laugh.

She turns to me in surprise. "What? I'm serious," she says. She sounds like a schoolgirl with a secret, and even though that secret is mine, and it's dark and irreversible, it feels just the littlest bit lighter now that she shares it, too.

"I know you are," I say. "Thanks."

"A secret," Ben says with a smirk.

"Yes, an unfortunate one," I say.

Ben's face loses any trace of humor and becomes serious. "I'm sorry, then," he says.

None of us say anything for a moment, and then Ben asks me gently, "So this is your spot back here?"

I nod, looking up at him. "And I'm sorry about that, because I think this part is technically on your property, though I'm not really sure because I haven't studied the map in a while."

"We can share it," Harper says sweetly.

I smile at her and then stand on tired legs. I walk slowly toward the edge of the cliff, the wind picking up as I get closer.

"Jesus, careful!" Harper says.

"It's beautiful, the water," I say to Harper. "You need to come look." I creep carefully to the edge, where the rocks line the lip of the cliff. I peer down into the water, at the rocky shore between the cliff's face and where the water starts.

And then my stomach drops before my brain processes what I see.

"Oh God," I hear myself say.

Down on the shore of the river is a body, splayed on the sand, white skin catching the moonlight, glowing.

"Ben," I shriek, covering my mouth, unable to take my eyes off it, and then he's beside me. "Look," I say, pointing down to the shore.

He turns back to Harper. "Call nine-one-one," he tells her, eerily calm. And then to me, "Is there a trail to get down there?"

"Yes, but it's steep."

"Show me," he says.

# TWENTY-THREE

*Clara*

I'm driving home from the fundraiser by myself, fury zipping through me, hands clenching the steering wheel. I never saw Evan again after I talked to Marlow; he texted me to say he couldn't find me and was heading home. Cole, Arden, and Camille are out—it's Saturday night, after all—which means inside my beautiful home sits my monster of a husband, all alone.

I turn right onto our manicured street and think about how Evan insisted we live here. He loved how neatly trimmed the lawns were, how the houses and properties were closer in style to the homes down county, and less wild than most of Sycamore Glen. I used to think his proclivity for uprooting and upgrading us into larger homes every few years was his way of providing for us, of sheltering us as best he could. He wasn't doing the day-to-day nurturing of the kids in the same way I was, and I thought the house thing was his way of showing care and protection. But now as I round the corner and our house is in view, everything feels insidious. Like the new-house thing is the same as the new-woman thing, and I was just foolish enough not to see any of it.

I pull into our driveway and leave the car outside, because my hands are shaking so hard I worry I'll ding the side of the house if I try to navigate the hairpin turn into the garage. I carefully climb the stone steps and stand outside our gleaming oak front door. I put a trembling hand on the knob, knowing it will be unlocked, because apparently nothing scares Evan enough to lock his family inside.

I open the door and step into the quiet foyer. Our entry table is stacked with art books and other carefully curated objects, and I wonder, really, what the point was of any of this; why did I buy these expensive things and hire a decorator to make a house filled with lies look so beautiful?

I walk softly across the foyer and feel stronger than I thought I would. Marlow wanted to come with me, but I promised her that I wouldn't confront Evan alone, that I'd wait until a shared therapy session or a public place, and I told her the last thing she needed to do was come to our house and be subjected to him. But now rage has ignited within me as I stand here in the house where I shelter my children, where I try to raise them to be good humans, where I try to do as good a job as I can while cohabitating with this criminal . . .

And, well, I forget everything I promised Marlow.

I slip off my heels and creep across the floor. I peek into Evan's study, but it's empty, so I stand very still, listening for sounds of him. All my senses feel finely tuned, like they've been waiting years for me to use them in this crucial moment, and now they've come to life. A shadow flickers in the double-wide doorway that leads from the foyer into the kitchen, and I head toward it, inching closer, feeling like an animal stalking her prey. I swear I hear the gentle *pfft* of a page turning, and then, Evan's voice.

"Clara?"

I freeze. The sound of him snaps me back to reality, deflates me, reminds me that I'm not a huntress, only the sorry wife of a man accused of drugging and raping her friend.

I put a foot forward and walk steadily into our kitchen, seeing Evan in the family room beyond it. He's sitting in his favorite chair, a light gray love seat, his feet up on the coffee table like he couldn't be more content with himself and his place in the world. His gray-framed reading glasses are on, and he's flipping through the *Wall Street Journal*.

"Hi," I say, startling myself, pleased that my voice still works in his presence.

"Hi," he says back. I expect him to compliment me on the fundraiser and gush over the planning of it, how well it went. He loves everything about how forward-facing I am at school and our golf club. But instead of saying anything, he considers me over his glasses like he knows something's wrong. A full beat goes by before he says, "Tonight was a success, wouldn't you say?"

"Oh, I *would*," I say, walking toward him, never breaking his eye contact. "I learned so much. It was truly an *enlightening* fundraiser."

I have his attention now. He's watching me round one of the sofas and take a seat across from him. I feel the cushions beneath me, grounding me. I put my feet on the floor for something solid. And then I say, "Marlow told me you drugged and raped her."

He blinks. Once, twice.

"Is this a joke?" he asks, his voice deadly calm.

"Yes, Evan," I say, my hands shaking so hard I force them into my lap to keep them still. "It's a joke. I love jokes about rape. Especially ones that involve my husband."

Evan snaps his paper shut. "You can't possibly believe her."

"Um, well, I do," I say, and my tone—my rage on display rather than sadness and tears—surprises me. I'm grateful for it.

"Marlow Patel is a lying bitch," Evan says.

I shake my head. "No, see, I think you're the liar. You never told me about sleeping with Marlow in the first place. A lie of omission. Let's start there."

"I made a mistake with Marlow. I didn't rape her. Isn't it obvious what's happening here?" When I don't have an answer, he continues, "Marlow wants you back in her life, and this is the only way. To lie about the circumstances of our affair."

"Did you put something in her drink?" I ask.

Evan looks at me like I've gone insane. "Of course I didn't. Do you seriously believe I'm capable of, what, procuring drugs on the internet and poisoning a guest in our house?"

This is the man I brought babies home with from the hospital. What do I *really* think he's capable of?

"I wouldn't have believed you were capable of drugging and raping a woman until I heard Marlow speak it tonight," I say, which is as close to the truth as I can describe with words.

He opens his mouth to defend himself, and I say, "I know you had sex with another woman in Miami, Evan. So please don't act like this was an innocent mistake you made with Marlow, or like this was the only mistake you've made in this marriage."

Evan goes very still. "What are you talking about?" he asks, but not in an incredulous way, or like he's proclaiming his innocence. He's asking it like he doesn't understand how I could possibly know about the woman from Miami.

"I followed you to Miami," I say. "To that swanky, flashy hotel you booked, the kind of trashy place that would have been awesome if you were a twenty-year-old going on spring break, which is so ironic, considering your classy persona up here in Sycamore Glen." And here I let out the darkest, most sorrowful laugh. "I waited for you at the bar, and when you walked in with a woman on your arm, I followed you upstairs and saw you go inside your room together, all cuddly. Kudos to you for getting some R & R."

Evan's mouth drops, and he suddenly looks like he's at a loss for words. I feel a slight thrill; it's the first time I've ever put that expression on his face.

"Can you put yourself in my shoes for even a second and imagine what it must have been like for me to see you with another woman, *twice*? Or are you so far gone that you're going to defend yourself?"

He's quiet. He looks down into his large hands, turning them over like he's written an answer on his palms. "I'm sorry," he says, his voice uncharacteristically meek. "I'm sorry that I cheated on you." He clears his throat, straightens, and then meets my gaze. "More than once," he says, his blue eyes shining with a sheen of what might be tears, but I have no idea, because I've never seen him cry. I stare at him, waiting for tears to fall on either of our faces, but they never do. He inches forward in his chair, close enough that our knees are almost touching.

"I have had affairs," he says. "I've been extremely weak, and wrong, and I know that you'll probably never accept an apology from me after what I've done. But I did *not* drug Marlow, and I didn't rape anyone."

"I don't believe you," I say. "I believe Marlow."

We're quiet for what feels like an eternity. I can see something pass over Evan's face: Resignation, maybe? Fear? And before I can say anything else, he changes tack. "I think I get it," he says slowly, calmly. "I think I understand what's going on here."

He says it so condescendingly I can't help but roll my eyes. "Oh, good," I say sarcastically. "I'm so glad you understand your affairs and violent proclivities."

"*No*," he says firmly. "I mean I think I understand why Marlow has this hold over you. She always has, hasn't she? And now, you believe what she tells you over your own husband, because Marlow, for all of her flaws, saved you during a crucial time in your life when you were lonely and so angry, when you were at home with the kids as babies, not in your best state, maybe even with shades of postpartum illness, and I was working too much."

"Excuse me?"

"When the kids were babies," he says slowly, like he's a teacher and I'm a child who doesn't understand. "Three kids under two, Clara. It was hard, and you were alone—I left you alone. And you were very sad, and then you met Marlow and she made everything better. She saved you, really, and I'll always be grateful for that, because it was my fault, too, for not realizing how hard it was to have three young children with no help."

"What are you *talking* about, Evan? I wasn't angry and sad home alone with the kids." My heart is racing—I know what he's doing, but it still gives me pause. I don't remember it that way—but is this seriously what he thought? Is this what I looked like to outsiders? "Obviously it was hard," I say. "That's what any mother with young children would say."

"You were losing your temper, Clara."

My palms begin to sweat. I feel frantic and confused, as though I've been plucked out of one conversation and dropped into another taking place in a foreign language.

"I'm sure I lost my temper sometimes," I say. "But it's not like I hit the kids or anything. I don't even understand what you're—"

"You yelled *a lot*. Marlow saw you at a playground, remember that day? And you were having such a hard time with the girls in the sandbox. They had to be, what, one and a half? And Cole was nearly three, and he'd thrown a shovel at Marlow's daughter, and it caught her cheek and drew blood. Don't you remember this?" Now his speech has picked up speed, the words pouring forward. "I remember Marlow telling me that you were a woman on the edge."

"What the fuck are you talking about?"

"*Exactly*, Clara," he says in a sickening, fake-soothing voice. "It makes you mad just talking about it. And I get it, trust me, I do. I see how hard it is for women raising young children, but I didn't understand it back then; I didn't realize how much you were suffering. I should have gotten you help, someone in the house, an au pair or something, but I didn't. And then there was Marlow, a trained social worker, and she was there to help you, and I was so grateful, I really was."

My mouth drops before I can stop it. "Marlow was my friend, you fucker. She wasn't my therapist." I lean forward, and for a second, the look on his face says he thinks I'm going to give in and agree with him.

Instead, I say, "Stop gaslighting me, you fucking rapist. I know exactly who I am as a mother, and without you, maybe I'll remember who I am as a woman." And as terrified as I am, a part of me relishes the moment right before I say the words I've been waiting two years to say. "I want a divorce, Evan. And I want it *now*."

# TWENTY-FOUR

*Sloane*

Ben is scrambling down the side of the bluff toward the body. I can't go any farther. It's too steep. I can hardly understand how Ben's still upright.

I hear Harper's voice from the top of the bluff, talking with the 911 operator.

When Ben finally descends the final twenty feet, he crouches beside the body and then searches for a pulse and confirms what I already know.

"It's Margaret," he yells up to me. "She's dead."

# PART II

# TWENTY-FIVE

*Margaret – the week before*

I n Mrs. Landau's creative writing seminar, Cole's staring at me like he wants to devour me whole, like if I let him, he'd put me on a sandwich and eat me for lunch. A dozen of us have our desks arranged in a circle (why is it so much easier to think this way?) and most of my classmates are shifting around in their seats, eager for the day to end. College acceptances are trickling in, making everyone excited and edgy and exhausted and devastated, and by the time school is over everyone just wants to go home and sleep or get high or get numb, or, in Cole's case, go to baseball practice.

"And how will the relationship between mother and son influence what your character ultimately decides to do?" Mrs. Landau asks me.

God bless Mrs. Landau. She doesn't shy away from darkness like every other creative writing teacher I've had here.

I tap my pencil against my desk. Everyone else here works off their devices, and I do, too, of course. But I still need a pencil in my hand to think. I answer Mrs. Landau the best way I know how: "I think when Pearl sees them together, she knows she can never compete with the love they have for each other. And her tragic flaw is that she doesn't think both relationships can coexist, because she's never seen love be expansive and unbridled; she's only ever seen it as a commodity that's doled out in portions and limited. And that's why she decides to kill the mother." Mrs. Landau uses a wrinkled finger to adjust her reading glasses. I wink at Cole as Mrs. Landau gives my short story a final glance. I think about Cole and his mom, Clara, because maybe their relationship is part of what inspired me to write a story about a mother and son, though I'd never tell him that. But their love *is* unbridled. Clara loves Cole without knowing half of who he really is.

"Well, Margaret, as usual, it's very well written," says Mrs. Landau. "I would advise you to ground your reader with sights, smells, and sounds when you make the transition from school to the mother's apartment, so that we really have a sense of where we are. But otherwise—"

The bell rings. And like robots, my classmates start to stand right in the middle of Mrs. Landau's sentence. "Rude," I say beneath my breath. I stay very still in my seat, staring at Mrs. Landau, in the hopes that she'll keep talking over them, but she doesn't. She gives in.

"I look forward to reading more," she says in the low, warbly voice that reminds me of my grandmother, my mother's mom, who overdosed on Seconal when my mom was a child. I only know what my grandma's voice sounds like because she was a jazz singer, an alto, and we have her records in our basement. To this day, my mother hates the arts.

Cole edges next to me as the other students filter from the classroom. "Ready?" he asks.

"As I'll ever be," I say.

He takes my hand as we leave Mrs. Landau's. His palm feels too warm and slick.

"Bye, Mrs. Landau," I say, and she smiles. And then, to Cole, once we're in the hallway and out of earshot, I ask, "Are we really doing this?"

# TWENTY-SIX

## *Sloane*

Somehow, I've managed to clamber back up to the top of the bluff to sit with Harper, my chest heaving, sobs racking my body. Harper has her arms around me, squeezing tight. She shushes me gently as I cry, but her attention is elsewhere. She's staring down at Ben and Margaret, transfixed. I follow her gaze to see Margaret's pale arm extended, and I begin to cry harder.

"Look away," Harper says, her voice cold and distant.

And then, the wail of sirens.

# TWENTY-SEVEN

*Clara*

Evan doesn't flinch at what I've said. He remains seated on the chair, and the stillness of his body infuriates me. I'm standing, trembling, and he looks like he's about to read the paper or ask what's for dinner. "You'll change your mind," he says evenly.

"I *won't*," I say. "I've wanted a divorce ever since I saw you in Miami."

There's a quicksilver flash of rage on his face, but he quickly tamps it down, his features morphing into something more palatable. My legs weaken beneath his gaze. When was the last time we held eye contact like this?

"You need me," he says.

Anger hums through my body, but there's sadness there, too. "The kids need you, Evan," I clarify. "Not me."

Is there any way I can salvage this? Not the marriage—the divorce. Is there a universe where we just quietly divorce and move on without each other? Or is every fear that's kept me awake in the middle of the night about to come true?

Evan's face is still, so still. "You've always needed me," he says cruelly.

The room feels like it's spinning. I try to pick a spot on the wallpaper, a tiny gray bird landing on a spindly branch—I stare hard at the bird in the hopes of stopping the spinning feeling. But it doesn't work. I try closing my eyes, but that makes it worse. When I snap my eyes back open, Evan's still staring at me, his features implacable.

"I'm going to lie down," I say. "I don't feel well."

He stands, slowly reaching out a hand. "Let me take you upstairs." He wraps his fingers around my elbow, his touch burning my skin, the bones in my arms. "You're not yourself," he says.

# TWENTY-EIGHT

*Margaret – the week before*

Cole and I started this whole thing to get back at his dad. And trust me—I get it. I'm currently in a huge fight with *my* dad, because I was working in his lab when his lab superstar, a post-doc named Carl, who always seemed off-kilter to me, accused me of stealing his idea about interferon signaling. And the problem is, I wrote about having that scientific idea as my college essay. And it was partly luck—a smart-*ish* inference that happened to be correct, but now Carl's making all this noise and accusing my dad of handling it unfairly, and my dad's freaked out that Carl's going to report it, and that anywhere I get in with that essay is gonna revoke my acceptance. Harvard just rejected me last week, and I barely applied to safety schools, so I'm not exactly feeling my best. But I didn't steal the idea. I've been working in my dad's lab at least twice a week for a year, and we've been trying to figure out if interferon gamma signaling was driving an anti-tumor response. And we were stuck, because you can't just measure interferon gamma in blood samples, it's too hard to detect. So one night I binged all this research online and realized that we could measure downstream chemokines as a back-door way to figure it out. I applied that to the molecule we were working on, we had a breakthrough, and my dad was genuinely happy with me for about five seconds before deciding for sure that this was what I should write my college essay on.

Anyway, my whole point: I get it about parents. But Cole's dad? He's on a whole other level.

Cole secretly *hates* his father. And more than anything I've ever seen drive Cole—including whatever sex and romance is between us—this supreme hatred of his father spurs him forward, sets him into motion, and drives his fate. Even if neither of us knows what that fate will be. He tends to his roiling hatred like a flame, oxygenating it just enough, tamping it down when it threatens to burn out of control. It's pure and unadulterated like a passion.

Now we're up in Cole's bedroom. His floral wallpaper has a fancy rich-woman vibe, but it doesn't seem to bother him in the slightest. Sometimes I wonder what the next girl he brings up here will think (we're eighteen—I'm not foolish enough to think I'll be the last), but maybe when you're six foot four and captain of the baseball team, you can pull off a bedroom cloaked in country-club-lady wallpaper. Maybe Cole won't think twice about screwing a girl surrounded by a paper garden full of daisies.

"Aren't you worried your dad will recognize your wallpaper in the photos?" I ask as Cole fidgets with a filter on his phone.

"Nah," he says. "He hasn't been in my bedroom in years, and the photos will be blurry enough that he won't notice."

"How is that even possible, Cole?" I ask, watching his brow furrow as he holds up the phone and tries to figure out how he wants to frame the shot. He's crazy good at taking pictures, even just with his phone, and also with the Nikon that Clara bought him. And he collects old things, including a Polaroid we break out sometimes, and those photos look vintage and stylish, like we've got a real point of view when we take them.

Cole meets my eyes. "Why would he come in here?"

"Because he's your *dad*."

"We don't exactly hang out. And if anyone cleans my room, it's my mom."

"That's lame."

"That my mom cleans my room?"

"Well, yes. But I mean it's lame that your dad never comes in your room to chat with you or just, like, check in. I think it's weird."

"*He's* weird. That's why we're doing this." Cole points to the center of his wall. "Stand there." And then, when he sees my face, he adds, "Please, Margaret."

I walk across Cole's floor, a little nervous. Not about getting naked in front of him—obviously I've done that plenty. It's Cole, after all, and I've loved him since we were freshmen in high school. We didn't start dating until fall semester this year, but I've had a crush on him since I was fourteen. Half of my creative writing assignments sophomore year were about him, and by junior year I was desperate.

But a lot has happened this year. I'll always love Cole and care deeply for him; he was my first real boyfriend. I lost my virginity to him at the start of senior year in a secret shed above the river, a place we used to sneak miles through the woods to find. But what I felt for him a year ago isn't there anymore. Now it's more like he's my best friend who I love and want to be close with, and whom I adore and still have fun messing around with. He talks about forever, and it's the sweetest thing, really, but it's not true. Even if he doesn't realize it yet.

College acceptances are rolling in this week for him and for me. There'll be the most natural breakup in the world at the end of the summer, clean and pretty—with no hurt feelings. He'll have a girlfriend by the time he returns to Sycamore Glen for Christmas break, but we'll still hang out and watch movies while his mom makes popcorn. At least, this is the picture I imagine when I think about all the ways it might unfold.

I can't stomach the idea of not being friends with him. And I can't imagine not being able to escape to his house and feel the ever-loving presence of Clara and his sisters. That's partly why what we're doing freaks me out—it's gonna blow apart his whole family.

"Okay," Cole says, "so stand there against the wall, and then in the shot, I want you to pose slightly turned, and then do that thing girls do with their hair when they want to look cheesy-sexy. You know that thing? Like this," he says, and he arches his spine, throws his head back, and fluffs nonexistent long hair.

I burst out laughing. "Oh my *God*, Cole."

"What?" he asks.

"That was very provocative."

"This is serious."

"You want me to be serious? Then how about you shut the door?"

"No one's home."

"*Yet*. Do you want me to take off my top when your mom could come home at any second?"

He gets off the bed and slams his door shut. When he turns to me, the set of his jaw reminds me of Evan's.

# TWENTY-NINE

## *Clara*

Evan's leading me up the stairs when my phone rings. I don't know why I'm letting him touch my arm. His fingers feel like a sunburn.

I stop on the top step as my phone trills from downstairs. "I need my phone," I say, turning around.

"Just ignore it," Evan says smoothly. "You should get some rest."

"It could be the kids," I say, aggravation soaking my voice.

"I'll bring it to you once you're in bed," he says. He pats my shoulder a little too hard, and I wonder what sick satisfaction he's getting from playing nursemaid. Him taking care of me is not the dynamic of our relationship, unless you count financially—which makes me wince to admit.

"Fine," I say, exhaling. "Please get it now."

The sight of my bed fills me with relief. I can shut my eyes and figure out what to do tomorrow. Cole's already eighteen, but we'll need to decide how we'll share custody of the girls, which was the entire reason I wanted to wait one more year—so that Evan couldn't say I was an unfit mother or figure out some other bullshit way to keep the girls away from me.

Evan stops at the doorway of my room and thankfully doesn't come closer. But I can feel him watching as I get into my bed and kick my feet beneath the covers.

And then he turns and disappears.

The hall is dark, and I look at the shadowy space where he was just standing.

*What happened to us? What happened to* him?

I close my eyes. What's he going to do to me in the morning when we wake up and he realizes I'm still planning to leave? The thought of telling the kids we're getting divorced is killing me; but the thought of them finding out who Evan really is . . .

Unthinkable.

I hear Evan's footsteps on the stairs, and then in the hall, stomping closer. I open my eyes to see him passing through the doorway and stalking toward my bed. He's got my phone in his hand like it's a bomb. "Why is Sloane Thompson calling you?" he asks, his mouth pinched, like the words are physically painful.

I shrug. "I dunno. Maybe to congratulate me on my stellar marriage."

"What the fuck is wrong with you, Clara? What's up with the jokes? Is this all a con—saying you want a divorce, accusing me of drugging Marlow, something I'd never do—"

The phone rings again. Evan looks down to see the name on the screen and then shakes his head at it. "I'm done with tonight," he says, tossing the phone onto the bed, narrowly missing my shin.

"Me too," I say, too softly for him to hear over the phone ringing.

I swipe the bar and answer, and right away I hear crying.

"Sloane? Is that you? Are you okay?"

"No, God no. Clara, I'm so sorry, I'm calling with something terrible."

My heart lurches.

"Margaret," Sloane says shakily. "Margaret is *dead*. We found her washed up on the shore behind my neighbor's house."

162

My breathing stops as my heart beats on, and it gives me the odd sensation of not being able to keep up with my body. *Margaret is dead.* Is that what Sloane just told me? But that can't be . . . "No," I say, my hand flying to cover my mouth. "No, no, no . . ."

I begin to sob and struggle for air. I curl my knees to my chest, and on the other end of the line, I hear Sloane weeping softly. Evan stands very still in the doorway to my bedroom. My eyes don't seem to be working right—I try to look at him, but he looks so blurry, like a ghost. And then he begins to walk slowly toward our bed. "Is it the kids?" he asks. "Is it the girls?"

I shake my head. "It's Margaret," I say, and his features finally unblur, coming into focus. "She's dead."

Evan's icy blue eyes widen. He runs a large hand over his face and then sits beside me. He takes the phone carefully from my hand and holds it to his ear. Into the phone, to Sloane, he asks, "What happened?"

# THIRTY

*Sloane*

I 'm shaking in my kitchen, a blanket over my shoulders. Harper's
making tea at the stove.

Ben sits next to me on the long wooden bench. His arms are
around me, holding the blanket in place, strong and sure. I have the
fleeting thought that I don't ever want him to let me go; I'm worried
that I'll fall if he lets me out of his embrace, that I'll sink onto the floor
and never get up.

Dave paces the kitchen like an animal. His usual frenetic energy has
been jolted into a new stratosphere ever since he saw the ambulances
and police cars parked in Harper's driveway and the swarm of officers
and medical personnel making their way alongside her house and into
the woods. Dave called me right away—and I'd answered, of course,
and told him about Margaret, and he begged me to come back to our
house where it was safe. But I didn't want to leave Harper and Ben and
Margaret's body all alone out there. I couldn't bring myself to leave, not
until the EMTs confirmed what Ben had already told us, that Margaret
was dead and gone. And then the police came in full force, cordoning
the area with tape.

"I don't get it," Dave's saying now, still pacing. He rakes a hand
through his hair. Harper hums quietly at the stove, like she's in a

different world from the rest of us. "Did she try to climb down the bluff?" Dave asks over Harper's humming. "That's not how she usually goes home. You know that, Sloane. She takes the trail behind the Larsens' house." He looks away from all of us, staring at a spot on the floor. "Should we not have let her take the trail? Were we careless with her? I mean, she's eighteen. She's an adult. She's eighteen, right?"

"She's eighteen," I say.

"Can't tell an adult what to do," Dave says inanely. As if whether we're at fault is what's important.

"What trail?" Ben asks, utterly calm. He didn't know Margaret, I guess—not for more than a few hours—and I suppose he sees death all the time, but still, his calm feels remarkable, like a force of nature. Like this is who he is and why he does what he does, like something bigger is at play.

"There's a trail from the far-left side of our lawn," I say. "It goes behind Mrs. Larsen's house and then descends toward Margaret's house. She's a runner; she does the trail in sneakers; she does it in Doc Martens; she does it all the time. She once told me nature calms her down. Not that that's so enlightening, or a clue or something. I guess it calms everyone down."

"Not me," pipes up Harper at the stove, her back still turned. She has a tea strainer in the water, stirring it jauntily. Her mood is so odd—she almost seems happy that we're all together, even under the circumstances.

"They're probably sending a police officer up here at some point to question Dave and me," I tell Ben and Harper. "Will you stay?" I really don't want to be alone with Dave and his anxiety.

"I'm sure they'll want to talk to us, too," Harper says, pouring the tea into two mugs. "I mean, they found her body on our property." Then, to Ben, "That *is* our property down there, right?" She brings the two mugs of tea over to me at the table, and the smell of chamomile flowers makes me want to retch. "Dave, tea?" she asks.

Dave ignores her. He's staring at Ben, an odd look on his face.

"Technically, yeah, it is our property," Ben says. "Though I never planned to go down there."

"You've never been down there?" Dave asks.

"To the bottom of the bluff?" Ben asks. "No. Why would I?"

"Coulda sworn I saw you down there the other day," Dave says.

Ben shrugs. "Don't think so, man. Must've been someone else."

Dave stares at Ben, and the silence feels like a thousand pin pricks. "Yeah," Dave finally says. "Must've been someone else." And then when no one else says anything, he adds, "I just figured you were down there trying to work out if you could build a dock. Everyone who moves into town thinks about it, but it's not allowed." Dave shakes his head, like everyone here is a fool except him. "People here are obsessed with the river. But not me."

Dave spent the first years of Daisy's life telling her stories about an underwater creature that lived deep in the river and swallowed little girls who went too close to the river's edge. I know he was doing it to protect her, to make sure she never went back there alone, but it was too dark. So many of his stories are.

Ben narrows his eyes at Dave and says, "They're not going to send a cop here who just gently questions all of us like last time. They'll call us down to the station individually, when they have detectives assigned to the case. It's not like before, when no one knew where Margaret was, and it'd only been a few hours she'd been gone. She's dead."

"I'm so sorry this happened, Sloane," Harper says softly. "You seemed like you really cared for her."

I give her a small nod. It's my loss, sure, but it's mostly Margaret's loss and the world's. Margaret was someone special, someone who was going to contribute and be kind and exist without hurting anyone. I don't try to say any of this out loud, because it will only come off as cliché. "What could have happened to her?" I ask instead. "Do you think she accidentally fell into the river, or tried to swim—or do you think someone killed her?"

Dave whirls around. "Why would someone kill Margaret?"

"I don't know, Dave, because sometimes things like that happen. And I've never known Margaret to go for a swim in the river at night after she babysits for us."

"I know, I just . . . ," Dave starts. "I guess I just thought if anything, that she'd, you know, maybe purposely—"

"I don't think so," I snap, uneasiness sweeping over me. It doesn't feel right to talk about Margaret like this, behind her back, when she's dead.

"Teenage mental health is at an all-time low," Ben says gently.

"I don't think that's what happened," I say, trying to be respectful to all of them, trying to keep any venom out of my voice. They're here, aren't they? We found Margaret together, and something has been forged between us. "Not that anyone can be sure of anything when it comes to someone else's mental health," I say carefully.

Harper sits on the other side of the bench and cradles her tea. "I think someone killed her," she says. She takes a swift sip, wincing like she did in the coffee shop with me earlier this week. Her gaze drifts out the French doors to the dark night, and I think about Margaret, and everything that's been lost.

"We should go," Ben says. Harper's eyes cut to him, and they exchange a look. When she stands and dutifully gathers her things, Ben's hand goes to the small of her back as he ushers her to the door, and it strikes me that it's the first time I've ever seen him touch her.

"Good night," I say, my voice so soft I'm not sure anyone can hear me.

# THIRTY-ONE

*Clara*

I'm holding my son as he cries, my heart breaking for him.

I texted Cole as soon as I got off the phone with Sloane, telling him to come home immediately and pick up Arden and Camille on the way. The three of them came cruising into the driveway and entered the house with their eyes darting from Evan to me like they knew something was very wrong.

And when we told them, the words felt like shattering glass, and immediately Cole crumpled.

I'm still holding him. It's almost two in the morning, and we're all together downstairs in the family room. Cole and I are on one sofa, and Evan's between Arden and Camille on the other. Arden and Camille are crying, too, but very softly, like they know this is Cole's singular pain, and they don't want to draw any attention from him.

I hold Cole's massive frame as tightly as I can. He's shaking violently, enough to scare me. Evan's watching him. He rubs the girls' backs mechanically, and they melt into him, seemingly comforted. For a fleeting moment I imagine what they would do if they heard what Marlow had to say about their dad tonight.

"I'm so sorry," I tell Cole repeatedly, but it's not like when he was little, and I could make anything and everything better. I'll never be able to make this better.

"I can't believe she's gone," Cole says. He looks like he's in a trance, staring hard at the edge of the sofa. Camille and Arden cry harder—it's awful seeing Cole like this. "Let me take you upstairs," I say, tugging at his shoulders. "To your room or mine, and we'll rest and recover for a bit." I need to get him alone. There's an energy to the three of my children when they're together; they love each other fiercely, they're protective of each other, but they also fight and egg each other on, and sometimes the collective emotion between them spirals like a cyclone. I need to try to calm Cole down, alone.

But then Evan cuts in.

"Cole," Evan says, right as I almost have our son standing. My hand is on his elbow, my other arm wrapping around his waist. Cole ignores Evan and starts to shuffle alongside me out of the family room. "*Son,*" Evan says sharply.

Cole freezes. He doesn't turn back to Evan; he just stands there very still, staring into the kitchen, away from all of us.

"It's very likely that you'll get called down to the police station to be interviewed," Evan says, his voice low.

Camille lets out a gasp.

"Yeah. I *know,*" Cole says, still not looking at us.

Evan turns to Camille and Arden. "Girls, please excuse yourselves and give us some privacy to talk with your brother."

"No, Dad," Arden protests in a whimper.

"Go upstairs to your room," Evan says, his voice much softer for the girls than it ever is for Cole. "*Now.*"

They listen. And when we're alone, Evan says to Cole, "If there's something you need to tell us, you should do so now."

When Cole finally turns to face us, his body moves slowly and stiffly, like everything hurts. "You think I have something to tell you?" he asks. "Something to *confess.*" He laughs, and the sound of it is eerie enough to wake up the hairs on the back of my neck. "That's funny," he says, his eyes holding Evan's. "Especially coming from you."

Evan stands. He's an inch shorter than Cole, but he comes off as larger and more ominous, like he could snap Cole in two by sheer will. "What are you talking about?" Evan asks, shaking his head sadly, the way he used to when Cole was a little boy and threw tantrums. He was always condescending with Cole, as though Cole wasn't living up to whatever impossible standards Evan had set.

"You seriously think I would ever hurt Margaret?" Cole asks, holding Evan's stare like he wants an answer.

"No, I don't," Evan says, which is maybe the kindest thing he's ever said to Cole. Even Cole looks surprised to hear it. "But I don't think you realize how bad this could get for you. Your girlfriend is dead. She may have fallen into the river or had some kind of accident, or someone may have hurt her. And the police are going to get very up close and personal with you and your relationship as they try to figure out what happened. So, if you have anything to tell us, now would be the time."

Cole stares hard at Evan, saying nothing.

"We'll have a lawyer beside you," Evan says, voice softer.

"He didn't do anything wrong," I say.

Evan looks at me like I'm the stupidest woman on earth. "This is *serious shit*, Clara."

"I don't need a lawyer," says Cole.

Evan shakes his head. "Your girlfriend is dead, and you don't think you need a lawyer?" And then he looks at me, like *I* said it. "How naive can the two of you possibly be?"

Dread washes over me, knowing that not only is there the indescribable tragedy of Margaret being dead, but that now Cole will be dragged into the murky aftermath.

"Let's go upstairs, Cole," I say. I know he's done nothing wrong, and holding on to that belief like a life raft.

# THIRTY-TWO

*Margaret — the week before*

I t's evening by the time Cole has edited and loaded the photos we took. I'm nervous Clara and the girls (or, God forbid, Evan) will be home soon and walk in on us, but Cole assures me that they're all at Arden's lacrosse game a half hour away, and we have time. Arden's trying to get recruited for lacrosse, and I remember how stressful that was with running. In the end, my times weren't fast enough to run at the schools I wanted to get into, and there wasn't a universe where my parents would let me go to a non–Ivy League school just so I could run on the track and field team there.

I'm constantly peering through the window onto their street, and maybe in a way it adds to the excitement of all of it—that any of them could glide into the driveway, enter the house, or call out our names. Maybe *excitement* is the real reason I agreed to do any of this.

"I think this is good," Cole finally says, turning his baseball cap so that it's backward on his head. His eyes are glazed, staring at the screen. We've loaded three photos of me into my profile, and the first one shows me from the waist up: I'm facing the camera wearing a see-through tank, and my head is bent so far forward that you can't see enough of my face to identify me. It looks artistic, as though the whole point was to obscure my face, which might turn off some people (including Evan) but it's not like we had a choice. The next two shots are sexy and revealing. The first one's taken from my chin down: I'm standing sideways in my bra and a tiny pair of shorts that may as well be underwear. The next is a full shot of my body from the back wearing the shorts and bra. My back is arched, per Cole's direction, and I'm lifting my hair so that you can see the curves of my body and the way my waist nips in.

It's funny how much sexier the photos look than I ever felt while they were being taken.

"You ready to write a description?" Cole asks. "You're the one who's good with words."

I angle the laptop toward me. In the section to input my name, I type Cassie, because I always loved that name when I was little. I used to tell my parents I wished they'd named me Cassie instead of something so old-fashioned.

I enter my height and weight, and mutter to Cole, "How disgusting is it that they ask this question?"

"How disgusting is the entire site?" asks Cole.

When I get to the section that asks what I'm seeking, I write: Just looking for a good time, no strings attached!

"Is that too cliché?" I ask Cole, but then I glance away from his phone to check mine, seeing a text from my dad. Where are you? Your mother and I want to talk about what happened. A lot of this could come back to haunt you, Margaret.

I ignore the text and put my phone away. If they only knew.

"I think cliché is the point," Cole says. "We need him to think you'd never be a stage-five clinger." He's quoting an old movie he once showed me, *Wedding Crashers*, to make me smile, but it doesn't work.

There's been this feeling that's plagued me ever since college applications were submitted last fall—something I'd felt before in tiny doses, but now feel more acutely and persistently than ever:

*Boredom.*

My childhood up until the moment I pressed send on my applications was filled with a never-ending academic obstacle course, a veritable Hunger Games scenario peppered with tests instead of physical challenges. Every Sunday night, my parents sat with Florence and me at our dinner table and went over upcoming tests or homework due, essays in need of editing, projects to be completed. I was exhausted, but also filled with adrenaline that coursed through my veins and spurred me from one academic event into the next, all leading toward this very finite goal of college acceptances. And then once I submitted my applications to every Ivy League school in the country, I felt the adrenaline wash from my system; I was shaky for a few days, sleeping too much, barely wanting to shower or see Cole. I felt dull without any pressure psyching me up or making me nervous, without a hurdle to jump. It was like my parents had turned me into a laser-focused academic beast, and without a challenge, I couldn't function. All there was to do was wait for the acceptances to roll in, but even that didn't make me nervous, because my college advisor said she'd never had a student who was such a sure thing.

And now it dawns on me that trying to lure Evan into a trap is the first time I've felt alive and excited in weeks.

"Let's make the profile live," I say. "Do it *now*, Cole, before I chicken out."

# THIRTY-THREE

*Sloane*

The next morning Daisy wakes me at six thirty. The sun is up, filtering into my bedroom with a gentle orange glow. I try to rub the exhaustion from my eyes, blinking to take in Daisy's sweet features. I think back to last night, to Margaret's body on the shore, and a shudder passes through me.

Daisy sits carefully on the edge of my bed. "What's wrong, Mama?"

I push myself up so that I'm sitting against my headboard and I can look straight into her eyes when I tell her. I open my mouth, and everything feels sticky, like I need gallons of water to be able to form these awful words. "Daisy, honey." I take her tiny hand. "Last night something terrible happened."

Daisy's blue eyes are all over my face, trying to read whatever it is I'm going to tell her. There's no way she could ever imagine that it's something this bad—she doesn't have any reference for a tragedy like this. "Margaret died," I say softly, and Daisy's little hand flies to cover her mouth.

"Oh no!" she cries. And then, she squeaks out, "*Why?*" as she begins to sob, a full-body shake overtaking her.

"Oh, sweetie, I don't know," I say, wrapping my arms around her. "I don't know what happened. I don't know if she tried to swim, or if there was some kind of accident. I just don't know, baby."

I squeeze my arms tighter as she cries harder.

# THIRTY-FOUR

*Margaret – the week before*

Cole and I sit opposite each other in the back corner of a diner one town over.

We know no one here, which is the whole point. An entire bowling league filled with dads who probably aren't trying to meet young women online sit at counter stools. Families tuck into booths, and the waitstaff buzz through the diner with coffee pots and steaming plates of food that all smells the same.

"You know we can't just wait for him to find you," Cole's saying, laptop open on the diner's Formica table. He's barely touched his burger.

I pop a fry into my mouth. "But isn't he going to be suspicious if he sees I just signed up for an account, and I immediately start messaging him?"

Knowing that someone like Evan exists makes me feel a lot better about my own dad. All my dad does is put a ton of pressure on me, which makes him nothing compared to the bastard Evan is. If you met Evan, you'd think he was a handsome and sophisticated version of a regular dad. This has been the first time I've really seen how deceiving looks can be. Evan would put any two-faced girl in my class to shame with the double life he's leading.

Cole realized it six months ago when he hacked into his dad's computer and found a super sketchy dating site filled with younger women where Evan had an active profile. Cole figured out a backend into the system that allowed him to watch what his dad was doing on the site from another room. Usually, his dad went on the site after Clara fell asleep.

It ate Cole alive, consumed his every thought. And even though I could sense something was very wrong, it took Cole weeks to tell me. When he finally did, I begged him to just tell his mom, not only because she had a right to know, but also because I was a little scared— not just by what Evan was doing, but by Cole's reaction to it, the way his eyes glazed over the more he talked about it, the way his hands trembled. All of it felt so dark, but rather than tell his mom or confront his dad, Cole stalked Evan's online activity for weeks, updating me through all of it and making me increasingly nervous, until Evan finally made a move and contacted one of the young women. And that's when things really tipped over the edge, because suddenly Evan and the young woman exchanged numbers, and from there, all their communication was presumably on their phones and off Evan's laptop, so Cole couldn't spy on it. And Cole basically lost it. We spent weeks obsessing about it. We stopped hooking up, and it was really weird to be in a relationship with someone and not have any part of it be physical. Sometimes Cole pecked me on my forehead, which is what my dad used to do when I was little, maybe second or third grade, before he started driving me into the ground.

And I guess maybe seeing Cole so despondent was why I agreed to this insane plan in the first place. Cole convinced me that we had to take it a step further, because if he only photographed or screenshotted Evan's communication on the site, it wouldn't work: Evan doesn't use his real name, so there would be no way to prove it was him, and Cole is convinced Evan would just find a way to talk his way out of it. So now, our plan is for me to use an alias and try to get Evan to meet up with me, in the hopes that we could arrange a meeting, and Cole would be waiting in the background when Evan and I meet, and he'd video all of it, and we'd show that video to Clara to take him down.

It sounds elaborate, I know. But it's not really. I have this feeling it's going to be like taking candy from a baby as long as we play our cards right. And it'll all be over soon, anyway, and then even though there will be massive fallout between Evan and Clara, maybe Cole will start feeling better, like a true hero instead of a thwarted one.

"Look," Cole says, angling his laptop toward me. There's an option to message Evan right on the screen.

I study Evan's profile pic. It's not a real picture of him, of course. It's only an avatar.

I'm about to tap the button when the waitress shows up and asks, "Can I get you kids anything else?"

"We're okay, just the check," Cole says gruffly. His nails are bitten down to the quick, and the diner's fluorescent lighting makes the circles beneath his eyes even darker.

The waitress leaves, and I click the message button on Evan's profile. Hey, I type. Want to meet up sometime?

I glance over at Cole, and in a way, I think I'm waiting for him to stop me. I think about all the things that could go wrong, the ways this could mess up my life. I don't think the site is illegal or anything, and I don't think colleges can rescind my acceptances just because I went on a dating site. But can you get in that kind of trouble for catfishing? Is that what this is?

"Are you sure you want to do this?" I ask. "You don't think we'd get in—"

Before I can finish my sentence, Cole angles the laptop toward him and presses send.

# THIRTY-FIVE

## *Sloane*

That night I'm with Dave and Daisy in our living room. Daisy's been crying on and off throughout the day, and Dave and I have taken turns snuggling and comforting her. Right now Dave has his arms around her shoulders. She's holding her bear, staring at the movie I just started.

Dave's barely speaking to me, as if I were the one who caused all this. My phone has blown up the entire day with messages from what feels like the entire town looking for information I don't have. The location of Margaret's body so close to our property has been leaked, and everyone seems to know she was babysitting here the night she disappeared.

"I need some air," I say softly to Dave.

Daisy turns. "Where are you going?" she asks.

"Just for a walk. I'll be right back, sweetie."

She nods, her eyes bloodshot from crying. I feel selfish for worrying about her health while all of this is going on, like it's a luxury to even have her here and be able to worry about her, when Margaret's parents no longer have that.

Outside, it's dark and cool. Harper and I texted earlier about trying to get together tonight if Daisy was emotionally stable enough, and it seems like as good a time as any to walk over. I head toward Harper's house, my eyes on the vegetation lining the side of the dirt road. Even in the darkness I can feel spring hanging in the air. Forsythia have begun to bloom; the wild grasses and foliage feel lusher. I turn into Harper's driveway and start to climb, the incline so steep it steals my breath. I stare down at my feet navigating the gravel. When I'm at the top, I finally look up, and it takes me a moment to process what I see.

Inside the screened-in porch, Harper is pressed up against a man who's blonder and shorter than Ben. The man's hands are all over her body, and when he lifts her up and carries her to a wicker sofa, I come to my senses and realize what I'm seeing. And then I freak out and stop watching. I whirl around and nearly trip as I race back down the driveway.

*What the actual fuck?*

My feet feel numb all the way until I hit the street and head toward my house. Halfway there, I stop, bending forward with my hands on my knees. I try to settle down, because there's no way I can enter my house like this—the last thing I want to do is blurt out what I saw to Dave.

I focus on my breath, the way my lungs gulp the air and push it back out again, and try to ground myself. What *did* I just see? Harper having an affair? She told me Ben was at work tonight; it's not like he's out of town. How nuts is she?

Unless . . .

Is there any chance they have some kind of arrangement? I stand there and breathe for a bit, thinking. Something's a little off about their marriage—I can't put my finger on it, but there's something between them that doesn't read quite right. I pace the road, turning it over in my mind, but the truth is I'm too tired and strung out to understand.

When I finally go back inside my house, Dave's in the kitchen, and I see that Daisy's fallen asleep during the movie.

"She's exhausted," Dave says, popping the top off a yogurt smoothie and taking a sip. "This isn't good for her, all this stress. When does she see Dr. Bhatt?"

"Tomorrow," I say. "And I was thinking the same thing." I'm relieved to be talking about Daisy and not Harper or Margaret.

But then Dave eyes me suspiciously. "Where did you just go?"

"Nowhere," I say, too quickly.

He raises an eyebrow. "I thought maybe you'd gone to your new friend Harper's." He doesn't say it sarcastically, or like he's making fun of me. He says it like he's concerned.

I ignore him. I move to the kitchen island and gather an empty yogurt container that probably belongs to Dave and not Daisy, because Daisy's pretty good about cleaning up. "You're really getting your calcium needs met," I say as he takes another sip of the smoothie and I throw away his trash. Dave ignores what I've said but continues to watch me as I move around the kitchen, tidying up. "I like her," I finally say. "Okay?"

"I don't like them," Dave says.

I look up at him. Maybe an hour ago I would have blown him off or argued, but now that I've just seen Harper making out with a guy who's not her husband, I'm curious. "Why?" I ask. Dave doesn't always have the best gut instincts about people, but I'm still interested in his take on them.

Dave shrugs. "I just don't."

"You can do better than that."

Dave averts his eyes, which is what he does when he needs to think. "He's too picture perfect, like he's playacting the part of a big, successful yet caring surgeon. And she's totally off, Sloane. I'm surprised you don't see it."

I blink, considering it. "I don't think she's off. I think she's artistic and different from all the cookie-cutter suburban types we see around here."

"That's not very *kind*," Dave snaps. "Isn't that your thing? *Kindness?* Isn't that what you're always trying to teach Daisy?"

"I don't know what my thing is anymore," I say, taking a sponge to the granite.

Dave says, "Those cookie-cutter women you're talking about are also your friends."

"Are they?" I scrub big, wide circles across the island. "I haven't really made a true friend here. I'm starting to think Harper's going to be the first."

Dave must know it's true. He paid attention when we were married. He wasn't the kind of guy who buried his head in the sand and only worried about his golf game. He noticed me, he still does.

"You have plenty of friends," he says tentatively, "like all those women who check in on you when Daisy's struggling."

"Yeah, but don't you sometimes get the idea that, in a way, our situation makes them feel good? It's every parent's nightmare, a sick kid, isn't it? And they're right up close to it, but they don't have to experience it. They can maybe even feel grateful it's not *them*."

Dave blinks, clearly surprised by what I've said. "I think you're being a little unfair."

"Nothing about Daisy's situation is fair. We have a child who will likely die before we will," I say, a stone lodging itself in my throat. "And neither is what happened to Margaret, not like it's even comparable. All of it is awful, sickening."

We're quiet, and there's a moment in which either one of us could pick an even worse fight. But instead, Dave closes the space between us and says, "Daisy's alive. And she has the best doctors." He puts his arms around me. "We're going to do everything we can to keep her safe, and here with us, where she belongs. I'm not going to let anything happen to her, Sloane. I promise."

# THIRTY-SIX

*Margaret – the week before*

We don't hear anything back from Evan on the app for an entire day. And then, in the cafeteria of all places, I get an alert and see a message.

Would like to meet up. When and where?

My stomach takes a plunge as I reread it. Cole and I made my profile look as though I lived in New York City, because we figured Evan might be more likely to go for it, since a woman from the city would feel far more anonymous than someone who lived closer to Sycamore Glen.

I live in the city, but in the mood for country life. I'll come to you, I type, but I don't press send. Cole and I rehearsed me answering with something like this—but I still don't want to send the message without him. I pocket my phone and lift my head to search the cafeteria for Cole, just in case he got here without me realizing, but I don't see him. The first person who grabs my glance is Robby Navarro, Cole's sworn enemy from some fight that happened on the baseball field years ago before Robby switched to lacrosse. Robby's sexy AF with dark hair and golden-brown eyes, and I secretly think he wants us to get together at some point, and maybe I would when Cole and I eventually end things, as bad as that would be for Cole.

Last week I said as much to my friend Ashley, and she looked at me in horror for saying something so traitorous to Cole, so I backtracked and said I was kidding.

I break Robby's stare and double-check that Cole isn't anywhere inside the cafeteria.

"I gotta go," I say to Ashley and the rest of my crew. Most of my friends barely look up. Everyone's stressed with college acceptances rolling in, and I don't expect much from any of them right now. One of the girls from my cross-country team gives me a little wave, and then returns to staring at her phone. I wonder what they would think if they knew what Cole and I were up to.

I sling my backpack over my shoulder and put my head down. The cafeteria smells like meat and milk, and suddenly I can't wait to be out of this school. I loved it here, but I need something fresh. Maybe every senior in the world feels this way.

I can feel Robby staring at me, and then his whole table starts staring, like maybe he just said something about me. I ignore it, but the back of my neck heats up with the attention. It's one thing when only Robby gazes at me a moment too long, but the gaze of all those guys doesn't feel good. I pull out my phone and pretend to be busy checking it as I walk past them, but then of course I see my draft message on the app, and I shove it back into my pocket. I just need to find Cole.

The air is a little cooler in the hallway outside the cafeteria, and I feel like I can breathe again. I head toward the art room, because that's the place I'll most likely find Cole. It's always cracked me up that his parents pushed sports so hard, because Cole is such a talented artist, and maybe if he had the space to do it more, he could have gone to art school. Now, instead, he's playing baseball in college, and I feel like he's going to do something that might not even make him happy, like major in business or sports marketing.

I avoid everyone's gaze as I trek down the hall and curve into the art room. Right away I see Cole in front of an easel. I glance around to make sure the room is empty, and it is. Cole studies what's in front of him for another breath, and then he looks up. "Hey," he says. He seems so tired.

"He messaged me," I say, and immediately Cole sits up straighter, like I just handed him a shot of espresso. He extends his hand for my phone, and demands, "Let me see," and I remember not so long ago when he used to hold out a hand like this all the time, seeking mine to hold.

I weave between art tables covered with half-made projects in materials like clay and papier-mâché. Ms. Chaudry, our art teacher, is the kind of person who everyone wants to be around, so often kids leave projects out and come in and out throughout the day to work on them. Even those of us who suck at art do it, just to be in the vibe of her classroom.

I tuck in with Cole behind his easel and hand him my phone with Evan's message on the screen. He scans it while I check out his painting: a watercolor, simpler than some of his other things, just a young boy in a field of wildflowers. It's beautiful.

"I love this," I say.

He grunts dismissively. He has an ego about baseball—I can tell he loves when I go to his games and shower him with compliments. But he almost never talks about his art; he doesn't seem to be looking for any exterior validation at all. Maybe that makes it purer, like a true passion. I guess I haven't really found a true passion yet, maybe because I've been so busy with schoolwork. I do love running, but I still think there's something out there waiting for me beyond all this. I like creative writing, too, I guess, and maybe that'll be my thing in college. Imagine what my parents would do if I didn't go into pre-med and instead told them I wanted to be a novelist.

Cole says, "I'm sending my dad your draft message," and when he does, there's a sinking feeling in my stomach—maybe because I wish Cole was even an ounce more worried about any of this.

"What if he doesn't want to meet in Sycamore Glen?" I ask. I try to lower myself into Cole's lap, but his leg is jiggling so violently that it makes it hard. I readjust my butt, and he finally chills a little and we sit together, both of us looking at the phone instead of at each other.

"Then we drive to wherever he wants the meeting place to be," Cole says. Finally, he looks at me. "I'm going to be with you the whole time, Margaret. You won't be alone with him. We'll snap a photo of his arrival to meet you, and then I'll text it to my mom before he can snatch away my phone. And then we'll leave."

"Yeah," I say, "but I guess I don't completely understand why you can't just screenshot his messages now and show your mom."

"Because there's no way we can prove it's really him. His name is nowhere on the account. We need the messages plus the photo confirmation of him arriving in person."

"But can't you just show your mom the activity you already found?"

"He deleted all of it, and I was stupid enough not to screenshot it. And there was no way for me to prove it was his account, other than his IP address matching his computer. But he could turn everything around and say it wasn't him, or that I was the one using his computer to do it. And he and that other woman exchanged numbers and must have started communicating that way, which meant I couldn't see any more. Just watch, Margaret. I guarantee he'll ask for your cell next."

"And what are we gonna do when he sees it's a Westchester area code and not a New York City one?"

Cole's face pales. "Shit," he says.

"Yeah, shit," I say, thinking of all the ways this could go sideways. "I'm tired, Cole," I say, and I mean it. All the adrenaline from earlier has washed from my system, and now all of this just feels sad.

"C'mon," Cole says. "I'll take you back to the caf. I need food. I don't think I've had anything today. And we'll get you a cappuccino or whatever it is you get in those machines." His tone of voice is fake; he sounds like a parent promising ice cream to steer a child in the direction they want her to go.

"Yeah, okay," I say as he leads me from the art room and into the empty hallway.

# THIRTY-SEVEN

## *Sloane*

An hour or so after seeing Harper doing God knows what with that random guy on her porch, I sit on the sofa in my living room and look out onto the street. I've already said goodbye to Dave, checked on a soundly sleeping Daisy twice, checked all the locks, and sent another unanswered email to Margaret's mother to see if there's anything I can do for her and Florence, even though I know there isn't. I can't even imagine the heartbreak ripping through their family right now. I've left most of my texts and emails unread, because the majority of them seem to be from people looking for information about Margaret's death, details about finding her that I don't really want to share with anyone. I wonder if Margaret's mom will ever call me back, or if she and her husband will just disappear to somewhere far away with Florence so that they never have to see Sycamore Glen again and all the things that remind them of Margaret.

I stare out the living room window, my hands in my lap, a slight shake in my fingers. Curiosity has gotten the better of me, and now I'm waiting to see when and if the man who was with Harper will leave her house, and if it'll be before Ben gets home. I flip through my phone, half watching the street, and then write back to Clara, who's been kind enough to check in on me even though I'm sure she's in crisis mode dealing with her son having lost his girlfriend. I'm pressing send on the text to her when Ben's car zips up the road. I sit up straight, panic rising in my chest. Is he about to walk in on Harper's affair?

I climb the stairs and creep down the hall to Daisy's darkened bedroom, where I have a direct view into Ben and Harper's home. I know I shouldn't spy on them—and everything about it feels wrong—but I can't stop myself.

Daisy's sleeping soundly, her blankets pulled tightly to her chin. I make my way to her window, where I can see Harper upstairs in her own bedroom, grabbing something from a dresser. The man from the porch sits in the kitchen as Ben puts his key into the front door.

Daisy's gentle exhalations sound from her bed, her breathing unlabored and reassuring. I press my fingers against the glass as Ben enters the house and shuts the front door behind him. He's out of view, and then appears in the kitchen. The other man turns from his seat at the table but doesn't stand. Ben's body remains still as a soldier, even as the other man begins gesticulating. They seem to be talking, but I can't see them well enough to be sure. Neither seems angry or shocked to see the other. And Harper must have heard Ben come in, but she doesn't seem in any hurry to go downstairs. She tidies a few things in her room, and a minute or two later leaves her room to join them, appearing in the kitchen. She doesn't physically greet Ben—no hug hello or kiss on the cheek. She doesn't touch the other man, either; she just makes her way to the stove. And then Ben leaves the kitchen altogether. I watch as the front door swings open, startled to see Ben head back outside and down the driveway. I back away from Daisy's window; I'm not feeling as guilty as I should, but I also don't want to get caught.

Moments later, I'm mindlessly picking up Daisy's bedroom when the doorbell rings. I set down the stuffed animal I'm holding and stand up straight.

Did Ben come *here*?

I descend the stairs feeling so unsettled—nothing in my house looks or feels familiar, including me; and nothing about the past few days feels grounded in any reality I've known.

I open the door to see Ben standing on the front step, his hands pushed into the pockets of his dark blue scrubs. A five o'clock shadow lines his face, and his deep brown eyes hold mine. He doesn't hurry to fill the air with words. He just looks at me the way you look at someone you've known much longer; the way you look at someone for whom you feel something inexplicable. All of it is confusing, adding to every uncertainty inside me.

"Come in," I say, and he does. I don't lead him into the kitchen, because it just reminds me of that depressing scene with Ben, Dave, Harper, and me sitting around the dinner table after we found Margaret. I step numbly back into the living room and sit on the sofa where I had just watched the street, waiting for Harper's lover to leave their home.

Ben doesn't sit next to me. He sits across from me on a love seat, and instead of pushing himself back and getting comfortable, he sits on the edge, bending forward so that his hands are on his knees. His body language makes it look like he has something to tell me.

"Are you okay?" he asks.

I blow out a breath. No one's really asked how I'm doing, not even Dave. Margaret's death isn't about me, but still, it's nice to be asked. "I'm okay, mostly," I say. "I've been focused on Daisy today, which has been a good distraction. Last night I couldn't really sleep at all. I just kept picturing Margaret back in the woods, so close to where our houses are, imagining what could have happened to her."

He nods. "Me too," he says softly.

"I'm sorry that you just moved here and all of this has happened. It must be a shock for you and Harper."

He nods but says nothing.

"Is she okay?" I ask.

Ben's face changes. His voice is less gentle when he says, "I worked all day and didn't talk to her very much because she's been busy entertaining an old friend I don't care for."

"Who's the friend?" I ask casually.

Ben's face gives away nothing. The set of his handsome features is very still, and even his broad jaw seems relaxed. "He's an art dealer. He gave Harper her start years ago in New York. He's a fine-enough guy, he's just irritating. He talks only about art in a language that's so sophisticated I can't even follow him. He just commented on our fruit bowl being inspired by the Dada era of art in Paris, and I'm pretty sure Harper got that bowl at T.J. Maxx."

I laugh for the first time since Margaret died.

There's a strangeness to Ben being here. We've only known each other for a few days, and I've only ever hung out with him when Harper's been there, too. And I need to change the subject, because I'm in over my head talking about Harper's guest and uneasy that Ben has no idea what she's up to and I do. At least, I don't think he knows what she's up to . . .

"I didn't realize you guys lived in New York," I say.

"I did my residency there," Ben says.

Yesterday, Harper mentioned a stint they'd had in Austin. I consider Ben carefully, sensing a vastness, like he contains much more than I can see on the surface—which is maybe true about every human but seems especially true about him.

My phone rings, and Ben stands slowly. "I can go, it's late," he says. "I really just wanted to see if you were okay."

I stand, too, the ringing phone in my hand. It's a local number, and I take the call as we walk to my front door.

"This is Detective MacAllister," says a deep voice on the other end. "Is this Sloane Thompson?"

"This is she," I say formally, nervous.

"I'd like you to come to the station for questioning tomorrow in relation to the death of Margaret Collins. Is it possible for you to arrive at twelve?"

I swallow hard. "Of course," I say, sensing Ben closing in behind me. "I'll be there."

# THIRTY-EIGHT

*Sloane*

The next morning I'm waiting at the bus stop with Daisy when I see Harper leave her house and head toward ours. *Jesus Christ.*

Do I admit to witnessing her affair? Or should I just shut up and mind my own business?

I hold tight to Daisy's hand. I wasn't ready to have her go back to school after what happened to Margaret, but she begged me. She wants to be out of the house and with her friends, and I get it; I don't really want to be in our house, either, so close to where Margaret's body was found.

I hear the chug of the bus from somewhere in the distance, and then Harper is there, saying hi to Daisy. Harper gives me a small smile, and I can tell she reads something on my face even though I'm trying not to look anything other than normal. She's perceptive, that's for sure. Aren't most artists?

The bus screeches to a stop in front of our driveway. The driver opens the door and smiles at Daisy, who gives her a small wave.

I watch as my daughter boards the bus and slips into her seat next to a neighbor from the bottom of Beckett's Hill. Daisy immediately lightens, her face brightening before my eyes, and I consider the idea that she needs a true friend just as much as I do. Which is why I don't want this thing hanging in the air between Harper and me. Maybe there's some kind of explanation.

Harper and I watch as the bus drives down the hill and around the bend, disappearing. I don't really want to ask her inside for coffee. "Want to take a little walk?" I suggest instead.

Harper smiles. "I do."

We take a right out of my driveway and begin a slow walk down Beckett's Hill, our sneakers light on the dirt. It hasn't rained in a while, and the dirt feels drier than usual. Dust kicks up around us.

"How are you?" Harper asks, nearly losing her footing in a deep tire mark. She rights herself.

"I'm okay," I say. "Devastated and anxious about Margaret, obviously."

"Yes, of course," Harper says.

We walk quietly a few paces, and when I open my mouth, I'm not sure of what I'm going to say until it comes out. "I need to tell you something," I start, and then there's the loud whir of a landscaping truck. It zooms past us, and when it's quiet again, Harper asks carefully, "Oh?"

"Last night I went to your house," I say, feeling more embarrassed than I've felt in a while, because how weird is it that I caught her doing something she never would have wanted me to see? "You and I had texted about getting together," I add quickly, to remind her that it's not like I went over entirely uninvited. "And I had Dave at my house with Daisy, and I just badly needed air all of a sudden. I probably should have texted you first rather than just walking over, but I didn't."

"You're always free to just stop by," Harper says serenely. "You don't need to ask me first. It's nice how we're just, you know, *comfortable* with each other right away. Like making a new friend who feels like an old friend."

I flush with relief. "I feel the same way, which is the reason I'm bringing this up. So that it doesn't stay unsaid and fester." Does she have any idea what I'm getting at? "I saw you with someone who wasn't Ben on your screened-in porch. In a private moment. And I want you to know that I saw it, so that I don't feel so weird not telling you that I saw it."

*Please, don't make me say anything more explicit.*

"Ah, yes," Harper finally says. She bends to pick a wildflower from the side of the road. "You saw me with Jacob, who happens to be my lover, and I'm sure you probably saw us in some kind of physical configuration that surprised you."

I nearly trip. "Um, yes," I say, trying to make my voice steady.

"But why?" Harper asks, twirling the wildflower between her fingers, the purple petals fanning out. "Why should it surprise you?"

I don't know how to answer her without offending her. "I think it would surprise most people, don't you?"

"But *why*?" Harper asks again, more gently this time. "Does it threaten you in some way? That I have lovers?"

She doesn't seem angry at all; she sounds genuinely curious. She tucks the wildflower behind her ear. "N-no," I stammer. "It doesn't threaten me. And it's your business. Well, yours and Ben's." Suddenly I don't want to ask anything else—I feel so childish, so ill-equipped to understand this, when I've only known marriage one way. I lived a freer lifestyle when I was a young artist in the city, and so did many people I knew. But an open marriage in the suburbs as thirtysomethings? I have no context for that.

Harper snaps her fingers like she's just had an epiphany. "Oh," she says, "I see. Were you concerned Ben didn't know I was seeing Jacob?"

I nod, heat flaming my cheeks.

"Oh, okay," she says. "So, here's the thing: I never lie to Ben about anything. Never have, never will. He's the only person who really knows me. Not Jacob, that's for sure, and not even most of my friends, because it seems like whenever I open up to people, I scare them. Maybe I'm scaring you right now."

My heart pounds as Harper stops walking and turns to me. I stop walking, too, and even though I don't want to, I turn and look her dead in the eye.

"Am I scaring you right now, Sloane?" Harper asks, an edge seeping into her voice, darkening her words.

I shake my head *no*.

"Oh, good," she says, the playfulness back. The change is startling. It's childlike, almost, the quicksilver change in mood. "Because I *want* to be able to be myself," she says, starting to walk down the hill again. "And this is who I am. There was a time I tried therapy, you know, because I can be impulsive, but it didn't really work. I find I do better when I just embrace who I am and find friends who get it. Which isn't easy, because we move all the time for Ben's job."

We round a bend, and the hill slopes dramatically downward. We're approaching Mrs. Larsen's house, and if Mrs. Larsen thought that me not being there to get Daisy off the bus and dressing her too lightly for winter was scandalous, I wonder what she'd think of Harper's marriage.

"Oh, shit," Harper says, looking at her phone. "We should head back. I have to go to the police station for questioning at ten."

"I go at noon," I say as we pivot. And then out of nowhere, Harper asks, "Do you think Evan killed Margaret?"

My heart stops. "What?"

"Well, he raped you."

"He raped me at a social event."

"Oh. Is that better?"

"No, *no*," I say quickly as we climb back up the hill. "I just mean it's not like he's walking the streets committing violent crimes against random women."

Harper laughs, and it's the first time I've ever heard her sound cruel. "Do you have any idea how foolish you sound?" she asks. "And offensive? Like it's a lesser crime to be raped by someone you know at a party? Or that it somehow means he doesn't commit other crimes against women?"

"I don't mean it like that."

"Evan Gartner is a violent sex offender," she practically shouts.

"Jesus!" I warn. "Keep your voice down."

"Why? Are you worried the sparrows will hear us?"

I exhale, hardly able to catch my breath. "I agree that Evan is a violent sex offender, okay?"

"Good," Harper says. "Because he is. And Margaret was dating his son, so he knew her quite well. Maybe it follows his pattern."

We walk in silence for a bit. And then I say, "It just seems so dangerous for him to do anything to his child's girlfriend. I mean, at least in my case, I was an adult at a party, and he could accuse me of getting drunk and coming on to him if I told everyone."

"I doubt he's thinking that clearly when he decides to rape women." Harper tilts her head and takes in her surroundings, like she's a thousand times more relaxed than I am, like we're just sitting around having tea and chatting about normal stuff, not powerwalking a hill talking about a rapist and a murder. "I'm going to pay him a little visit, I think," she says.

"What?" I ask, downing a gulp of air in a big, dramatic breath. "Don't you think you should leave it to the police?" I feel a little dizzy, not sure I'm understanding her correctly.

"Nah," Harper says. "I don't. I have a sixth sense about these kinds of things, Sloane. You'll see."

We walk the rest of the way in silence. There are so many things I want to say to dissuade her from going anywhere near Evan, but I have a feeling that would only make her want to do it more.

# THIRTY-NINE

*Margaret – the week before*

Evan messaged on the app with an actual place to meet tomorrow night, and I honestly can't believe we're going through with this. The restaurant he suggested is an hour west of here, and now we're driving there as the sun sets to get the lay of the land, like a dress rehearsal, so that we know exactly what we're getting into and we're as ready as we can be for tomorrow night.

I can tell by the way Cole's hunched forward toward the steering wheel that his back is sore. He messed up a disc playing baseball, and sometimes it acts up when he sits for too long. We drive in silence past a row of townhouses and a yellow-brick apartment complex, and I try to force myself to eat a granola bar. I haven't eaten anything since breakfast because my stomach's been in knots. I manage to get half of it down, and then I say, "I just wish there was another way we could do this, like just talk to your mom—"

Cole slams on the brakes too far in front of a red light. "How many fucking times do I have to tell you that we can't prove he's the one sending the messages?"

I don't want to start crying, but I can't help it. Cole's never talked to me like that. "What the *hell*, Cole?" I whimper, sounding so weak. "Why are you yelling at me?"

He's sweating. I can see it along his hairline, on the skin of his neck, dampening the front of his shirt. His knuckles go white against the steering wheel, and it's this moment that I realize, without a doubt, that this is going to ruin us.

"We could stop now, is all I'm saying," I say, tears on my face. "We could call it quits and tell your mom what we know, and she would believe us, even if we couldn't prove it."

Cole taps the wheel, sniffs. The light changes to green, and we cruise forward. "Maybe you're right," he says slowly, and I can tell that even though he's pissed, he's considering it. "But what if my mom tries to leave him after we tell her, and he tries to destroy her. Wouldn't it be better if we had real proof she could use?"

I can't argue with that. Both of us are quiet, and then my phone announces we've arrived at our destination. Cole curves into the bumpy parking lot of a run-down lodge that barely looks like a restaurant, more like a motel.

"We may as well just check it out," I say, opening the car door and slamming it behind me.

Cole stands in the lot and surveys the restaurant. It's got a log cabin feel. You can't really see inside because the windows are small and located high on the exterior wooden walls, which is probably good for our plan, because Evan won't spot us waiting for him.

Cole turns to me. "You sure?" he asks, and I nod. For the first time, Cole seems hesitant. He says, "What if he's in there *now*, checking it out for tomorrow, just like we are?"

I shrug. Funny how when someone else finally shows concern, it makes you let go a little, like you can loosen the reins and be the careless one for a moment. "If he's in there," I say, "then he's the guilty one, not us. It's not even a bar. We're allowed to go for drives and eat at random places."

"He would know we were following him, though," Cole says. "He's smart, Margaret. How else do you think he hasn't been caught yet?"

204

"You don't know he hasn't been caught," I say. "Isn't there a chance your mom already knows?"

Disgust overlays Cole's face. "My mom would never stay with my dad if she knew he was cheating on her."

"Wake up, Cole," I snap. I'm tired of him tonight. He suddenly seems too young, too sheltered. Maybe what I really need is to get to college and be around older guys who don't say naive things just because their mom is involved. "You don't think women stay in marriages where their husbands cheat?"

Cole's mouth tightens. He's tired of me, too—I can feel it. "My mom would never."

"Let's go, Cole, okay? I don't wanna fight with you anymore." *And I don't really want to be dating you anymore,* I think to myself. I'm not going to be able to stay with him until the end of the summer.

I let go of a breath as Cole and I walk across the parking lot. I just need to get through this messed-up field trip and get back to my house. I promised Florence I'd do her spelling list with her tonight. She stays up way later than any fifth grader should, but we still need to hurry if I want to get back in time.

Beneath the ever-darkening sky, you can see moths circling the light above the door. Cole pushes the door open, and inside the restaurant, four guys play pool, a man and a woman play darts, and everything looks sticky: the bar, the floor, the tables.

"God," Cole says. "I wonder what they think of my dad when he strolls in wearing his fancy suits."

"I doubt he's been before," I say. "He can't go to the same place twice when he does this kind of thing."

"But I'm sure he came here at some point to check it out, don't you think?"

"Maybe," I say, a dark feeling passing through me. Everything that used to be exciting about all this—the plotting, the planning, the hushed chats Cole and I had late into the night—now that we're about to put it into practice, it just feels scary and wrong.

Cole looks at me. "Should we sit and eat?"

I shake my head—I need to get out of here. "There's nothing else for us to see. If you want to meet him here tomorrow, then let's just do it. I'll wait there," I say, pointing to the bar in the center of the restaurant. "He shows up after we do, and he'll start looking around for me, or for the person who looks enough like my profile picture, and then you take the video of him being here, and you need to text it to me and your mom right away, because he could grab your phone when he realizes what we've done."

I shrug, giving the restaurant a final glance.

"Let's get it over with," I say.

# FORTY

*Sloane*

Detective MacAllister is staring at me over the table in the
precinct. I've never been inside Sycamore Glen's police station; I don't recognize any of the officers I've seen so far
today, and why would I? Sycamore Glen is the definition of *sleepy*. In
our local newspaper, the biggest piece of crime news generally happens
around Halloween, when a kid gets too carried away with a prank, or
once after prom, when a high school kid drove into a mailbox. The kid
wasn't even drinking.

I've been here for an hour with the detective, going over every
detail I can remember about the night Margaret babysat Daisy, and
then every horrid detail I can remember about finding her body with
Ben and Harper. But even as I recount it, the night we found her feels
fuzzy, as though my brain is trying to protect me from what I saw. I can
remember everything Ben, Harper, and I talked about in my kitchen
with Margaret, but the details of where we were when we first spotted
her body, what it was like for Ben to descend the bluff, and how we
waited for help to arrive—all that feels murkier. I'm trying hard to get
it right, for Margaret's sake, but going around and around like this
is maddening, making me feel like I'm misremembering. Or like I'm

missing an important detail just out of reach, one that would help them figure everything out.

"And these neighbors of yours, Ben and Harper," the detective says, straying from the topic of Margaret for the first time. "Interesting folks, yeah?" he asks.

He's been mostly tepid this afternoon. Nonthreatening. He's middle-ish, everything about him, average height and weight, average build, light brown hair with matching eyes. He doesn't seem overly excited to be here talking with me; he's got a bland way of speaking without any cadence to his words. But the moment he mentions Ben and Harper, I can see the smallest light within him flicker. He has a job to do, and he likely knows how to do it. All of us would do well to remember that.

"They're interesting, yes," I say, not sure what he's asking.

"Yeah, wow," he says, shaking his head with wonder. It comes off fake. "So, let's see. Let's start with Harper. An artist, is that right?"

Unease skates through me. And then I do the thing I found myself doing days ago: I distance myself from them, from *her*, mostly, by saying, "Yes. I think. I've known them for barely a week."

"But you're close with them, that's what your husband, Dave, tells me."

"Dave is my ex-husband."

"Ah, yes," he says, looking at his notes. I'm not sure why he's bothering to play like he's a little slow, when I can tell that he's not. He goes on, "And is your ex-husband correct in his observation that you're close? He tells me you've spent an inordinate amount of time with Ben and Harper over the past week of becoming acquainted with them."

*Inordinate?* Is that really what Dave said?

"Is that a crime?"

The detective lets out a flat, unnatural laugh. "Oh, not at all." And then he clears his throat. "Margaret's death is a crime. And that is why we are here."

My heart presses hard against my chest wall, jamming itself against skin and bones. Margaret was just in my kitchen, living, breathing. My voice is small when I ask, "You think she was killed?"

"What do you think?" he asks, an eyebrow arching.

"I don't know what to think," I say. And maybe the sight of my tears softens him, because his voice is a little easier when he tells me, "I believe Margaret's death was a homicide for reasons I'm not at liberty to say. And because you cared about her, I'm telling you my professional opinion, so that you'll cooperate in any way that might help me find out who killed her."

I swallow over a hard lump. "What do you want to know?" I ask.

# FORTY-ONE

*Margaret – the week before*

R-A-B-I-D," Florence spells that night after Cole drops me off at home. The memory of the dimly lit restaurant is sticky against my skin, making me feel nervous.

Florence's tiny legs are crossed on her twin bed. We're sitting together on her star-printed blanket, practicing words for the spelling bee. We almost always get time alone together at night, because my parents have to go to bed early to be in their labs by seven. We eat dinner as a family, but Florence and I have been getting ourselves to bed and onto the bus in the morning since she was in third grade. I love my sister—everything about her. Our seven-year age difference means there's never been any competition between us, only affection. She's always been precocious, like she was trying to be my best friend by the time she was in kindergarten, and I was in seventh. And in a way, she *is* my best friend.

"These words are too easy for you," I say.

"No shit," says Florence.

"Language," I say, and then she cracks me up by spelling, "L-A-N-G-U-A-G-E."

"You need to go to bed, it's late."

"Will you sit with me?" she asks, and I do. I lean back against her wall, my phone glowing in the dark. Her breathing is starting to slow when I get a text from Robby.

Hey. Come out tonight? Party at Perez's house.

My heart thumps. We have each other's numbers from a project we did together last year, but he's never texted me.

I stare down at his message. I'm exhausted from going to that horrible restaurant with Cole, emotionally wiped from the tension between us and the thought of what we're doing tomorrow night to his dad. Maybe a party with kids my own age, who aren't cheating psychos like Cole's dad, is exactly what I need. And I still have a few hours until my curfew.

Sure. Cool. Text me the address. Xx.

I press send.

# FORTY-TWO

## *Sloane*

What do *I* want to know?" the detective asks somberly, reflecting my question back upon himself. And then he says, "Well, let's see," and his fingers go to the paper cup of water in front of him. I have a matching one, sitting untouched. "I find it interesting that, including Margaret's death, there have been three mysterious deaths on record on the same streets where your new friend Harper Wilson has lived during her lifetime. One occurred when she was a child, so I probably can't fault her for that one." He smiles sadly, like he says things like this all the time.

"In Spokane?" I ask, barely able to get the words out. My breath feels like razors in my lungs, remembering what Harper told me about the neighbor whose head she smashed with a rock. The one who she told me was still alive.

"Yes, in Spokane."

I kick myself for mentioning Spokane—what if the detective asks if she told me anything about it?

My heart pounds as he opens a folder and glances over the contents. "Roger DuBois, age forty-one at the time of his death. Died from a traumatic head injury. Case was never solved." He chuckles to himself, like this is fun, and says, "Like I said, she was a child, only twelve at the time, so I doubt she took a heavy object to his head and killed him."

I'm going to be sick—I'm sure of it. I'm about to excuse myself to use the bathroom when the detective flips to the next page, and says, "And then, in San Francisco, where she and Ben were just living . . ." And here he looks up at me and says, "Listen, I take all of this with a grain of salt, because San Francisco's an urban area and there's crime there . . . but if you look right here, there's a Mark Adler, himself with a criminal past peppered with sexual assault charges, who happened to live on Harper's street, and dead as of six months ago from blunt trauma. Harper was questioned but never charged. Same for Ben. Now, what are the chances?"

My heart thrums. "You think Harper killed these men?" I manage to ask, choking on the words. "Or that maybe Ben killed the one in San Francisco?"

"Ben could've killed the one in Spokane, too," the detective says.

"What do you mean?" I ask.

"Ben was fourteen," says the detective. And then his eyes hold mine, considering me very carefully. "He was living with her in Spokane, too. Ben and Harper are brother and sister. You didn't know?"

# FORTY-THREE

## *Clara*

This morning I insisted Arden and Camille go to school, telling them we needed time alone with Cole and his lawyer before his interview today. Being surrounded by friends will be good for the girls—our house is beyond depressing right now; all anyone did yesterday was cry. Marlow texted to see if I wanted to go for a walk, which was exactly what I needed, but I told her I couldn't, because I didn't want to leave Cole alone with Evan. And now the lawyer's here, and the tension between Cole and Evan is still nearly unbearable, even in front of the lawyer. They've never been close, obviously, and I've accepted that unlike his relationship with the girls, Evan and Cole never seemed to be able to make it work. But now the tension between them borders on physically painful for me as I shuttle back and forth, bringing them food and water, sometimes coffee. It doesn't feel like disconnection or misunderstanding between them now as it always did before; it feels like hatred.

The lawyer, who introduced himself as Chris Scoffield, told Cole and me that he was one of Evan's old college friends, which is odd considering I've never heard his name before. I can't seem to sit still, but I make myself, pulling up a chair at the table once I've served everyone drinks.

Evan's staring at Cole as the lawyer asks him questions, but Cole won't meet Evan's eyes. He acts like his dad isn't even here, and I think about genetics, about all the things from Evan and me that have shaped our son. "Margaret and I were in love," Cole tells the lawyer for what feels like the tenth time. "I would never, ever hurt her."

# FORTY-FOUR

*Margaret – the week before*

At the party, everyone's smoking pot, and even though I don't smoke, it still feels good to get lost in the pungent, earthy smell of it. It's so heavy and suffocating I can barely think about anything else, and tonight, that's a gift. Tonight, I want to be anywhere other than with Cole, driving home from the restaurant in silence, the quiet of the car and the end of the relationship like a blanket over my head.

I'm playing pool with Robby, who's nursing a beer. We move around the pool table like a dance. Cole taught me to play pool in his basement, and now I'm showing off, sinking balls left and right, feeling good.

"Not bad, Collins," Robby says as I sink a striped ball in a corner pocket. I forgot how last year, when we did that project together, he always called me by my last name. It's sexy the way he says it, and it makes *me* feel sexy, which I haven't felt in a while. I can feel my heart race at the feeling of being wanted.

My friend Ashley's watching me from a corner of the party, her eyes like knives cutting into us. She's always had a crush on Cole, and I feel stupid for not realizing it until the past few months.

The party is packed, and other than Ashley, no one seems to be paying any attention to Robby and me. I sip a High Noon and feel myself loosen, the alcohol making my shoulders release their permanent tightness. I imagine what it would be like to be someone else—to be the kind of carefree girl who flirts with a boy like Robby even when she has a boyfriend. I imagine what it would feel like to kiss him, to have his hands on me, pulling me closer.

Robby purposely misses his final shot, and it makes me laugh—the transparency of it all. He throws up his hands and says, "What?" as though he didn't just purposely shank the ball to give me another chance.

I set down my pool stick on the table. "Wanna call it a tie?"

"I don't know, maybe?" Robby says, stretching out an arm like it's sore. He's got a build like Cole, solid and buff from so many seasons of high school sports. "Let's talk about it outside, it's too hot in here."

He puts a hand on the small of my back and right away I'm nervous, because I know this is trouble. I'm not going to do anything with him tonight because I wouldn't do that to Cole, but I can feel that this is the start of something, and he and I both know it, and there's magic to the knowing: a fiery zip that runs through me, a flush of excitement that leaves me light-headed.

We leave the crowded room together and make our way through the kitchen where kids are doing shots of Fireball. And then we head out onto the deck, a small wooden rectangle that overlooks the woods.

Nobody's out here. My house is only a mile away, and I imagine Florence's twinkling night-light somewhere beyond the trees. I feel nostalgic thinking about her sleeping alone in her bedroom; it's hard to believe we'll be separated this fall when I'm away at school.

Robby puts his elbows on the deck's railing. His arms are tanned after a few weeks of afternoon practices. "So, you and Cole," he says, cutting right to it.

I stare at him, nervous, but excited, too.

"Me and Cole," I say easily, and everything feels fluid, like I could melt into the night and take flight.

"You're getting into Princeton, right?"

"Ha. Maybe. I think so." I don't tell him I got rejected from Harvard. Because I have this feeling about Princeton—like I'm gonna get it.

"And then?"

"And then *what*?" I ask, even though I know what he's getting at. I want to hear him say it.

"What happens with you and Cole?"

*We break up.*

"I think we'll decide to see other people at school," I say carefully, feeling like a traitor for telling him the thing I know to be true before I tell it to Cole. But Cole must agree with me, right? He must see it coming.

Robby turns so that he's not looking out into the woods; he's looking right at me. "Maybe you should trial run that situation now," he says with a smile. "So that you're ready for college."

I scrunch my toes inside my Converse, more nervous than I've been in a very long time. "Maybe not right now," I say, my voice steadier than I feel. "But maybe sooner than later."

Robby moves a little closer, smiles, but from the corner of my eye I see Ashley in the kitchen, moving toward the sliding glass door that leads to the deck. I take a step back from Robby, trying to put space between us, but then his hand is on my wrist, warm and solid. I catch Ashley's gaze right as he gives me a gentle tug. Her eyes narrow, seeing us like that.

"Robby," I whisper-hiss, pulling away. "We have an audience."

He takes a step back, but it's too late. I look again toward the sliding glass door, but there's only the flicker of the party, a swarm of kids that moves and breathes like a living thing.

Ashley's already gone.

# FORTY-FIVE

*Sloane*

I don't bother going home after the police station. I head straight to
Harper and Ben's and pound on the door, and I'm surprised when
Ben answers instead of Harper. I figured he'd be at work, but he's
standing there in Adidas shorts, looking half-asleep.

"I'm sorry," I say. "Did I wake you?"

"I got called into the hospital last night," he says, only half answering my question. "And then I had my interview at the police station this
morning, which kinda wiped me out."

We stand there, staring at each other. I'm not sure what exactly
this feeling is inside me; it's beyond morbid curiosity or fascination. It's
more like a force driving forward into a landscape I don't understand
but want to.

"Come in," Ben says, opening the door wider. When I close it
behind me, he asks, "Want to sit on the porch?" but he doesn't wait for
me to answer; he's already turning and heading in that direction. I stare
at his broad shoulders as we walk through the living room, his large
hands curling at his sides, his gait easier than usual. Now that I know
about him and Harper, I let my gaze linger on him longer than I have
before, trying to figure him out, to really *see* him. Before now, it always
felt dangerous to look at him too closely, like staring into the sun.

On the porch, we scan the furniture like we're trying to decide where to sit, and I picture Harper in the embrace of her lover just last night in this very room. I let go of a breath, unanchored and nearly frantic with indecision. Like picking the right sofa will steer this ship in the right direction.

"Are you okay?" Ben asks. He doesn't sit, either. The gentle twitter of birds filters through the screens.

"Not really," I say. "Are you?"

Ben shakes his head. "It's been an extremely strange week."

"It has," I say. He looks down at his hand, and when he finally looks back up, we stare at one another. Neither of us moves to a sofa. I'm still standing when I say, "The detective told me, among other things, that you and Harper are brother and sister."

Ben blinks. He shifts his weight, and the quiet moments that follow feel like agony.

"We are," he finally says, holding my gaze.

"Why didn't you tell me?" I ask. My voice is nearly a whisper. All the serene greenery and nature blooming right outside make the room feel sacred, a good place for secrets.

Ben's voice is quiet, too, when he says, "We didn't tell you we were married, or that we *weren't* brother and sister."

I can't argue with that. "Okay, sure," I say, with an ease I don't feel. It's his business, after all, but the truth is he knew I was under the assumption they were husband and wife. I'm quiet for a moment, and then I say it:

"You let me assume you were a married couple. Why?"

Ben's shoulders tense. "We didn't mislead you," he says, a new edge in his voice. I want to sit, because I feel so unsteady standing like this, but we don't. We just stand there, staring at each other. And then Ben says, not unkindly, "You came to your own conclusions on our living arrangements. We didn't put on a charade—we didn't act married. We never do."

"Other than living together," I say.

"People often have roommates they're not married to, wouldn't you say?"

Now it's my turn to shift my weight, to absorb the uneasiness of his question. "But why not tell people from the start, then?"

Ben lets go of a breath. "Because no one ever gets it. When we were younger, early twenties, it wasn't a big deal to be roommates; but as we got older, everyone looked at us sideways when we told them we were family, until finally we just stopped saying anything, and let people assume what they wanted. We move around a lot, and sometimes it doesn't really feel worth explaining."

I realize I'm holding my breath, and I try to let it go slowly. "*Why* do you move around so much?" I ask. I know I'm not owed an answer, but I also get the sense that Ben trusts me enough to tell me.

He waves at the air between us. "Maybe partly because conversations like these, no offense. And partly because both Harper and I get antsy very easily."

I swallow, feeling the real things I need answers to clawing right below the surface of our conversation. When I ask, "Why *do* you live together?" there's a sliver of fear in my voice.

"Do you really want to know, Sloane? Because if you do, I'll tell you."

A chill sweeps across my skin, warning me that I'm about to push this too far. But there have been so many times in my life when people haven't told me the truth, the biggest offender being Dave. Dave saw *something* that night Evan raped me—I know he did. And that knowing was there for months before we separated, heavy in the undercurrent of our marriage, poisoning the water.

"I want to know the truth," I say.

"Fine, then." Ben exhales, sitting down on the longer sofa, and instead of sitting across from him, I sit beside him. Our bodies tilt toward each other, knees almost touching. When Ben starts talking, his voice is low and filled with worry. "Harper has some destructive tendencies I like to keep an eye on. She's sexually impulsive, for one, which she told me you witnessed the other night in this very room. She also has a propensity for violence. And without getting into too much detail, my desire to protect Harper—or at least, this is the understanding of myself I've come to after years of therapy—goes way back to when we were children, and I didn't protect her from a violent man. I'm aware she told you about him, our neighbor in Spokane, and as for the rest of what I'm telling you, I'm asking you to keep it between us."

I nod, swallowing hard.

"I love my sister," Ben says. "I always will. And if living with her helps me to keep an eye on her and keep her under control, and in therapy, and on the medication she needs to keep some of these impulses and destructive tendencies under control, then so be it. I owe her that, at least. After what I've done."

"What you've done?" I say carefully.

"Maybe not what I've done," Ben says. "But what I failed to do. I was only a child, and I didn't know any better. And as someone who treats children now, I know from a logical perspective that I wasn't at fault. But still, on my darker days I blame myself. And this is part of what I do to make my guilt livable. Can you understand?"

I lean back against a gold cushion, my eyes never leaving his.

"I can," I say. We're quiet for a few moments, everything we've said settling between us. When I speak again, my voice is soft. "The neighbor in Spokane . . . Harper said she bashed his head in with a rock. Is that true?"

"Yes," Ben says, and then more defensively, "but she was a child. You can't possibly blame her for protecting herself."

"But then the police told me about a neighbor in San Francisco that was killed."

"Yes. Mark Adler. A sex offender who died tragically. But no one ever linked that to Harper or charged her with anything. We were both questioned because we lived near him. The cop here, your Sycamore Glen detective? I'm sure this is the biggest thing he's ever seen happen in his career, and now he's digging around in our pasts because Margaret coincidentally died on our property. Probably murdered by someone she knows quite well in Sycamore Glen. Not by us."

"So, Harper killed *only* the neighbor in Spokane," I say, wincing at the snap in my voice.

"That was a tragic accident."

I nod. "What happened to Harper when she was little was a tragedy," I say. "And I'm sorry that it happened—sorry for both of you, the pain it must have caused you then and still causes you now. It must be unimaginable."

Ben reaches out like he's going to touch me but doesn't. He puts his hand back on his own knee.

"Harper is your little sister," I say, trying out the words. "I didn't see that one coming, and I have a big imagination." I give him a gentle smile. "It's not about me, Ben. Your past is yours. And I understand sexual abuse, too, as an adult. So, going forward from tonight, you won't get judgment from me, okay?"

"Okay, cool," Ben says. "Because this is going to blow up for me at work, so it would be nice to maybe have one person besides Harper in my corner. Surgeons don't usually live with their sisters and have people die on their property the first week they move to a new town to start a new position." He tries to smile, but it's so very sad.

"I don't really understand how this hasn't come out yet," I say. I can't imagine the implications for his life, what it's meant to try to keep all of it under wraps.

Ben shrugs, looking tired, like this conversation has drained whatever else he had left after this week. "Sometimes Harper and I kept separate residences even though she always stayed with me. We never really got close enough with anyone for them to care very much about what we were doing."

"I'm sorry," I say.

"Yeah, and I kinda promised Harper it would be different here. I think that's why she was so excited when she met you and really liked you."

"I was excited, too."

"And are you still?"

"I'm overwhelmed and needing to think, is what I am." We sit there quietly for a moment, and the silence feels easier than I thought it would. "Thank you for trusting me with all of this," I say softly.

# FORTY-SIX

*Margaret – the week before*

Cole finds me at track practice the next afternoon. I take one look at his face, and I know Ashley told him.

The weather took a turn today, and I'm bundled in a sweatshirt and freezing, even though I just ran three miles. My hands are stuffed inside my pockets, and I'm as still as a statue watching Cole close the distance between us. I'm standing with my track friends, but the look on Cole's face scares everyone off; they quickly mutter their goodbyes and head toward their cars. There are still lacrosse guys on the field—no Robby, thank God—but some of his teammates were at the party last night, and now they stare at Cole like they know what's coming. I've got to get Cole out of here—I don't want to do this in front of everyone.

"Don't you have practice today?" I ask when he's close enough. I just talked to him a few periods ago, and he didn't seem pissed at all. But he had math with Ashley last period, and I knew she wouldn't be able to keep her mouth shut about Robby and me on the deck last night.

"Ended early. Is it true that you and Robby were hanging out last night?" he asks, a riptide beneath his words.

"Yeah, we were. At a party. With lots of other people there, too."

"Playing pool together, getting cozy on a deck, alone. That's what I heard. That's what everyone saw. Is that right?"

"Yeah." I shift my weight, toying with my key chain. "But nothing happened, if that's what you mean."

Cole looks incredulous. "You're not even going to deny it? You're my *girlfriend*, Margaret. We've been together a fucking year. And of all the guys in the world you want to be with behind my back, you pick Robby?"

"I didn't hook up with him."

He inches closer to me, his face contorted with anger. "But you wanted to. Say it, Margaret. You wanted to."

"Don't be disgusting," I say, tears pressing against the back of my eyes, knowing he's right. Why did I do things this way? I should've just properly broken up with him when I started feeling like this. "Please, can we not do this here, in front of everyone?" I turn and see two of Robby's friends staring at us with their stupid lacrosse sticks on the ten-yard line, like we're on a movie set. I hush my voice. "We have things to do together tonight, Cole." I imagine that dingy restaurant where we're supposed to meet Cole's dad, making myself feel sicker than I already do.

"Not anymore," Cole says. "I don't need your fucking help anymore. Forget I ever asked."

"You can't be serious," I say.

"We're *done*, Margaret," Cole says. "You betrayed me. Why is it that no one in my life can stay faithful?"

"Are you seriously comparing me to your dad?"

Cole rakes a hand through his hair. "I know it's not the same. But you hurt me, and even if you don't want to admit it, you know that you betrayed me last night with Robby, even if you didn't technically do anything with him. Ashley told me what she saw. And I believe her."

I start crying, and maybe that's the answer right there.

Cole shakes his head. "I can't believe you'd do this to me," he says softly, and it's like a knife in my gut. "Goodbye, Margaret." He turns and walks away.

# FORTY-SEVEN

## *Clara*

The lawyer has left our house, off to do some work while we all sit around and wait for Cole's five p.m. questioning at the police station.

Cole sits at the kitchen table with his head in his hands. Evan's a few chairs away on his phone, and I'm cleaning the kitchen, scrubbing places that don't need to be scrubbed.

So, when a shadowy figure shows up on our deck, feet from where Evan's sitting, I assume it's the lawyer, back with a question for Cole. Though I'm not sure why he would come to the back door; it seems like no one walks around the side of houses anymore—it's too intimate.

The figure knocks gently, and Evan turns. I come closer and see that I'm mistaken—it's not the lawyer, it's a woman, and then Evan opens the door and reveals the pretty woman from the fundraiser. Harper, Sloane's friend.

"Hello," Evan says coldly, which shocks me a little, because Evan's fake-polite to everyone he meets at first, especially women. And that only changes if the person does something Evan deems a slight. "Can we help you?" Evan asks, his voice slipping into a lower register, a little more neutral than before.

"Oh, hi!" Harper says. "Can I come in? I tried the front door . . ."

That must be a lie—even if she didn't ring the bell, I would have heard her knocking.

Evan steps aside and lets Harper into our kitchen. Cole looks up, considering her. Does he know Margaret was found dead on Harper's property? I have no idea if anyone would have told him that.

I don't say anything, which is nearly impossible for me, because I'm so trained to be the perfect hostess. But I don't want to start any small talk because I'm worried it'll go in that direction, and Harper will prattle on about nothing and never leave. I wait, silently, for her to tell us why she's here.

Harper smiles at Evan. Then at me. She seems to have zero problems with the awkward silence.

"I'm very sorry about your loss," she says suddenly to Cole, as though she just remembered why she came. "I'd only met Margaret once, on the night she disappeared, and she was lovely. And I'm so torn up about her being found on *our property*. You can imagine—I've just moved here, and it's quite unsettling."

Cole narrows his eyes. He's still sitting at the table, his large frame hunched. He looks like someone else. "You knew Margaret?" he asks Harper, emotion in his voice. "You saw her that night?"

"I did. She babysits for my new friend, Sloane, and I saw her at Sloane's house and spoke to her when Sloane and I returned home from the spelling bee your mother so masterfully planned."

I swallow, embarrassed, like she's playing a joke on me, even if I can't yet figure out the punchline.

"You live in the Tudor next to Sloane's?" Cole asks, suddenly alert.

"I do," Harper says, and then she turns and smiles at Evan in the oddest way, like she's truly interested in his presence, even though she's talking to Cole. Evan's staring back at her, and for the briefest second, I see something unknowable pass between them.

"Do you know that there's a trail from your property that goes all the way up over the ridge to a little red shed," Cole says, "a mile away maybe, near the cliff's edge? Margaret and I used to sneak through your lawn and hope the old lady who used to live in your house wouldn't catch us. I just told the lawyer about it."

"I didn't know that," Harper says, returning her gaze to Cole. "I've only just started going into the woods, because, well, to be honest, they totally freak me out."

Cole stares at her, saying nothing. I move to the cabinet, grabbing a glass, thinking I'll pour her some water, because I honestly have no idea what else to do. It's so odd that she's here.

"Margaret and I first had sex in that shed," Cole says, out of nowhere, and my mouth drops.

"*Cole,*" I say.

Cole turns to me. "What?" he asks.

"Stop talking, Cole," Evan says.

"Fuck you," Cole says, and I nearly drop the glass.

"Cole!" I say.

Evan goes deadly still. Harper looks from Evan to Cole like she's watching Netflix.

"It's not like I'm slandering Margaret by saying we had sex," Cole says.

"I don't know what's gotten into you," I say. "But I don't think—"

"Well, his girlfriend was murdered," Harper interrupts, almost nicely, like she's trying to explain it to me. "That's probably what's gotten into him."

I turn to her. "Can we help you with something? Is there a reason you're here, other than to tell us you find it unsettling that our son's girlfriend was found on your property?"

Harper shrugs her tiny shoulders. "No, that's it," she says, and then she turns and looks Evan dead in the eye, like she knows him, like she isn't just new to the town or meeting him for the first or second time. She seems so comfortable with the silence, but Evan frowns, annoyance flashing on his face. "I was just trying to be a good neighbor and offer my condolences," Harper says, still only looking at Evan. Her green eyes are blazing when she says, "It's such a tragedy when a young woman gets hurt."

Evan's features contract, and he suddenly looks pissed and done with whatever this is. "Thanks for coming by," he says, and then he opens the door and makes it clear she should leave.

She smiles at all of us, and it's so unnerving that I grab the counter to feel something solid and familiar. "Please let me know if there's anything I can do," she says breathlessly, like all of this is exciting. And then she smiles even wider at Evan and leaves the way she came.

# FORTY-EIGHT

*Margaret – the week before*

That afternoon after track, I manage to help Florence with her spelling list without crying or telling her that Cole and I are over. I don't want to distract her, because she cares about winning this thing, even if she pretends she doesn't. She's downstairs in the kitchen now, fixing herself a sandwich, and I'm lying in my bed staring at my phone. Cole won't return my texts or calls, and I've made several. I've apologized and asked him to talk, and now I just feel filled with regret, wishing that all of this went down differently. I want to see him and explain, and I consider going to his house, but I have to get to Sloane's house because she's volunteering at the spelling bee and I'm babysitting Daisy. Obviously the plan had been for Cole and me to drive out and meet Evan in that awful restaurant at midnight tonight, but apparently Cole no longer wants my help catching his dad in the act. Or at least that's what he said. But we did so much work to get to this place—to trick and lure Evan to Cutty's tonight—and as freaked out as I've been about it, throwing it all away seems insane.

I pull up my phone and check the dating app. It's not like Cole can stop me if I want to go, and I try to imagine what it would be like to drive there myself and wait for Evan. Would that be the stupidest thing ever—or would it be heroic?

I take a breath, adrenaline surging through me. What if this was how it was all meant to go down? To spare Cole the pain of seeing his dad in action—but to get the job done? Couldn't it be like one final gift for Cole, a way to tell him I'm sorry, and I'll always be there for him, even if we're not together?

Can I do this by myself?

I tap my messages.

Confirming tonight, I write to Evan, staring hard at the screen before adding: Midnight at Cutty's?

Before I can chicken out, I tap send, and right away there's a reply from Evan.

See you there.

I picture Evan in his house, in that grand office with a leather wing-back chair, scrolling on his phone, betraying his family, about to enter a trap he doesn't see coming.

It makes me feel happy for the first time all day.

# FORTY-NINE

*Sloane*

That night around five, Dave and I are sitting at the kitchen table while Daisy packs her overnight bag upstairs. No matter how much she loves him, Daisy's always hesitant about staying at Dave's, even though we've been sharing custody of her for years.

Dave's a mess, sitting in front of a cup of coffee, his hands shaking. "They were intensely questioning me," he says about the police. "Like I'd done something to Margaret."

"That's their job, Dave."

"Were there two detectives in your interview?" he asks, and I shake my head. "They were hammering me, Sloane. The two of them, just going at me." He looks down at his hands. "I just don't get it," he says, and then he shifts gears. "Why would a brother and sister act like they're married?"

This seems to be the topic he can't get enough of. "They actually don't act like they're married," I say. I'm mindlessly arranging some of Daisy's papers, adding a sheet of her math problems into my throwaway pile, and then a drawing of a bird into the pile of things I intend to keep. "They act like roommates," I go on, trying to sound reasonable. "It's just that a lot of married people act like roommates, so we don't even notice anything strange about it."

Dave chews on that for a minute. At his core, he's not a black-and-white thinker. His brain has space for this, even if that won't be the case for many residents of Sycamore Glen once the word gets out about Ben and Harper's living arrangements. When Dave's still quiet, I say, "Think about how many nonsexual married people there are out there."

"Yeah, but they were sexual at some point, presumably."

I shrug, my eyes roving over a drawing Daisy did of a tall, thin girl with long dark hair. Margaret.

"Maybe sex isn't everything," I say. "Or maybe it is at some point in the relationship, and then it falls away. People stay in marriages that aren't really marriages all the time. Maybe Ben and Harper just never tried to find that, and this made sense for whatever reason."

"But *why?*" Dave asks, like he thinks I know more than I'm saying.

"I wouldn't tell you even if I knew," I say.

Dave rolls his eyes. "I still don't like them. And this only adds to the murkiness."

I put Daisy's papers in a final, neat stack and meet Dave's gaze. "Someone killed Margaret. Maybe we should focus on that."

"Maybe Ben or Harper killed Margaret."

I try not to flinch at what he's said, like nothing about this is chilling. "Or maybe not," I say, but Dave doesn't let it go. His dark eyes are angry and scared when he asks me, "And you're fine just crawling into a lion's den with them?"

"I like them, Dave. I've liked them since the moment I met them. And I trust them. I don't think they killed Margaret." But there's doubt in my words. Could it be that I'm just so desperate for a true friend that I'm overlooking something?

Dave shudders, as though he's afraid not only of our neighbors, but of me, too. "You don't know them," he says softly. He's not wrong, and I feel worse by the second, like this conversation is slipping away from me, like I'm losing a fight I didn't even know I was in. And so maybe it's desperation that makes me say, "But I thought I knew *you,* and I didn't. So how well do any of us even know each other? Don't we all take a leap of faith?"

Dave's dark eyebrows narrow. "What are you talking about? You know me, you always have."

I feel my bare feet against the floor, and I try to ground myself, to feel the earth beneath me, reminding myself that I'm part of something bigger and stronger, something that can bear the weight of this even if I can't. "We have to keep our voices down," I say. "I don't want Daisy hearing us. But at some point, even if not tonight, we need to talk about that night at Evan's party eight years ago, when he was sponsoring us to get into the club, when I got really drunk at his party, and you walked in on us."

Dave's face goes ashen. "What are you talking about, *walked in on you?*" Adrenaline surges through me. I can't believe I'm doing this. Dave reaches across the table and grabs my hands. "Are you talking about that awful Fourth of July party when I found you upstairs with him?"

I nod. "How well do you remember it?"

"I thought you . . . well, that maybe you and Evan . . . I thought you wanted to be alone with him, or that you'd gone up there together . . . but I didn't walk in on anything *happening*, Sloane."

I've never seen Dave this uncomfortable, and a part of me relishes it, that this night was critical to him, too, that it scared him to find us together. And that I was right—he *did* walk in on us in some shape or form.

"What did you think happened in that bedroom?" I ask, my voice coarse. I've waited so long to talk about this, and now that it's happening, I wonder why I didn't do it sooner. Maybe nothing feels hard considering what's happened to Margaret, certainly not a conversation.

Dave says quickly, defensively, "I thought you'd gone up there with him, and I knew you were too drunk to be thinking straight, but you weren't physically together when I went up there. You were on the bed, and Evan was busying himself near the closet, telling me he had to get someone's coat."

"Why would anyone wear a coat to a Fourth of July party?" I shake my head. "I don't even remember setting out to get that drunk."

"Everyone was wasted at that party. And I thought you got wasted and went upstairs with Evan."

My hands are shaking, and the coffee cup makes a clattering sound as I set it onto the table. I lower my voice to say, "*He raped me, Dave. And you walked in on the aftermath.*" We blink at each other, Dave's eyes like saucers. "Sloane," he says, his mouth barely moving. He looks woozy in his chair, like he's about to pass out. But still I can't help myself from saying, "*And I think you knew it.*"

Dave leaps from his side of the table and comes to stand beside me. He crouches, putting his arms around me. "I didn't, Sloane," he says, his voice shaking. "I could never." We hold each other for what feels like a very long time, certainly longer than we've embraced in years. And when Dave says, "I'm gonna kill him," his voice is distant, like he's imagining it.

"You're not," I say, "for so many reasons."

He pulls back and looks at me, and his features twist as he considers my face. "I don't get it," he says. "Did you seriously think I'd walk in on someone, anyone, raping my wife and not stop it or call the cops or do whatever any sane person would do in that situation?"

"I thought you knew," I say. "I was lying there, and Evan was tucking his shirt back in. I thought you could figure it out."

"I swear to God I didn't," he says, and tears fill his eyes. "How could I blame Evan for anything when I didn't see anything? Would you blame someone for rape if you saw them in the same room, fully clothed, with your fully clothed friend?"

I put my head in my hands. "I wasn't your friend. I was your wife."

"I will never forgive myself," Dave says, putting his arms around me again, holding me even tighter. I can't believe we're here inside the moment I've dreaded for so long. I pull away and make him look me in the eye when I ask, "But why didn't you ask me what happened? The next morning, why didn't you make sure I was okay?"

"I don't know," Dave says, fully crying now. "Maybe I was too scared to know the answer. And maybe my thinking was backward. I knew you were drunk, way too drunk to do anything consensual, obviously I knew that. But I didn't know what happened with Evan, and I thought maybe you wanted to be upstairs alone with him. I thought maybe I'd walked in on the start of something horrible, not the end of it. I'm so sorry, Sloane, I . . ."

I stare into his deep brown eyes and wonder how we got here.

"There are things that have happened since," Dave says, his voice careful. "Things I've seen and heard that have made me realize Evan pushes too far past the lines of legality, of right and wrong. You've seen me pull away from him, Sloane. But I never thought—"

"I don't care about your relationship with Evan," I interrupt. "I care about all the ways this ruined us. You never made sure something hadn't happened to me in that room. And I think, more than anything, that was the thing I couldn't get past. The thing that finally ended us."

Dave blinks, incredulous. We're quiet, until he says, "I'm sorry, Sloane. I'm so very sorry."

# FIFTY

*Margaret – the week before*

Earlier, right before I went to Sloane's to babysit Daisy, I got my acceptance from Princeton, and I still can't really believe it. Even though I was jaded and thought it wouldn't be that exciting because my counselor was so sure I'd get in, I still felt really good when I read the letter—better than I thought I would. And that feeling of *good* almost kept me from going to meet Evan, but a promise is a promise—a promise to *whom*, I'm not sure, it's not like Cole even knows I'm going. But tonight feels like something I have to do.

So now it's nearly midnight, and I've been sitting at the bar at Cutty's for a full hour before Evan's scheduled to show. I tried to stand so I'd be more agile, ready to spring into action and take a photo, but I'm too nauseous and shaky. Guys at the bar are staring at me. It's too late—they're too drunk—why did Cole and I set such a late meeting time? What was the point of making all this even seedier?

I tap my foot against the leg of my stool. I'm surprised they're letting me sit at the bar—I don't look twenty-one. The bartender makes drinks and ignores me. He took my seltzer order around eleven, but then didn't return to ask if I wanted another.

A few tables are filled with people in their twenties, but most of the clientele are middle-aged men drinking or playing darts.

I chew the last small ice cubes in my glass. I don't know what I'm going to do when I see Evan. Do I stand and just take the photo right away? Because if I try to do anything else, like talk to him or something, he's just going to turn tail and disappear.

My eyes are glued to the door. I'm terrified to see Evan, scared to think about what will transpire between us, what he'll do when I take his picture, when he sees me, and when I bury my head in my phone to quickly text it to Cole . . .

I'm so consumed with those worries that it takes me a moment to realize I recognize the person walking through the door of the restaurant, and it's not Evan.

# FIFTY-ONE

*Sloane*

The rain pounds outside.

My house feels desolate and empty without Daisy here. Shadows creep across the floor, and everything that once felt quiet and peaceful feels ominous.

I'm upstairs in my closet, reading work I'd stashed away a long time ago. I haven't read my plays in years, and I want to blame it on the lack of time, but that wouldn't be entirely true; I could have found time, even while caring for Daisy. Other women do. I think it's just felt too painful to remember who I once was before Dave, and before Evan. Before Daisy, even.

The work is lush and electric—dramatic scenes meander this way and that, always with a through-line of feminine longing, love, and family drama. The scripts are *good*, even the plays that were never produced. And the ones that were produced—as I sit here and reread them, I remember what it used to be like to see the actors on stage saying my words, making them their own.

Why did I stop writing?

I know deep down it wasn't only becoming a mother or becoming a mother of a sick child. Some of it was sheer exhaustion from the trauma and stress of being raped by Evan, the way it spun me out trying to make sense of what had happened, blaming Dave, blaming myself. How it felt even harder, after the rape, to fit into my idyllic town with its unknowable inhabitants. It killed something inside me, something I'm desperate to bring back to life.

The doorbell rings and I drop the papers.

I head down the steps to the foyer and open the front door to see Ben. "Hey," I say softly. And then, curiously, "Where's Harper?"

"Just me tonight," he says, the smile he usually gives me gone. A pulse of thunder pounds beyond him.

"Come in," I say, but he shakes his head and says, "No." And then, "You come with me." His body takes up nearly the entire door-frame, but behind him I can make out the rain falling in silver slits. "To the woods," he says, extending his hand. "There's something I need to show you."

# FIFTY-TWO

*Clara*

Cole and I drive through the thrumming rain toward our house. My hands clutch the steering wheel, feeling like the car could spin out of control at any second.

Cole's lawyer and Evan are in the car behind us, all of us putting as much space as we can between ourselves and the police station. We fly over the black pavement toward the safety of our house to debrief about what happened during Cole's questioning at the station, but Cole is so agitated he seems like he's going to jump out of the car. I check twice to make sure his seat belt is on.

"They know we were in a fight, Mom," Cole says. "Margaret's teammates told the police, and some of the other guys on the lacrosse team told them, too, and I'm sure Robby told them. And we *were* in a fight; we were breaking up, even though that was the last thing I wanted, no matter how pissed I was at her, so I just tried to explain that to them. And they basically acted like that meant I killed her!"

"Cole, slow down."

"This isn't *fair.* My girlfriend's dead and my life is ruined. You realize I'm probably never leaving Sycamore Glen, now, probably not playing baseball in college, probably not going to college, probably never dating anyone else again because they'll all think I'm a murderer. That'll be my reputation from now on."

"No one said anything about you not going to college." But in my head, I think about how much he sounds like Evan. His *reputation*? When has Cole ever been worried about his reputation?

"And there's this thing, Mom, this thing Margaret and I did. I'm not allowed to talk to you about it, not yet, because I'm sure the police think you'd alert Dad, even though I know you wouldn't." He's talking a hundred miles per minute. "It was this website we were on . . ."

Anxiety surges through me. "What aren't you allowed to tell me?"

"It has to do with Dad, actually . . ."

"What are you talking about, Cole?" I have to force myself not to turn and look at him, to keep my eyes on the road and the storm.

"Mom," Cole says urgently. "Margaret and I fought once, about this random thing, and I just need to ask you something."

I turn to glance at him. He's peering out the window into the rain.

"You'd never stay with Dad if you knew he was cheating on you, right?" he asks, still not looking at me.

The words hit me like a punch. "Why would you ask me that?"

He shrugs lazily, like he's losing steam, even though just moments ago he seemed manic. "Margaret said the craziest thing once, and I told her I knew you wouldn't do that." He finally turns to me, and I swear I see the smallest smile on his lips when he says, "I think our entire family is about to lose our reputation . . . not the girls, of course. But you, me, and Dad."

"You're scaring me, Cole," I say, fingers white against the steering wheel. A car stops short in front of us, and I slam on the brakes. "Jesus Christ," I say beneath my breath, watching three deer cut across the road and disappear into the dark cover of the woods.

# FIFTY-THREE

*Sloane*

I take Ben's hand as he tears through the downpour toward the back of his lawn. My heart pounds inside my chest, my sneakers splashing, my clothes already soaked. "Back here," Ben says as we enter the trail. "Harper told me about . . ." Then his voice is silenced by the rain. Along the trail we go, half running, half stumbling. "There's this shed," he tries again, louder, "and we think . . ."

He doesn't finish his sentence. Our bodies jostle against each other as we maneuver the trail, his hand never leaving mine. Right at the spot where the trail splits to go toward the bluff, Ben turns, about to plunge us along a smaller trail I've never traveled. We go on forever that way—at least a mile or so, dodging holes and shifting to single file when the trail narrows. I swear I make out a light in the distance—I suppose it could just be starlight, a gentle flicker. Rain soaks us, and I'm out of breath when I say, "Ben, wait."

He turns to me, and I can just make out his beautiful face in the darkness. I put a hand on his chest, feeling a heady mix of desire and fear descend upon me. I don't know what comes over me as I stare at him, but all at once I rise onto my tiptoes and press my mouth against his.

He's startled. At first, he pulls back and looks deep into my eyes. I give him the smallest nod, my blood on fire, and then his arm is on the small of my back, pulling me against him. He kisses me like I've never been kissed before, devouring me until my knees go weak. The rain runs over our faces, but Ben's mouth never leaves mine, and I can feel every ounce of myself wanting this like I haven't wanted anything in a very long time. It makes me feel unearthly, as though I'm floating outside myself and none of this is real. Ben's hands travel over my skin and I can feel how much he wants this, too. But then a voice cries out:

"Ben? Are you coming? Do you have her?"

I pull away and look into the distance, realizing the light I saw before is a flashlight. In the darkness, the beam flickers.

"Shit," Ben says. His hands are still on me. "It's Harper. We have to go, Sloane. The shed," he says, as out of breath as I am. "There's something we have to show you."

# FIFTY-FOUR

*Margaret – the week before*

I can't believe it. Walking into the restaurant is Harper Wilson, the woman I just met in Sloane's kitchen. What the hell is she possibly doing here at Cutty's? She scans the place and spots me easily. My heart pounds as she moves toward me, a look on her face that could only be described as fury.

# FIFTY-FIVE

*Sloane*

<br>

Ben clutches my hand, practically dragging me along the trail. Another fifty yards or so, and I can make out Harper standing in front of a dilapidated structure.

She's holding a flashlight up to her face, looking scary lit up that way. What happened to her fear of the woods?

The structure is some kind of shed, to use Ben's term. Maybe a small barn. It might be painted red, but it's hard to tell in the dark. "What are you doing back here?" I ask, freaked out about whether she could see through the trees well enough to see Ben and me together. I have no idea if she'd view that as some kind of betrayal of our friendship—I have no idea what she'd think of it at all. All I know is that my body feels like it's half here and half back there, getting kissed in the rain.

"Sloane, come, I need to show you something," Harper practically shouts. She gestures with her hand for me to come closer, and I do, soaked leaves softening beneath me.

Harper opens the door to the shed, bending to flip on a battery-powered lantern on the floor that scatters light in shadows across the interior. Beautiful blankets that don't look old or tattered are piled on the floor. Candles line the room, with a few matchbooks scattered next to the candles. Three hardcover books sit on top of one of the blankets, and I recognize one of the books as a novel Margaret was reading weeks ago. And then I see what Harper and Ben are staring at, what they're waiting for me to see: In the corner of the shed, dark and unmistakable, is a pool of dried, flaking blood.

"Oh no," I say with a gasp. I turn to them, my eyes probing theirs. "What is this place?" I ask.

Harper shuts the door behind us.

# FIFTY-SIX

*Margaret – the week before*

Harper's staring right at me as she crosses the restaurant's
sticky floor. Her gaze is so piercing I don't bother trying to
stand or make a run for it. What would be the point?

Her dark curls hang loose around her shoulders. She finally
stops staring at me; now she's perusing the restaurant's clientele like
she's trying to assess what kind of situation we're in. Most of the
people here seem to have noticed her arrival, probably because she's
beautiful, but also because she seems to be aggressively surveying
them, like she's an FBI agent looking for clues. Finally, her gaze
returns to me, and then she closes the distance between us, sidestep-
ping clusters of people. When she's a few feet away, emotion twists
her face. She opens her mouth like she wants to say something. We
stare at each other, and when she finally speaks, everything comes
out timidly.

"I think we should probably get you out of here, kiddo," she says,
much less animated than when she was talking to me tonight back at
Sloane's. "It's almost midnight. Isn't that the time you were supposed
to meet the guy from the site?"

"What are you talking about?" I demand, trying to sound like I'm in charge, but my voice is a dead giveaway that I'm lying and scared.

"Trust me, I've done worse," she says. "So, you don't need to pretend you just happen to be here at this random place at midnight on a school night." She glances down at her watch, the tattered leather band that holds it in place at odds with the rest of her sophisticated clothing. She looks back up at me. "Seriously, let's scram before he gets here, don't you think? Who is he, anyway, the guy you're meeting up with? That site you're on looks kinda fucked up."

I don't say anything.

"Who is he, Margaret?" she asks again, but her voice is kind. Adults are always trying to sound like they understand you, like they're not judging you. But they usually *are* judging, even if only a little. Maybe not Harper. And something about her understanding and empathy makes me burst into tears.

"Don't cry, it's okay," she says, wrapping her arms around me. "Let's take your car home, and we'll chat, okay? And I'll Uber out here tomorrow and grab my car. You shouldn't be alone right now." She smiles gently, looking entirely out of place here at run-down Cutty's, like an ethereal creature who's gracing everyone with her presence and sure to be gone in a flash. I smile back at her, flushed with gratitude that she's going to get me out of here. I let her guide me through the restaurant, and then off we go through the exit and into the darkness of the parking lot. My limbs are shaking. I don't really know this woman at all, or how she figured out what I was doing, but all at once I get this rush of endorphins, maybe from the release of crying. I feel so much better being outside that horrible place. Beneath a sky twinkling with stars, I have a feeling of openness, like so many possibilities exist now that I've abandoned this charade. Maybe I can still help Cole—I can talk to Clara with him and tell her what we've done so far, and all the reasons we're sure it's Evan behind that avatar and username.

"I'll drive," Harper says in the parking lot, and I pass her my keys—I'm crying so hard I don't think I could drive anyway. I lean back against the seat, closing my eyes, listening to Harper's soothing voice telling me everything's going to be all right.

I want to believe her. I want to believe in all the possibilities that await me, but a small, nagging part of me warns me she's lying.

# FIFTY-SEVEN

*Sloane*

T"oday in Clara's kitchen, Cole told me about a shed in the woods," Harper says. She turns off her phone's flashlight, and the golden beam from the lantern on the floor is enough for us to see each other and the blood, even though I wish we couldn't. We're all just standing there, breathing heavily, the air wet and dank.

"Why were you in Clara's kitchen today?" I ask, my thoughts scattering. It's not like Harper knows Clara—she only met her once at the fundraiser, as far as I know.

"Because Harper is obsessed with Evan Gartner and has been for days," Ben says. "I've obviously told her to stay away from him, but she hasn't listened."

Harper ignores him. To me, she says, "I haven't been totally honest with you, Sloane, because the police told me I couldn't be. They literally told me I'd be obstructing justice if I told anyone what I knew, and they kind of freaked me out." Rain pounds the top of the shed so hard I can barely hear her when she goes on: "And now I'm even more scared that I'm going to be the one in trouble, because this shed is only accessible from our property, and it's freaking covered in blood that's probably Margaret's."

She strikes me as overdramatic for the first time since I've known her. If she didn't do anything wrong, then what's the problem?

"I'm assuming you're not both just bringing me out here to show me a murder-scene shed without having already called the police?" I ask, and when I see her face, I say, "Harper! Call them *now*. You have to. Or I will."

"We're going to call the police now," Ben says, "but we—"

"Well, forgive me for freaking out," Harper interrupts, "but they already seem so insanely suspicious of me because of the guy who died on my street at the last place I lived."

"And the neighbor in Spokane," I say, so she knows I know. We have to be honest with each other—it's the only way we're getting out of this.

"And the neighbor in Spokane," Harper repeats, standing straighter, like she'll defend herself if she needs to.

I stay quiet, waiting for her to go on. She gives a little sniff and says, "When Margaret was babysitting for you on the night she disappeared, I checked her phone."

"*What?*" I ask, and I must look incredulous, because she blurts, "She literally just left it lying out, in the bathroom," like that makes it okay. "Okay, sorry, Sloane," she says. "I'm not exactly perfect."

I feel the heat of Ben's gaze, and I can tell that he already knows all of this, and that they've been waiting to tell me, or maybe they've been trying to decide whether they should.

"Margaret had a message up on her phone," Harper says, the golden glow from the lantern casting oblong shadows across her skin. "I bummed around on the app she was on, and it was super shady, like a dating app but more of a hookup thing. And some guy had messaged Margaret with a meeting spot for that same night at a restaurant. I thought about telling you, but I'd only just met you! And anyway, I have experience with this kind of wayward, fucked-up behavior, so I decided to go there myself, basically to get Margaret out of a bad situation and try to talk some sense into her. I found her at the restaurant. It was an hour away and a total dive, and I honestly have no idea what she was thinking. Every guy in there was leering at her, and she wouldn't tell me who she was meeting. I have no idea if the guy was there or not. I drove her back to Sycamore Glen in her car, and she let me talk to her. She was pretty quiet, but mostly nodding along when I listed all the reasons she shouldn't be doing this, that she could end up dead. And she told me about the adrenaline rush she got while doing it, which of course I totally understood, and then she told me more about her parents, and how her dad has been on her about some mishap that happened at his lab while she was working there, which sounded kind of bad, like she was worried her college acceptances could be revoked because some guy accused her of stealing his idea, which I also told the police about. The science was a little over my head, but anyway her dad sounds like an *asshole*, which is what I was trying to tell that retired officer who was a friend of her parents' that night in your kitchen. And I went to the real police that night after I left your house and told them what I knew." Harper takes a huge breath, and I try to connect the dots as she goes on. "Margaret got back into the driver's seat at my house and left, and Ben and I went to get my car at the restaurant the next day. I told Ben, obviously, and like I said, we went to the cops with all of this as soon as she disappeared. But no one has Margaret's phone, it's lost, probably at the bottom of the river somewhere, so waterlogged no one could ever track where she was. Her online footprint is nowhere, or it's yet to be found, or the police have it and they're not telling me. But they're pushing on me *so* hard. I was the last one who saw Margaret, and she's dead, on our property. And now, this shed. I mean, come on. They're gonna think it's us."

I shake my head. "You're not thinking clearly, Harper," I say, my voice sharper than I mean it to be. "I'm sure they suspect the older guy from the app—wouldn't it make more sense for them to be trying to find *him*?"

"They *are*," Harper says. "I'm sure they are, but they haven't found him, and they're riding me." She looks at me, her eyes plaintive. "I didn't hurt her, Sloane. I've done things in my past; I've been violent with men who've hurt women, but I would never—"

Ben's eyes cut to Harper, a warning glance so fleeting I could have missed it if my every sense wasn't on such high alert.

"—I swear to God, I would never hurt Margaret," she says.

# FIFTY-EIGHT

*Margaret – the week before*

At Harper's house, I switch into the driver's seat and watch her climb the steps into her new home. I give her a gentle wave and back out of the driveway, but I can't bear to go to my house yet, so I drive my car farther up the hill to a secluded spot beneath pine trees. It's where Cole and I used to hide our cars before sneaking to the back of Harper's lawn to take the trail to the shed. The old woman who lived in Harper's house turned off her lights by nine, so we always chanced it and hoped she was sleeping and couldn't see us scuttling through the dark. The risk was part of what made it so fun.

I open my phone and text Cole.

I went to Cutty's, I write. It's one in the morning, but Cole is a night owl. And this is the only thing I can think of writing that will get his attention.

It works. He doesn't even bother texting back—he calls me right away. My car idling beneath me, my phone buzzes in my hand. I decline the call. Instead, I text him: Can't talk. Meet me at our spot.

Now?! he texts back.

Yes, now, I text. I cut the ignition and open my door, stepping soundlessly into the night.

# FIFTY-NINE

## Clara

Inside my kitchen, after his teammate sent him a screenshot from a text chain between kids at school discussing whether he killed Margaret, Cole is in a rage. He throws a chair across the room, and the girls and I watch, wide eyed, as it clatters pathetically against the floor. "My life is over," he screams at me, "and you don't get it!"

I'm backed against a wall, my arm across Arden's chest. Camille whimpers beside her. I want to go to Cole, but I'm scared.

"Cole, please," I cry, but the shattering of a plate against the window drowns out everything, and then Cole picks up a water glass. "Don't!" I say, and I try to step closer to him, but Arden and Camille pull me back.

The door from the garage slams, and moments later Evan finds us in the kitchen. "What the hell is going on in here?" he asks. Cole winds his arm back like he's pitching a baseball, about to hurl the glass across the kitchen.

Evan lunges at Cole. "You're hurting him!" I cry as he wraps his arms around Cole's shoulders, restraining him.

"He was about to hurt *you*."

"He *wasn't*," I say, sobbing as Cole fights like an animal to get out of his dad's grip. "He would never."

# SIXTY

*Margaret — the week before*

I'm pressing through the woods toward the shed to meet Cole when my dad calls.

"Sorry, Dad," I say, a little breathless, more from emotion than anything physical. "I'm sorry," I say again, "I can't talk. Is everything okay?"

"*You can't talk?*" my dad hisses, like I told him to fuck off. And then he says, "I thought you were coming home, so we could talk about this," and even though he's royally pissed, he's talking quietly, which means my mom is still sleeping. Last she knew, I was sleeping at Cole's tonight, but my dad doesn't always know what she and I agreed upon. He's usually never up this late, which freaks me out. He's still so upset about his labmate saying that my idea about interferon signaling was stolen from him. I thought it would blow over, but now it doesn't seem like it.

I don't say anything—I don't want to give myself away. I'm still not supposed to be out this late and in the freaking woods. I turned off my location tracking earlier, when I went to Cutty's, even though I don't think my parents ever bother checking it. But what if my dad talked to Clara and knows I'm not at Cole's?

"Do you have *any idea* what all of this could mean for us?"

"For *me*," I correct.

"It impacts me, too, *Margaret*." He says my name like it's a curse word. "It could impact us greatly."

I still haven't told them about the Princeton acceptance, and the truth is that's partly because I'm worried it will make everything he's talking about *worse*. Because then there really will be something to lose if Princeton gets wind of my dad's labmate accusing me of stealing his idea, the idea around which I based my entire essay.

"Carl called me again, Margaret," my dad says, even softer.

"But I didn't do anything wrong!" I say. "I didn't take his idea, Dad. You know that better than anyone else. It's not even a proprietary idea. I just got lucky that it worked."

"Well, he's saying it was his suggestion, and that you took it and claimed it as yours."

I try to focus on the dark trail passing beneath me. We've gone over this so many times.

"Everything I wrote in my college essay *happened* to me, Dad. In your lab. I didn't make it up."

"He might take this further, Margaret. He might officially report it," my dad says. "And that is untenable for me."

"What do you want me to do?" I ask, feeling worse than I've felt in a very long time. I can just make out the shed in the distance.

"I want to talk with you alone tonight. I want to go over everything that happened in my lab, and I want you to tell me the truth. And if you don't, things might get very, very bad for you." My fingers tighten against my phone, and when I don't say anything, my dad says, "Come home *now*, Margaret. Or I'll come find you."

He hangs up on me. I stare down at my phone, feeling like the walls are closing in. I bypass the trail to shed and head toward the cliffs.

# SIXTY-ONE

*Sloane*

Harper stays in the shed to make the call to the police, but I can't be in there any longer, not with the blood and the rest of the evidence of Margaret.

Outside in the rain, I start crying. Ben pulls me into his arms again, this time kissing me gently on the head.

"Who do you think killed her?" I ask Ben.

"I honestly don't know," he says.

I lean my head against his chest, closing my eyes and listening to the rain. Before we know it, sirens sound.

# SIXTY-TWO

*Margaret – the week before*

At the very edge of the cliffs, I look down into the black water. How is it that everything's gotten this complicated? A heaviness settles around my shoulders. My feet are too close to the edge for safety—I know that, I do, it's just that I want to feel something bigger than myself, and whether that's fear or nature or the vastness of it all, I'm not sure. My parents never raised me to think about God or something larger, but I experience something close to that feeling whenever I run, or whenever I'm in these woods. Florence and I used to come back here when we were little, and I felt it then, alone with her and the dirt and the trees. I don't know when we stopped coming here together, but I wish I could bend time and get it back.

My phone buzzes, and I look down to see a text from Cole.

I'm here. Where are you?

At the cliff's edge, I text back. Meet me.

# SIXTY-THREE

*Sloane*

The rain has mercifully stopped. Ben, Harper, and I stand on the wet ground together. Maybe under different circumstances it would be awkward how close we're all standing, but right now it feels necessary. The police sirens have quieted, and I imagine the officers have parked either at my house or Harper's and are now trudging through the woods to find us.

I turn to Harper and realize she's crying. She leans into Ben, and he puts an arm around her shoulders.

# SIXTY-FOUR

*Margaret – the week before*

Cole bursts into the clearing and walks toward me. "Come here," he says, reaching out an arm to me. "You're too close." I stand my ground. "I'm really sorry," I blurt, and even though I've cried so many times tonight, more tears come. "I'm really sorry for everything I did."

"Did you see my dad?" Cole asks, giving up on getting me to come closer, instead stalking across the clearing to stand with me near the cliff's edge. The river rushes below us.

I'm crying harder, and I want him to console me, but he doesn't. "Tell me what happened," he says, and his voice sounds strangled, like he's trying to stop himself from shouting.

"I didn't see him," I say. My shoulders start shaking, and I drop my head into my hands, wiping my eyes. Finally, I look back at Cole, and say, "It was crazy. I went there, and then one of Sloane's friends must have followed me or something. I don't even know how she knew I was there. And she basically said we had to leave, and she promised she wouldn't tell Sloane or anyone."

"Sloane's *friend?* Holy shit," Cole says, shaking his head. "She followed you? Who is she?"

"It's this woman, Harper. But I swear to God, I didn't tell her anything about our plan to trap your dad, or anything like that. She just thinks I was there meeting someone. She has no idea it was your dad."

"But I don't even understand why you went alone. We called it off, Margaret."

"Don't be mad at me. Please. I'm so sorry for what I did, tonight, but especially for letting things get messed up with us."

Cole shakes his head gently. "I can forgive you for the Robby thing. But it seriously can't happen again."

I shake my head—I have to tell him. "I wanted to do this thing tonight for you with your dad, I really did. But I don't think this can work between us. I think we lost our way."

Cole looks at me like he can't believe what I'm saying. "Are you fucking serious?"

"Yeah, I'm serious," I say, but he blinks like he doesn't believe me.

"I can't believe you're doing this."

"Well, I just think—"

"Is this because of Robby?"

"No, it's not. I've been feeling like this for a little while, and . . ."

My voice trails off. The wind has picked up back here by the cliffs, whipping across our faces.

"And *what?*" Cole snarls. "You've just been pitying me, not wanting to break up with me, stringing me along, flirting with Robby and embarrassing the fuck out of me?"

"I don't know what's gotten into you," I say, surprised that he's this pissed. "I'm sorry, but people are allowed to break up."

"Don't say sorry like that, it's patronizing," he says, his fists balled.

I'm so flustered, I almost say I'm sorry again. Instead, I swallow, barely able to meet his glance. I shake my head, tears falling. "I love you, Cole, but we're over." I start to cry harder, hating every moment of this. "Can you please just give me some privacy?" I can feel myself about to lose it. "I think I need to be alone."

But he doesn't leave. Instead, he says, "No one will ever love you like I do."

Anger twists his face into something unrecognizable. He steps toward me, and I have the vague sensation that we're too close to the edge. "Cole, *careful*," I hiss, but he keeps coming.

# SIXTY-FIVE

## *Sloane*

Two plainclothes detectives arrive at the small clearing where Harper, Ben, and I are standing, flashing their badges. One is MacAllister, and the other is taller and more austere-looking. "Detective Jameson," he tells me as he shakes my hand, gripping too hard. Their flashlights scatter the woods, casting shadows and spotlighting the private details of the forest: the hollowed-out tree trunks, the gentle dips and curves in the dirt, the exposed roots and gnarled bark. The trees loom and sway above us and there's something in the air, a feeling of reverence, maybe. A moment descends when I can feel Margaret warm-blooded and alive, in my kitchen, caring for my daughter, pressing onward in a life that I thought was supposed to be hers. But it passes, and then it's just me again in the woods facing a harsher reality.

Harper presses herself against Ben, and when he wraps an arm around her, our eyes meet. Everything passes between us.

"This is it?" asks MacAllister, gesturing toward the shed.

"This is it," Ben says.

MacAllister pulls on gloves and opens the door of the shed, shining his flashlight in the direction of the blood. He turns to Detective Jameson, his face unreadable. "Call for backup and forensics," he says.

# SIXTY-SIX

## *Clara*

I'm not going to hurt anyone," Cole says as Evan pins him against the kitchen island, his voice rasping.

"Then *calm down*," Evan says. "Get control of yourself."

*Control.* As if Evan understands the meaning of the word. Cole's breath comes fast, and he leans against Evan, something I haven't seen him do since he was a small child. And then Evan lets him go at the very moment Cole needs him the most.

I shake my head, unable to disguise my disgust.

Cole staggers across the kitchen toward me. I throw my arms around him, and he starts to cry. "Mom," he says quietly enough that only I can hear him. "I need to tell you what I've done."

# SIXTY-SEVEN

*Margaret – the week before*

Y ou're throwing all this away?" Cole asks, coming too close. I
don't want his embrace anymore. I just need to be alone—to
think about how I want to handle my dad tonight when I go
back home. I need to tell my father I got accepted to Princeton and go
over all the things that happened in his lab, step by step. Worse comes
to worst, can't we just call Princeton and explain things before that guy
can mess everything up?

"I'm sorry, Cole," I say over the whoosh of river water below us,
trying to rein in my sobbing. "And I'll go with you to tell your mom
about your dad, whenever you want to do it. I'll tell her about my part
in everything, what I saw, so that you don't have to do it alone."

Cole shakes his head sadly. "I loved you, Margaret," he says.

"I loved you, too," I say, meaning every word. "Go, Cole, go back
home and get some sleep. And then we can plan how to get your mom
alone. Tomorrow. Once we've both had time to chill and think. I've
gotta deal with my dad tonight, anyway," I say. "I'm going home."

Cole nods. He reaches out and gives me a solid hug, and it almost
makes me cry how we already feel like just-friends. It's what I want, but
it's a loss of something I held dear.

"Goodbye, Cole," I say softly.

"Goodbye, Margaret," he says, pressing his lips to my cheek. He pulls away, and then gently touches the gold locket at my neck, the one he gave me for Christmas. He had it engraved with my initials, and glued a photo of himself on one side, which I found a little embarrassing at the time, even though I loved it, and glued a photo of Florence on the other side. He could be so thoughtful when he wasn't consumed with his dad.

I blink away tears as I watch Cole step back from the edge of the cliff and disappear into the woods. A part of me wants to follow him, but I don't. I give him a minute or two before starting along the trail myself. The tears fall over my cheeks, and I'm so sad and exhausted about everything that happened tonight that all I want to do is sleep. I veer left and head to the shed Cole and I loved so much. I can't imagine I'll be coming here anytime soon now that he and I aren't together, and I want to grab some of the books I stashed there. I'm nearly at the shed when I hear a branch snap. I whip around, squinting in the darkness.

"Cole?" I call tentatively, but no one answers. I step forward, rounding the side of the shed and unlatching the door. I slip inside and close the door behind me—I don't need any wild animals trailing me inside—and then I flick on the lantern we keep by the door. The shed is the same as we left it last week, the interior feeling much more like an oasis than the dilapidated exterior. We made it that way, Cole and I, decorating it with pride, like it was our first apartment or something.

I kneel into a cluster of blankets, and I'm retrieving a hardcover when the door to the shed swings open—I can hear the latch click and the door creaking. I turn around to see Evan.

Fear shoots through my entire being. I'm on my hands and knees and still I feel as though I could pass out from the terror of seeing him here. I rear back into a sitting position, pushing myself against the wall.

"Hi, Margaret," Evan says, his voice calm and cool. He's wearing dark black gloves, and his hand rests against the door for a moment before he shuts it behind him. I press my spine into the hard wood of the shed. "Hi, Mr. Gartner," I say, so scared that I can barely get the words out. "What are you . . ."

"He was so easy to follow," Evan says casually. "My son. Leaving the house in a love-struck fury." He laughs a little, like Cole's a loser—which is exactly what Cole thinks his dad thinks about him. "So was Cole the one who put you up to all this?" he asks.

"Um, I . . ."

"I saw you at Cutty's tonight, at the meeting spot I'd arranged before realizing that you'd been the one communicating with me."

My heart races, fear zinging through me. "I didn't see you there," I manage to say.

"Oh, I think you did."

"I *didn't*," I cry, feeling blood drain from my limbs, knowing how much trouble I'm in now that he knows it was me.

Evan laughs. "Well, I guess it doesn't matter now, because I just *told* you I was there. Silly me."

I want to be sick. What kind of horrible game is this?

"It's too bad that woman came to rescue you, Margaret," Evan says slickly, and I flash back to Harper's kind face in the restaurant. "If she hadn't, maybe we could have had some fun together."

Bile rises in my throat. I cover my hand with my mouth.

"So, am I right—does my son know? I can't imagine you've been up to this all by yourself."

I'm so scared I can't answer—I can't seem to get my mouth to make words.

"You need to tell me the truth now," he says, his voice eerily calm.

"Um. No. It was just me," I manage to get out.

Evan makes a clicking noise with his tongue. I shift my weight and feel how soaked my pants are. I'm so scared I've peed myself.

"See, here's the problem. Even if you're lying to me, and Cole knows something, he still wasn't there tonight at Cutty's, now, was he? He never saw me. And he isn't privy to this little conversation we're having. You, Margaret, are the one who can tie me to a site linking me with other women, and you're the one who can tell people I tried to meet up with you. So, we have a very, very big problem."

He steps toward me, his hands reaching for my body. I scramble back, but there's nowhere to go.

"And really, there's only one thing to be done about it," he says as I begin to scream.

# EPILOGUE

## *The Woman from Miami*

## *Two and a Half Years Later*

I come in through the screen door soaking wet and freezing. Evan's sitting in the kitchen inside the new house he bought me, the one with a kidney-shaped pool and marina views. I flick the switch to turn on a string of Christmas lights on the screened-in porch. I grew up in Minnesota for the first fifteen years of my life until my mom moved us to Miami. There was more money in Miami than in our tiny town and more people looking for housecleaners. But celebrating Christmas in warm weather always strikes me as depressing, no matter how long I've lived in Florida. The holiday is only a few days away, and I still don't know if Evan's going to spend it with me or go back up north and try to see his kids.

Evan has his reading glasses on, his eyes glazed as he stares into the folded newspaper. I'm a little surprised that he doesn't even look up as I saunter across the kitchen.

I'm almost thirty, and I'm trying to tell myself that getting a house from a man is almost the same as getting a ring. But my mom is breathing down my neck, even more so than a year and a half ago when Evan and Clara's divorce became final. That's when I finally told her about Evan, and she Googled him and found out about his delinquent son Cole being on trial for his girlfriend's murder, and about the rape charges brought against Evan by his ex-wife's friends. (Which made *no* sense. Trust me, if you saw Evan, you'd know he'd never need to drug anybody to have sex, and the grand jury didn't indict him. But imagine trying to explain that to your mom.)

Cole got acquitted, but still. Evan thinks his son killed his girl-friend, and of course, so do I. Listen to a few true-crime podcasts, and you'll learn pretty quickly that it's almost always the boyfriend. Cole's DNA was in a shed where his girlfriend's blood was found, and she'd just broken up with him that afternoon. Practically their entire school saw them fighting.

"Hi, babe," I say to Evan. At the sound of my voice, he finally lifts his head. His lips move into the barely-there smile he gives me lately when he's annoyed. But is he annoyed because I interrupted his reading? Or is it because I'm tracking wet footprints across our kitchen? I hope it's not because he's getting bored of me. We have an entire lifetime to spend together, and I've already done enough sickening things to be with him—things that make me hate myself. The worst was when we first got together, when I was cocktail waitressing at a restaurant where Evan and his work friends went. I was only twenty-five then, and the first night we hooked up Evan wasn't wearing a wedding ring. We exchanged numbers, but I didn't have his last name when I put his number in my phone. It's still saved that way, just *Evan*. After a few more meetups, I got wise enough to get his last name and stalked him online to learn exactly who he was, and that's when I realized he was married, and he had an entire life in upstate New York: a pretty wife, three kids, and a golf club that always posted his picture when he won a championship. But by then, I was already in too deep, totally in love with him and sure we were meant to be together. Maybe a stronger woman would have cut things off, but I didn't. And now here we are.

Evan's still sitting at the kitchen table with that half smile on his face, but I'm not an amateur at dealing with his moods, and I have ways to snap him out of it. Like this: While standing in front of him in my bikini, I ask, "Whatcha reading about?" And at the same time, I slowly untie the top of my suit.

He closes the paper and sets it down on the table. He looks at me, and I revel in his gaze. I always love the moment his eyes travel over my body and it's obvious that he likes what he sees. Clara had never put out, according to Evan. I guess she probably used to at some point, but as soon as she found out he was seeing other women behind her back, not so much. And who could blame her? Well, I mean, I *do* blame her for plenty of things. She keeps the kids from Evan, for one. I've never even been able to meet them. And considering we're hopefully going to be getting engaged soon, that seems a little unfair. (Obviously, I'm nervous to meet Cole after what he did, but he's still Evan's son.)

With Evan gazing at me, I untie the bottom of my bikini and shimmy out of it. I stand in front of him completely naked, and he puts a hand on the curve of my hip. "Come closer," he says, and then he tugs me into his lap so I'm straddling his legs. I can't believe he doesn't care that I'm still wet from the pool. Usually, he's anal about that kind of thing.

I take his reading glasses and set them carefully on the table, and then I run my fingers over the tanned skin on his face and into his light hair. I lean forward and kiss him, and he kisses me back. I'm never happier than in moments like this one. Evan's not perfect, but I love him, and it's been hard lately with him constantly traveling up north for work. I try to think of this house as *our* house, but, the truth is, I'm not sure which place Evan considers his home—here, or his house in Sycamore Glen, the place he tells me he can't give up because of work. He's flying out later today to go back there.

Evan pulls me so close that the pressure he's putting on my back starts to hurt, but I don't say anything. As we kiss, I think about his overnight bags packed upstairs. I finally pull away and ask, "So you'll be back for Christmas, right?" I try to make my voice sound shy and girlish because usually that's how I can get what I want from him. "I was thinking we could wake up together and then go to my mom's."

Evan frowns. *Ugh*—I never should have mentioned my mom. How dumb am I? I can feel myself redden as he stares at me. "I don't know, babe," he says evenly. "I have children I need to see."

I almost snap that his children probably won't want to see him. Last year Evan showed up to Clara's house on Christmas, and his daughter Camille shut the door in his face.

But if I say that, it'll be a huge fight. So instead, I remind myself that my friend Jenny who works at the mall told me that while she was on break getting a smoothie, she saw Evan at Kay Jewelers looking at rings. A proposal *has* to be right around the corner. In fact, maybe the ring is here in the house somewhere. Maybe Evan's whole plan has been to wait until Christmas to propose.

I give Evan a small smile and press my lips against his once more. And then I get an idea.

## Clara

I'm decorating the library's Christmas tree when I see the back of Margaret's little sister. I'd recognize Florence's blunt bob anywhere. She's in eighth grade now, all slender limbs, Doc Martens, and navy-blue nail polish. Years ago, a close friend of Margaret's mom told me that neither she nor Margaret's dad believed that Cole killed Margaret. I hold onto that with everything I have and try to keep my head high when I cross paths with them.

Florence hasn't spotted me yet. She's looking down at the tower of fantasy novels in her hands, barely able to balance them. Usually, one of her parents is with her at the library, helping her with the stack she checks out every few weeks. They seem to act so differently with Florence now that Margaret is gone. They watch her with a look of reverence on their faces, like they're grateful for each minute with their only surviving daughter. Florence told one of the librarians that she wants to be a poet, and the librarian told me that Florence's mom checked out half a dozen poetry collections and a handful of books about writing poetry.

"Florence?" I ask tentatively. I'm always nervous around her.

She turns and catches my eye. "Let me get you a tote for those books," I say, moving quickly to the stack of canvas bags I keep behind the checkout desk.

Florence stands there mildly, seemingly unmoved by my knight in shining armor routine. "Here," I say, moving toward her again, opening the tote so she can dump the books inside, which is exactly what she does.

"Thanks, Mrs. Gartner," she says politely, a little like a robot. But then she slings the bag over her shoulder, and instead of turning around and heading to the door, she lingers for a moment.

"Merry Christmas," she finally says.

"Merry Christmas to you, too," I say, and she gives me the smallest smile before turning and walking out of the library. I swallow over a hard lump in my throat, making my way back to the Christmas tree and picking up the strand of popcorn I left dangling over the fake green branches. I try not to think about Florence and Margaret's parents as I decorate the tree. Instead, I try to focus on how much I'm loving having my girls home from Villanova and Cole home from Bucknell. But it's nearly impossible not to think about the Collinses celebrating another Christmas without Margaret.

As close as my girls are, they probably wouldn't have gone to the same college if Cole hadn't been on trial for Margaret's murder, and if, during the trial, it hadn't come out that their father had been sexting and meeting up with numerous women, including Margaret. (Which the prosecution tried to use against Cole, as if Cole and Margaret were the problem for trying to catfish Evan.) And then there were the rape allegations from Marlow and Sloane, and all of it meant that Arden and Camille needed to stay close to each other.

Cole was right in a way—what happened to Margaret did ruin his life, at least partially. He tanked emotionally after the trial, but eventually made it to college, two years late and without a spot on the baseball team. He's keeping his head above water now, double-majoring in business and art, maintaining a very small but tight-knit group of friends. Everyone still looks at him strangely, and at the girls and me, too—the deep suspicion and fascination certainly followed Arden and Camille to Villanova. It's like a dark blanket has been thrown over the four of us, like even though Cole was acquitted, people will always think he had something to do with Margaret's death.

The negative attention made me take a step back from PTA life and hunker down and get closer with a small group—some mothers I know from school, but mainly Marlow, Sloane, and Harper. They all know what I know: Cole didn't murder Margaret, and Evan did. It was all we talked about for months after Margaret died. We'd sit around my living room and rehash everything we knew—every crime and transgression Evan had committed against us and others. But even with the evidence from the dating site, there still wasn't enough to charge Evan with Margaret's murder. The evidence all stacked up against Cole: There was the timing of Margaret breaking up with Cole hours earlier; and Cole's own admission that he snuck out to meet Margaret in the woods on the night she disappeared. And then there was Cole's DNA in the shed where Margaret's blood was found, not Evan's. Not to mention Harper's testimony that she and Margaret left the restaurant where Margaret and Evan were supposed to meet, before the meeting time and without ever seeing Evan.

But I remember the way Evan looked at Harper when he met her at the fundraiser later that week. It was with recognition, like he'd seen her before. It made me sure that Evan was somewhere on the restaurant's premises when Harper came and got Margaret. I would bet my life that Evan saw Margaret waiting for him at the restaurant, and realized that she was the person he'd been communicating with; and once he knew Margaret had evidence of his dirty little secret, he killed her.

Evan was so confident that Cole would never get convicted—and he was right. But how did he let it go as far as it did—how could he ever let his son take the blame for a crime he committed?

Even after everything came out about Evan, still he walked the streets of Sycamore Glen with his chin held high, as though daring anyone to say a word. He moved into a 1950s bungalow even closer to Main Street. To the outside observer, he behaved like a man who'd done nothing wrong. To me, he behaved like a ruthless killer who'd gotten away with murder. And the town seems split on what they believe actually happened. Some of Evan's old friends distanced themselves, but some shored up their loyalty, insisting that the man they knew never would have done the unspeakable things that Marlow and Sloane accused him of doing, and leaning into the idea that without a grand jury indicting him, there must not be a real case behind their allegations. Evan still gets invited to things, and he's still a member at the country club. How he's been able to get away with so much and have his impeccable social standing only slightly altered is mind-blowing, but when I started looking deeper into other rape cases involving men like him, I realized that it's happening everywhere.

About a year ago, Evan opened an office in Miami and got a girlfriend there—or at least, that's my best understanding about what's going on. A few of the women at the club have shown me pictures they've seen Evan's redheaded girlfriend post, and I know there's a chance she's the same redhead I saw him with in the hotel that night in Miami, but I never saw the woman in Miami's face clearly enough to be able to tell. And I'm certainly not going to ask Evan. I do wonder if this is his pattern: Needing a forward-facing wife or girlfriend to play house with while he does whatever he wants behind her back.

Cole and Camille won't talk to their dad—Cole is convinced Evan killed Margaret, and even though the girls remain less sure about who killed Margaret, the rape charges and the fact that Evan was having affairs and seeking out sex behind my back were enough to forever alter their relationship with him. It didn't stop Evan from trying—especially with the girls—by showing up to Villanova with flowers and apologies until finally Camille threatened to take out a restraining order. Surprisingly, Arden, my no-nonsense daughter, is the one who caves and still sees him from time to time. She tells me she can't fully break away, and I don't judge her for it, but for weeks after she sees Evan, it's like she's drowning in a river of despair, and nothing I do can pull her out of it. It makes me hate him even more.

I'm lost deeply enough in my thoughts that I jump when Maryanne, the head librarian who officially hired me last year, comes to stand beside me. I try to tear myself from Evan's narrative, but it's hard when my brain goes down this route.

"The tree looks beautiful," she says.

"It'll be a lovely holiday," I say. My mind flashes back to all those years ago at our annual Christmas party when Evan raped Marlow, and a shudder passes through me.

I force a smile at Maryanne and carry on with my work.

## The Woman from Miami

I wave to Evan from the lawn as his Mercedes backs down the driveway. At least he's bringing his car to the airport—that gives me hope he's coming back in time for Christmas. Whenever he has a driver take him, those trips are usually the longest.

I'm wearing a short silk robe, and I can feel the neighbor next door staring at me. I turn to see a frown of disapproval on her face. This neighborhood is so hoity-toity. That's the word my mom used to describe the vibe when Evan bought me the house, and the more I live here, the more I realize she's right.

I turn away from the neighbor and try to lock eyes with Evan through his windshield, but I see him staring at the neighbor, too. He seems to register her look of disdain, and then he looks back at me. And he's frowning now, too, and all at once I feel like a stupid, chastised child. I wrap the robe tighter around me, tears burning my eyes as he reverses onto the street and drives away.

I head back to the house, tucking my head, willing myself not to look at the neighbor or say anything. I don't need any trouble, not when I'm trying so hard to make it work here.

Inside, I lock the door behind me and race up the steps. When we first moved here, Evan convinced me he needed a safe for work. I've never tried to open the safe, but I guarantee the combination numbers are his daughters' birthday. He's obsessed with his twin daughters. And I know their birthday because he always spends weeks trying to figure out what to buy them, and he always asks me what I think college girls would want, which I find a little creepy. It's like he wants to remember me as someone much younger, the sexier girl I was when we first met.

In Evan's closet, I get down on my knees and level with the safe. If he's bought me an engagement ring, I know it's going to be in here. The other day I saw him staring into the open safe, admiring whatever was inside with a look on his face like he was really pleased with what he saw. And then when I got closer, he slammed the safe's door closed and gave me a sly smile.

My hands travel over the numbers that make Camille and Arden's birthday, but it doesn't open. *Crap.* I almost try Cole's and Clara's birthdays, but I'm so sure he'd pick the girls' birthday that I give it one last try and enter the numbers backwards, and yup, *click*, there it goes, popping right open.

I pull the door open and look inside the darkness.

## Clara

On Christmas Eve, Cole blasts Christmas music from his phone. The sound of Mariah Carey belting "All I Want for Christmas Is You" filters through our living room. Daisy's the cutest thing, holding her eggnog like it's a microphone and singing along to Mariah while Arden videos her, and Camille gives enthusiastic stage directions. Harper stands off to the side, smiling as she watches the three girls together. Harper and Sloane are still inseparable. I invited Dave and his new wife, who's lovely, but they decided to do Christmas Eve with her family so they could do Christmas Day with Daisy and Sloane.

A few months after Margaret died, Sloane told me that Evan was Daisy's biological father. It blew me apart, the sheer force of Evan's violence and far-reaching consequences beyond anything I ever could have imagined. But when I recovered, the truth that Daisy was the half-sister of my children, and therefore my family, too, made me love her and want to build a relationship with her. And though Sloane and Dave haven't told Daisy, they plan to at some point, and once Daisy knows, I'll tell my children, too. But in the meantime, I want them all to spend as much time together as possible, so that when they learn Daisy is their half-sister, they'll already have spent years building that bond.

Ben watches Daisy sing, a nostalgic look on his handsome face. Daisy's health took a nosedive earlier this year, but she rebounded on a new medicine, and all of us are just so grateful she's okay. On one side of Ben is Marlow, whose children are down in the basement playing ping pong. On the other side is Sloane, her fingers laced through Ben's. At one point Ben turns and watches Sloane as she watches Daisy, and the way he feels about her is written all over him.

Right when Daisy is about to finish the song, the doorbell rings. I'm not sure who it could be because all my guests are here. I move through the foyer and open the front door to see a beautiful young woman standing on the steps. She's maybe thirty or so, underdressed for the weather in a long-sleeved thermal shirt beneath a puffer vest. Her blue-green eyes are deep set, and her porcelain skin is covered in pretty clusters of freckles. Her red hair is long and loose over her shoulders.

She looks just like the woman from the Instagram photos.

"Can I help you?" I ask.

The woman nods. "I think so," she says. "Are you Clara?"

I nod, steeling myself.

She shifts her weight. "Do you know who I am?" she asks.

"Should I?"

I sound tougher than I feel.

"I'm Lucy," she says quickly, and it seems like she's trying to make her voice sound confident, too. "I'm the woman you saw with Evan in Miami. In the hotel. The night you followed us."

My stomach plummets. My breathing comes quickly as my eyes travel her face, looking for something I can recognize from that awful night in Miami. I suddenly feel way too warm, like I'm going to faint. Why would Evan even tell her I flew down and followed them? *Why is she here?*

Marlow is the first to sense something's wrong. "Clara?" she calls from the foyer. And then she moves to the doorway and stands beside me. "Who's this?" she asks.

"This is Lucy," I say to Marlow. "Evan's *girlfriend.*"

Marlow doesn't flinch. She just studies the woman with dark, unblinking eyes. And then Sloane comes to stand next to Marlow, and from inside the foyer I can hear Harper asking sweetly, "What's going on?" followed by Cole's deep voice: "Mom?"

Now everyone's crowding the door like they can smell blood. But Lucy doesn't look intimidated—she looks profoundly sad. "There's something I have to give you," she says to no one in particular. There's a tremble in her thin fingers when she reaches into her pocket and pulls out a rose gold locket engraved with the initials *M.C.*

I recognize it right away as Margaret's—I remember when Cole gave it to her so many Christmases ago—and my heart pounds to see it dangling in front of us. A deep and guttural wail sounds, and at first, I think I've made the sound, but then I realize the cry is coming from Cole. "*That's Margaret's necklace,*" he says, his words choked.

Sloane's hands cover her mouth, and Harper's green eyes are as wide as I've ever seen them. Ben rakes a hand through his hair, watching as Lucy passes the locket to Cole. Cole stares down at it, and then, as if to confirm that what he's seeing is real, he opens the locket to see a photo of himself on one side, and a photo of Florence on the other. His hands are trembling, and he looks up at Lucy. He opens his mouth, but nothing comes out.

"Where did you find this?" Sloane asks Lucy. She holds Daisy tightly against her. Arden and Camille are next to Daisy; Camille cries softly, and Arden looks terrified.

"In Evan's things," Lucy says. "In his safe. In *our house*."

The way she straightens her shoulders when she says *our house*, like a part of her is still proud of her life with him, takes the breath out of me because she's no doubt blowing up her life by bringing us Margaret's locket. "*Why are you doing this?*" I ask, trying hard not to cry, so overwhelmed I can barely get the words out.

Lucy shrugs, her body hunching forward again. She looks pained as she says, "Because I've done a lot of things I'm not proud of, but I could live with those things." She shakes her head, wringing her hands together. "But not *this*. The locket wasn't the only thing I found inside the safe. There were other things—ugly things. *Tokens*." She starts crying, and I can't help myself—I reach out my hand and take hers. "I called the police," she says, her fingers cold and limp in mine. "There was a dead phone in the safe they were able to get running and analyze, and it's definitely Margaret's. There was more jewelry, some of it definitely not Margaret's—a class ring with a graduation date on it that means it must have belonged to someone a little older than she was. And Evan kept Rohypnol inside the safe, and the police have that, too. And they're going to try to match the jewelry with its rightful owners and piece together what else he might have done."

I turn to catch Marlow's eyes. She shakes her head almost imperceptibly.

"I've followed the news," Lucy says. "I know the police never found Margaret's phone, and that they thought maybe it was in the river, or that whoever killed her took it or hid it. When I found the phone and saw the initials on the locket, and then the photos inside the locket—I knew Evan wasn't the man I thought he was."

Cole's shaking beside me. I drop Lucy's hand and pull him close to me.

"I shouldn't have taken the locket," Lucy says quickly, as though that's why we're upset. "I know that, and I'm sorry. I just felt like it belonged with you instead of inside an evidence bag."

Arden puts a hand to the doorframe to steady herself. Camille's eyes are already puffy, her cheeks bright red.

Lucy drops her gaze to stare at the space between her boots, and she suddenly looks so tired, like this night has taken everything out of her. "They're headed to your country club now," she says.

"*Who's* headed to our country club?" Arden asks, her voice steely.

Lucy turns to look at Arden and Camille like she's just realized they're there. She studies them for a moment, and then says, "The police. They're arresting your dad."

Camille lets out a breath, and Arden's hand flies to cover her mouth.

Cole straightens. "They're arresting him?" he asks Lucy. "You're sure?"

Lucy nods, still looking away from us like she's ashamed.

Something inside of me comes alive again—a fire, roiling in my gut. I turn to my children and my friends. "Let's go," I say. "Let's go—*now*. I need to see it."

~

We don't even bother grabbing our coats.

Lucy's in the front seat of my car as we drive to the club, and she's the only one still crying. All three of my children sit silently in the back, like the electric quiet before a storm. Sloane, Harper, and Ben are driving in a car behind us. Marlow stayed back at my house with Daisy, assuring us that Daisy didn't need to see the things we were about to see. Daisy tried to protest, but Sloane kissed her gently on the cheek and promised she'd be right back.

In the parking lot of the country club, the seven of us scramble out of our cars. Six police vehicles fan out from the entrance to the club. There's frenetic movement inside the club—an abnormal amount of people mill in front of the windows near the front of the club's main dining room. I quickly realize that the members know something we don't, that they're pressing themselves up against the windows to get a closer look at what's about to unfold on the lawn.

A moment later, the grand oak front doors fly open, and two officers emerge with Evan, gripping his arms, trying to get him down the stone front steps. Christmas music filters from the open doors into the cold, frosty air. Evan's trying his best to get out of the officers' grip—straining hard against them, but they're too strong for him. His thick blonde hair is a mess, and he must look unrecognizable to the other members, drenched in rage, his carefully controlled exterior cracked. "*Get off of me! I didn't do it!*" he shouts to the officers, and then, "*Let me go!*" But they only manhandle him more firmly, guiding him over the snow toward the police car as he flips the fuck out.

Braver members, many of them old friends of ours, have started exiting the club for a better view. At first it's just a few—but then nearly everyone seems to pour outside until it seems like the entire Christmas party is out on the snowy lawn. Maybe a hundred or so people watch as Evan lets his body go slack and then starts kicking, and a third officer has to approach the chaos. Some of the women gasp and shake their heads in disbelief as the three police officers drag Evan to the car like a petulant toddler. He's screaming obscenities now, and no one seems to be able to look away. Right before the cops throw him into the backseat, Evan lifts his head, and his eyes catch mine. He blinks a few times at me, like he can't believe I'm really standing there with our children. But where else would I be?

We all watch as the police cars speed away. Harper's hands cover her mouth, and tears of what must be relief stream over Sloane's cheeks.

When the police cars are gone, everyone turns their gaze to us—the family Evan tried to destroy but couldn't.

Snow falls in thick flakes. Sloane leans into Ben, and Harper and Lucy stand close, still staring into the wake of the police cars. Arden takes my hand, and Camille presses herself against me. I look at Cole, and see he's standing a little taller, his light blue eyes blazing. I think of Margaret, hoping that wherever she is, she's looking down and seeing all of this.

Christmas lights inside the club twinkle, and I feel warmth running through me, not only because of what happened tonight, but also because my three children—all I've ever really needed—are right beside me.

I exchange a glance with Sloane and then Harper. I kiss Cole's cheek and squeeze my daughters' hands. And I pray that with any luck, this is the moment when all of us start anew.

# ACKNOWLEDGMENTS

Thank you to Katie Clark and Jessica Clark, my aunt and my cousin, two loving and brave women who died from primary pulmonary hypertension at ages thirty-eight and twenty-two, respectively. Thank you both for showing our whole family what bravery and faith can look like. This paragraph is too small to describe what you meant to everyone you loved and who loved you. You are profoundly missed.

I'm very grateful to every reader who spent their time in this book's pages. Thank you!

Thank you to the incredible team at Amazon Publishing, who treats me and my books like gold. I am very grateful for everything you've invested in making these books shine and helping readers to find them. Thank you especially to Carmen Johnson and Faith Black Ross, for their keen editing eyes and unwavering dedication to making this book the best it could be.

Thank you endlessly to Dan Mandel, who guides my career with a steady hand, unparalleled skill, and the utmost faith in what we can do together. I am so lucky to be one of your authors.

Thank you to fairy-book-godmother Zibby Owens, who champions my books and the work of so many authors, and who creates a community that makes writing feel a lot less solitary.

Thank you to all my early readers, who are generous enough to read my books and give me terrific feedback. During the writing of

*You Must Be New Here*, more than for any book I've written before, I relied heavily on readers to help me choose between two very different endings for these characters. I was shuttling manuscripts and different epilogue options across town, and I'm so grateful to live in a community where everyone is always so up for it all. Special shout out to Alex Padden, who got on the phone with me, helped me brainstorm, and is the entire reason the epilogue exists as such. Thank you to Isabel Murphy for being the final word and my true north on so many things, certainly on this epilogue. Thank you to especially to Melissa Mendez, Ali Watts, Rachel Patino, and Olivia Reighley, who were subjected to many emails and many revisions and so generously gave me their time and feedback! Thank you to an extraordinary book club who read *You Must Be New Here* over the course of a week and met in my kitchen to hash out how they felt after reading different ending options: Molly Felde, Lauren Schwarzfeld, Fran Hauser, Emily Winograd Leonard, and Rebecca Rivard. Thank you to insightful readers Joan and Jeff Miller, Artika Loganathan, Megan Mazza, Andi Ahrens, Caroline Moore, Bob Schewior, Julie Dumke, Chrissie Irwin, Nina Levine, Liv Peters, Lauren Locke, Janelle Lika, Barbara Harm, Ally Reuben, Annie Manning, Antonia Davis, Wendy Levey, and Julia Kelly. Thank you especially to Melissa Mendez, Dr. Audrey Birnbaum, and Jeremy Randol, who never cease to amaze me with their attention to detail, making me wonder if they were professional editors in another lifetime; I cannot express my gratitude enough to the three of you for the selfless way you devoted yourself to this project. Thank you to my aunts, Joan, Posie, and Angela, and my godfather, Bill, who love me, support me, and always read my books and give me the best feedback. Thank you to my sister, Meghan, my best friend and toughest (but fairest!) critic, who pushes me to make each book better with her edits. Thank you to Meghan's husband, Roby Bhattacharyya, my amazing brother-in-law, for his feedback and general greatness, and to their incredible children, Rose and Owen. Thank you, Meg and Roby, for answering my science questions for this book and others. Thank you to my awesome brother, Jack Sise, and his wife, Ali, who always reads everything I write and gives me the kind of great feedback only voracious readers can. Thank you to their amazing kids, Jack, Darcy, and Schuyler. Thank you to the Hawes family in San Diego. And thank you to early reader Erika Grevelding, for being the kind of close friend Sloane was looking for, the one she mentioned who helped her get through adolescence unscathed. That was you for me.

Thank you to investigator James Castiglione, for his help on this book and my previous books with crime scenes and police procedure. Thank you, James, for answering my fictional questions about very sensitive issues with such thoughtful responses. All mistakes are mine.

Thank you to lawyers Megan Mazza and Joe Sise for answering my legal questions for this book; and again, all mistakes are mine. Thank you also to Megan for her friendship, and to Joe for his constant love and support.

Thank you to Carole and Ray Sweeney, for all their love and encouragement always. Thank you to Bob and Linda Harrison, for modeling the kind of life that is filled with curiosity for learning and reading and writing. Thank you to my parents, for being wonderful in every sense of the word, and for loving me and supporting me and cheering me on all the way, and especially for teaching me the value of kindness and hard work.

Thank you to all the booksellers, librarians, reviewers, and the book bloggers and communities on social media who spread the word about my books and many others.

Thank you to my children's teachers! And to their coaches, especially Olga, Bob, Seth, Dinah, Brad, Akash, and at school, Coach Dossena, Coach Ludwig, and Coach Shannon.

Thank you to all the teachers from whom I've been lucky enough to learn, especially as I tried to make my way creatively. Thank you to all my friends, you know who you are! Special thanks to Lorena,

Isabel, Jamie, Caroline, Brinn, Claire, Tricia, Megan, Jessica, Kim, Jesse, Chrissie, Sarah, Nina, and Fran.

The biggest thanks goes to my husband, Brian, and my children, Luke, William, Isabel, and Eloise. The five of you are my big loves and my whole heart.

# ABOUT THE AUTHOR

*Photo © 2022 Jennifer Mullowney*

Katie Sise is a bestselling author of seven novels, including *The Break*, *Open House*, and *We Were Mothers*. Katie is a former TV host and jewelry designer and lives outside New York City with her husband, four children, and a golden retriever who has finally calmed down. For more information, visit katiesise.com.